Depths

ANN DENTON

Copyright © 2021 Ann Denton

All rights reserved. No part of this publication may be reproduced, distributed, or transmitted in any form or by any means, including photocopying, recording, or other electronic or mechanical methods, without the prior written permission of the publisher, except in the case of brief quotations embodied in critical reviews and certain other noncommercial uses permitted by copyright law. For permission requests, write to the publisher, addressed "Attention: Permissions Coordinator," at the address below.

Le Rue Publishing

Le Rue Publishing
320 South Boston Avenue, Suite 1030
Tulsa, OK 74103
www.LeRuePublishing.com

ISBN: 978-1-951714-16-1

To everyone who's ever wished for more...

OKEANOS

KREMOS

PSILOS

SKY STONES

SYSTROFI MOUNTAINS

PALATI

KELP FOREST

REEF CITY

SHELL CASTLE

NAVAGIO

NOWHERE

UMRA DESERT

PROLOGUE

Raj

I WAITED in a line of imbeciles, hovering in a street in the middle of the ocean, miles beneath the surface of the water, between two rows of mottled green glass buildings housing shops that sold everything from barnacles to bells. The light drifting out from the shops gave all the men on the streets sallow coloring as they swam hither and yon, baskets on their arms as they completed their shopping. Idiotic mutterings filled the water around me, and I was tempted to slaughter the sea people in line just for talking.

"Did you see the price of eel last week? Outrageous! Mad, I say!" a siren with pink hair complained to his friend.

"Indeed. Where they getting it from that makes it so precious, then, the river in Rasle?" the siren with a robin's egg blue top knot replied.

"Remember that vendor—Bale, I think it was—who tried to sell 'uman dick that one time?"

"Oh, right, after that shipwreck! Ha. Yes. Scavenged those sailors."

"Smallest eels that shifter ever sold!"

"I remember hearing the rumor it was nasty, creamy gristle. Too chewy."

"Bet the idiots who bought it off him couldn't wait to wash that taste out of their mouths!"

They laughed, their long, thin forms looking waif-like in comparison to the burly merman who was in front of them. Their golden skin turned a spring green color in the light shed by the nearest shop's glass walls. They almost looked human but for their ethereal beauty and the fact that they could kick their feet so fast they blurred when they swam. Sirens. Such fools. Most of them spoke prettier than this pair did. But clearly, these two were a special sort. They were not the golden-tongued stereotype of the siren courtier. They could hardly be called intelligent lifeforms. I twisted the black ring on my finger, breathing slowly and carefully out my mouth to try and calm myself down.

In normal circumstances, I'd have had a servant wish up a scimitar and slowly skin them, then perhaps roast them while my musicians played a song and I forced some shuddering peasant to bathe in their blood. But these weren't normal circumstances.

Idiots have a purpose, I reminded myself. They were excellent arrow fodder in a war, bodies to distract the archers from better targets, or here, in the kingdom under the sea, great to draw out the attacks of the aggressive bull sharks the soldiers rode. The fool in front of me had particularly long pink hair, which would make it easy to grab so that I could swing him around in a giant arc and toss him at the bloodthirsty predators before making my own escape. A small smile played about my lips at the mental image.

I'd witnessed a glorious fight just last night when I'd first entered the capital city, Palati. Two men had been flung out of a five-story blue glass tavern, and they'd shifted right before my eyes. Their brawling fists had turned to gnashing teeth and fins versus tentacles as they'd mutated into a shark and a squid, shifting right in the middle of a jeering crowd. I'd watched in amusement as one bit the other's head off, literally.

It was a pity that most of the kingdoms on land had banned the sea shifter battles years ago. I recalled that, as a young man nearly eight centuries past, I'd loved watching the huge tank brought into the palace in

Cheryn and set in my father's sandy fighting pit. I had stared raptly as two men climbed in, shifted, and fought until the water was streaked a glorious red. I'd give these sea shifters that, they did know how to battle. They did know how to make the blood pump and nerves sing, how to make you rise on your tiptoes in anticipation of that final moment. They gave death the flair it deserved.

Sirens, unlike sea shifters, were practically useless. Their voices didn't entrance the sea creatures in the same way they did humans, so they were practically magicless down here. Thus, easy to kill. Dull. At least mermen were stocked full of muscle and made good soldiers, even if their memory modification powers failed to work under the waves. Most of the soldiers at the registration table up ahead were mer.

I glanced around me as the two siren dolts in front of me continued a conversation so exaggeratedly stupid that it only felt fit for the stage. Their golden faces stretched wide as they went on about some seal fight that they'd attended and bet upon the prior week. I tried to distract myself from the urge to simply wish for their heads to explode, by looking about.

Wishing for that would be a waste of my magic. It would also put those idiotic royal guards on high alert. I didn't want high alert. I wanted to slide into that underwater castle in the distance undetected.

I glanced over at it—my destination. The palace was a magical feat of wonder, a crystal clear base with twisting green glass spires piercing the ocean as it glowed like an enchanted peridot gem under the water. My gaze grew hungry, but before a desirous expression could cross my face, I looked away. I had to stay in character, practice the part I was about to play.

Unfortunately, a couple fishwives caught my eye, saw the grin that had been forced on my face when I'd removed that sarding curse set upon me—or had it partially removed, the stupid smile was a side effect I found difficult to get rid of—and taken it as an invitation. They swam forward to ply their "wares." Some had actual goods to sell: shell combs, algae cure-alls, amethyst glass potion bottles with any elixir one could desire. Other women just came up to sell themselves. And with the ratio of men to women in the entire world at approximately five to one, these ladies were quite expensive.

"Eight sand dollars for a quick suck!" the man behind me exclaimed. "I could eat for two weeks on that!"

"Not my pussy, you couldn't." The nubile young mermaid winked at him and flicked her pink tail.

I heard him moan in longing before digging foolishly into his purse.

Apparently, that tail flick was an attractive thing. I tried not to roll my eyes at the pre-mating ritual taking place behind me. I hadn't really figured out where mermaid pussies were located. I had more important goals right now.

Like vengeance. Like destroying the enemies who had cost me the war against Evaness and humiliated me in a way that meant no punishment was bad enough. Blinding fury rose in me again at the knowledge that the queens of the sea and Rasle, my allies, were both dead. I couldn't believe we'd lost our bid to take that country. Even more, I couldn't believe that I'd lost my own standing as Sultan. I'd lost my crown in Cheryn. I was the strongest djinni ever to live, and still ... that upstart of a girl, that weak excuse for a queen, Bloss, had found the single chink in my armor, armor I'd spent centuries building. She'd made a wish for my happiness. My eternal, orgasmic happiness. She'd made me into a moaning, mindless fool! A laughingstock. She'd defeated *me*, the endless king. She'd unseated my mind, made me lose my crown, changed everything.

Black fury seethed in my stomach like tar, a bubbling pit.

Though the world had toppled onto its head, these idiots around me went on as though nothing were wrong. As if the world weren't *wrong*.

I focused on my fury instead of satisfying my menial curiosity about anatomy as the man behind me abandoned the line, following the maid with the pink tail. Then the line ahead of me moved, and I shoved the golden-skinned siren in front of me when he failed to swim forward.

"Hey, watch it!" he said.

"Sorry." I showed him my teeth in what might have looked like a smile or—if he were smart enough to recognize it, which I doubted—a threat. "Just anxious to sign up." I let my eyes drop so that I hid my violent desires.

"Yeah, well, this is late sign-ups for the royal tournament to wed that new Queen Avia. I 'eard she's a looker. I'm excited me-self. You 'eard the speculation that we'll be asked to wrestle a puss? Eight-legged blighters, they are." He clicked his tongue. "That will be a bit of a rush. But this late sign-up has no guarantees." The siren scoffed as he turned to face me fully and looked me over for the first time, unaware he didn't speak in proper sentences, painfully unaware he was missing the letter *h* entirely. "What the 'ell are you wearing?"

I didn't bother to answer. I hadn't stripped myself down to heathen level like the imbeciles who paraded shirtless around me. I wore decent breeches and a full shirt, and I didn't need to explain myself. Though I'd probably need to blend at least a bit in the castle. My hand closed over my ring, and I nearly twisted, nearly wished this idiot's head to expand like a puffer fish until it popped. But I couldn't use my wishes so freely any longer. Not without giving myself away. I had to practice restraint and only use them in the most needful of circumstances.

The line moved again. Good, they must have quickly rejected that last ass. The merman hung his head as he swam off from the table.

Idiot number one in front of me, the siren with pink hair who'd gone on about eels, approached the wooden table where a handful of royal guards floated, spears in hand, full armor reflecting the little magical bobbing ball of glass that was tied to the corner of the table. Inside that little sphere, an enchanted, waterproof orange flame flickered. On the table sat some water-sealed parchment and an inkwell. And a large black box.

"Good day, I'm 'ere to sign up for the tournament and *marry that queen*." The siren smiled brightly.

I watched in mute pleasure as the guard in charge, a mer fellow with a blue tail, merely said in a dull voice, "Sign your name here to prove you can write, and pay the ten sandies."

"Ten! I heard it was five!"

The guard didn't bat an eye. "It was five, three hours ago. But we've got nearly eighty applicants right now, so we've had to narrow it down a bit. You have to sign your name, pay the fee, then answer a question."

"What kinda question?" The siren curled his lip in offense.

"We don't ask until you've paid the fee," the guard replied with a sigh. "We only have so many questions. So we don't want to use them on men who aren't serious."

"Sarding hell, this is ridiculous! Riptide robbery!" The siren stormed off and, to my delight, his dullard friend followed.

Guess eels *and queens* were out of their pay grade.

I grinned and swam forward, digging into the sealskin pouch at my waist. I took out eleven sand dollars and pushed them across the table. I couldn't knock the stupid, enchanted grin off my face even though I was internally seething about the fact that I had to stoop to peasant levels. *Disguise,* I reminded myself. *This is all just practice for your greatest deception, your greatest triumph.*

The burly, blue-tailed, blue-haired guard shoved one back. "Only ten."

Hmmm. So, he was a fair one then. Or at least, not a cheap one to bribe. Duly noted. I'd kill another few mermen tonight and steal their sand dollars to bulk up my purse. I signed the name I'd created for myself on the parchment and then looked up with a grin. "I'm ready for your question."

"Who is the current queen of the land realm of Evaness?" the guard asked, reading off a list before his brown eyes flicked to meet mine.

It was ironic that was the question I got, because that *bitch* was the very reason I was here. The very reason that I'd sworn to compete in this foolish tournament for a queen. Because I owed Bloss Hale a debt of revenge. And I was going to make her little sister pay it … in blood.

The guard cleared his throat expectantly. "Look, if you don't know the answer, you need to move along."

"Queen Bloss Hale," I responded quickly, not wanting to give him the chance to dismiss me. It was difficult, but I managed to say her name without cursing, without breaking something. Without giving myself away.

The guard sighed and nodded, folding back up his list of questions and making eye contact with me. "Your name will be entered into a drawing. Two random competitors will be chosen to fill our final spots. The names will be posted in the town square in two days' time."

His "Good luck" was flat and insincere.

But I gave a wide grin anyway as I reached for the ring on my finger and twisted it. "Oh, I wish you'd choose *me*."

1

Many men understand the thrill of murder. Many don't understand the thrill of crushing a person's soul while they still live and breathe.

—Sultan Raj of Cheryn

Avia Hale

A SHAFT of sunlight pierced the ocean and shone down on me, giving light but no warmth—like an empty promise. Like everything thus far in my life. False. Appearing one way but actually another.

They'd said my rule would be graciously accepted. After all, I was the true heir to the most powerful sea sprite between the shores. It shouldn't have mattered that I was raised on land. I'd still been raised in a castle, taught to rule, navigate courtiers, create treaties, encourage trade.

Lies.

"False queen!" A woman's voice smacked hard like an oar and cut through the dull ripples of conversation.

"Air lover!" a man growled.

"Sky breather!" some unseen figure bellowed.

I blinked as a chilled wave darted across my back, raising goose bumps on my skin, which had absolutely nothing to do with the curses being hurled my direction from the crowd below. Or so I told myself. But I fought the urge to scratch at my arms uncomfortably. I *hated* when people didn't like me. My smile grew brittle, but I kept it in place, hoping it might soften one or two of my citizens below.

Honey, not vinegar, I reminded myself. *If it works to attract flies, it'll work for fish, right?*

I stood twenty feet above a crowded mix of sea people, on a palace balcony made of the glass cut to reflect like a prism. My body was encased in a shimmering golden dress stitched with as many earth walker gold pieces as the seamstress could manage. I jangled when I moved, like a coin purse or a wind chime. The effect was enchanting, a dress that blinded as much as it sparkled.

It reflected my heritage and signaled the riches I could bring the sea kingdom through trade, or so the seamstress had said when she'd stealthily pitched her idea for the gown I should wear to today's tournament opening ceremony. The thing weighed as much as a shipwreck. If I tripped, I feared I'd crack the glass floor of the castle.

The ocean floor in front of the palace was packed tight with sea people of all stripes and sizes. There were shark shifters who chose to retain their dorsal fins even in human form. There were mermen and mermaids, the bright colors of their hair and tails like flashes of rainbow amidst the rest of the crowd. There were small mer children with silver fins who hadn't developed their final colors yet, constantly trying to swim up and away from their parents, many of whom grabbed their little ones by the tail and held on, making the children bob in the water like birds might bob while clinging to a clothesline on a windy day back in Evaness. Back home.

Some of the children waved their hands in time to the music that began to play; the castle's orchestra had arrived just after the verbal jabs and was currently smoothing over the discontent with a jaunty song mocking sailors. The crowd perked up and started singing along as soon as they recognized the tune. I'd discovered this was common. The ocean people were very musically inclined.

You know what only a fool would do? Would do? Would do?

Only a fool would ride a tree

Thinking that he could cross the sea

With nothing but the wind to blow him

Naught but a plank to stow him

I think that we should show him

That a fool will dro-o-own, down, down in the sea

As the song grew more raucous, my eyes traced over hermit crab shifters, whose red hair gave them away and who looked decidedly uncomfortable without their giant shells protecting their backs, shells which hadn't been allowed onto the castle grounds for security reasons. Or so Felipe, my personal guard, had told me earlier. At least I wasn't the only one who felt awkwardly exposed.

Off to one side, a group of unearthly beautiful sirens stood a head taller than most of the others, their magically selected hair colors on display standing out in the crowd. They could alter their hair at will. Most of them had chosen to make their hair white blonde today, but some had midnight black locks to contrast with their golden skin. All of them had beautifully shaped curls floating around them in gorgeous waves that made me envious. My hair only ever knotted if the current caught it, which was why I'd had my own golden locks carefully plaited today, and layered the braids in elaborate swooping designs beneath my shell crown.

A few half-rotted faces were scattered here and there amongst the crowd, some of Posey's friends from the undead army who hadn't left with my sister, Bloss. The soldiers stood apart from the people, judged by them, but they were merely mercenaries who'd fought the evil Queen Mayi and helped to liberate the sea kingdom from her rule and to keep me from becoming her puppet. To me, they were heroes, saviors. They'd stormed under the water, their ability to exist without breathing an asset as they marched across the depths and stormed the castle, sweeping away the reign of the monster who'd kidnapped me. I thought I saw a familiar decaying face among them, but it moved before I could be certain it was Lizza, my sister's newly appointed castle mage, who had stayed behind in the sea to help me. Beside that face, I'd sworn I'd seen a brunette. *Perhaps it was merely a trick of the eyes,* I told myself. Wishful thinking since part of me wanted my sister here to hold my hand, even while another part of me rebelled against such childishness. I gave the undead a grateful smile before my eyes swept on.

There was also a tight knot of people with jellyfish-like tentacles for hair. They danced eerily in the current, and their skin was a soft lavender. It was difficult not to stare. Near them, swordfish shifters with sharp, elongated noses stayed in fish form, all except for one, who looked almost human except for the lethal-looking protrusion of his nose, like a dagger had been stuck onto his face. I wondered briefly if he ever smashed into things with a nose that long. Did it get caught in doorjambs?

Before he caught me staring, I let my eyes roam again.

I made the mistake of making eye contact with one of the sirens, and his resulting wink and grin had my grip tightening on the glass railing. Dammit. I'd broken one of mother's cardinal rules. No. Not mother's. Queen Gela's. I still had to remind myself that the woman who'd raised me was no mother of mine. People always said life changes in an instant. My life proved that saying true.

One moment, I'd been Queen Gela's human, second-born daughter. Rare, but not special in a world that had few women but a lot of magic. Lacking the latter, I'd been nothing more than a spare princess. But, the next second, I'd been snapped up by a dragon, who'd delivered me to a monstrous sea sprite. The sprite had told me that I was her daughter, stolen shortly after birth, that I was months older than I'd thought I was and eighteen already, and I'd discovered I was incredibly magically powerful. Everything I'd ever believed about myself had drowned a slow, painful death, swirling like a whirlpool, slowly sucked under.

The pain of that betrayal, the discovery of the fact that the woman I'd loved with all my heart, the woman who'd kissed away my scraped knees and bruised elbows, pressed at me. Each memory—our silly tea parties, the way she'd always caressed my hair—felt like a stone set onto my chest, compressing it further so that I couldn't breathe.

Before my emotions could catapult me down into a deep chasm of hurt, a cheer rippled through the crowd like a riptide, yanking me out of that depressing trajectory and forcing me to focus on the present.

I snarkily scolded myself. *Come, Avia, no time for pouting. Every royal family has an entire wing of skeletons hidden in the castle. You're just one of the many bones.*

I focused outward. The orchestra had just swum up higher, so the crowd could better see them. Once they were above the heads of even the tallest, the royal musicians started a new song and performed a complicated little swimming formation as they played, moving in synchrony, forming circles and shapes with their bodies. I realized, with the wide-eyed clarity of someone last to understand a joke, that the orchestra had just spelled out the name of the sea kingdom: Okeanos. It was a name only spoken by residents, considered sacred. Secret.

It was a name I'd only learned about a week ago, when I'd decided to claim my birthright and accept my place as sea queen.

I smiled, glad the orchestra seemed to have changed the tide. The people weren't shouting hatred anymore. I raised my hands to clap for the musicians, but a sea sponge smashed into my cheek, laden with squid ink. The dark ink billowed out in a foul-tasting cloud around my face, temporarily blinding me until I pulled it away, realizing that it had darkened my skin to a deep blue-black.

Apparently, the shouting protests had escalated to projectiles. Wonderful.

Felipe, my bodyguard, cursed beneath his breath and quickly pulled open the door behind me, barking at one of the mer attendants there. I didn't look back, I simply kept smiling as though I hadn't realized I looked a horrible fright. Embarrassment grated at my stomach, shredding it. The only action I took was a slight wave of my hand behind me as I summoned my guard back, wanting to counteract whatever angry order he was issuing. "Felipe," I called softly.

He immediately swam closer, and I felt the water grow warmer around me as he radiated heat like a furnace.

"Yes, Your Majesty?" His tone was dark and decadent like a bass note on a cello. I glanced over briefly but quickly back out at the crowd, giving a cheery wave despite, or to spite, my detractors. I found it hard to look directly at my guard. Felipe was just too handsome. He was stacked with muscle in a burly, intimidating, and grumpy sort of way, with a big square jaw and a scar that sliced through one of his thick, dark blue eyebrows. He had a tattoo of a wagon wheel over his left pec that I was insanely curious about but too shy to ask about, especially when faced with his burning brown eyes. Despite his surly manner, I did find I trusted him, though I probably irritated him at least fifty times a day. Like I was about to do.

"Invite the protesters to the ball," I instructed, trying not to spit as I realized a bit of the ink had gotten into my mouth. It was sour and disgusting, but I swallowed it down with a stilted smile.

"Majesty?" His tone was mystified, as though I'd just suggested we put the protesters on fishing hooks and suspend them from the ceiling in the throne room.

While my birth mother might have taken that approach, I'd always taken a different route. "I'd like them to come, meet me, and discuss their grievances in a civilized manner," I told him. "Please go deliver my invitation."

I heard and enjoyed the barest of teeth grinding as my guard battled over his resistance to my order and sought a way to counter it. "I'll have someone else deliver it," he finally grumbled.

"Wonderful." I agreed to his modified plan. Sometimes, I'd learned, you had to make concessions to allow others to feel like they had some power over a situation, particularly men. Bloss always said being born with a penis was a handicap because men were required to spend so much time stroking their own egos that there was hardly any brain power left for anything else. Of course, she said that years ago just before she fled from her fiancés. Still, she had a point.

I gave a quick nod to Felipe, and his deep blue tail flicked as he swam back over to the door of the glass castle behind us, no doubt to change his earlier angry order to forcibly remove the "sea scum"—his pet name for nearly everyone.

I returned my attention to the crowd gathered below me.

It was high noon, so the sun was straight overhead and provided the greatest amount of illumination, aided by glowing sea lanterns, orbs brimming with orange magic dotted around the peridot-colored glass palace behind me. Even so, the ocean was cool at this depth. Add a swift current, which we had today, and it was uncomfortably so. I longed to bundle up in a thick, warm shawl. But a queen couldn't show petty weakness. A queen was a figurehead, an idol on the altar, some forgotten god's messenger to earth. Petty things like warmth or squid ink couldn't bother me.

It was all bullshite.

The crowd gathered today didn't care about me, as a person or their queen. Some outright despised me. I doubted most gave two shites about this tournament I was hosting to find myself some husbands, a horror I was not ready to endure but apparently had to undergo. For Okeanos' sake, the eighth kingdom of Kenmare.

The herald on the small balcony separated from mine by only a low, waist-high wall shuffled forward a step, his formal shell armor clinking. He raised a large, gold-covered conical shell and spoke through it so that his voice was magnified, "Her Majesty, Queen Avia, is delighted to open the Syzygos Tournament to all contestants brave enough to face her challenges."

My heart faltered slightly at the thought of husbands, and I swayed where I stood. I was merely eighteen. I'd only ever kissed one man. Now thirty men would compete for my hand, most at least a decade my senior. And though the marriage itself wouldn't take place until I was ready, *if* I survived...

I splayed the wing-like fins on my back a bit in order to maintain my balance at that dizzying notion. *If.* It was utterly scary and made me stumble, mentally and physically. My heart pulsed weakly, showcasing the reason I wondered *if.*

"Chin up." Next to me, a siren named Sahar spoke through her teeth, her smile stretched wider than natural. I hadn't noticed her join me on the balcony, but she was one of the more popular of my advisers. Perhaps she'd decided to dissuade any more sponge attacks by standing beside me. If so, I was in favor of her decision. "Flutter your fins. Give them a little show," she instructed. An older siren, in her sixties, Sahar was genteel and refined in all the best ways. She'd lost that competitive gleam in her eye that women often get toward one another. Instead, it seemed like wisdom radiated from her very gaze. She was absolutely the best person in the entire castle, if not the kingdom.

But it was easy for her to say flutter. She had no idea that my chest was currently being pinched by a vise. In fact, it felt like a giant thirty feet tall had taken my heart between two fingers as thick as tree trunks and squeezed. Pain radiated through my center.

Sard her and her good intentions. The bitter thought popped into my head before I could quash it.

I fought the urge to bring my hand to my chest and curve my body protectively around the poor quivering organ.

My heart had been injured irreparably by my own stupidity. I'd made assumptions about other people's magic. I'd expected my sister and her husbands to swoop in and save me from the monster of a mother who'd trapped me and bound me to her. I'd stabbed myself in the chest in a bid to escape her magical ties and carve her heart from my body. I'd been saved ... in a limited fashion, by Lizza, my sister's mage. But my own heart ... it stuttered again as it struggled to pump blood through my body, no doubt weakened by the cold water all around. My heart had been injured and would not last. Not if I kept it.

I blinked hard and fought not to stumble a second time as my heart trembled. *Shite. Play it off. Do what Sahar said, put the wings out fully and give a huge wave and smile,* I told myself.

I flared my wings, two semi-translucent betta fish fins that resembled fairy wings but could slice through the water and propel me along. As I flapped them slightly, creating gentle waves, I could see the orange glow of the lamps behind me illuminate them so that they became luminescent. I gave a wave, letting the pearlescent scales that lined the outside of my arms get caught in the light as well, reminding the people that I was of the sea, just like them. Despite my golden hair and soft human facial features, I was sea-born. My little gesture earned me cheers from the crowd.

There. Overripe berries turned into delicious pie. Something nearly ruined made right again.

Next to me, a herald blew his spiral shell again, releasing a blast of sound before speaking through it. "Welcome to the tournament!" he shouted into the shell. "Today, the bravest among you will begin a quest for Queen Avia's hand!"

I waved, but the announcement spurred the protesters again.

Insults floated up from the crowd and pummeled my ears, crashing down on me like massive waves.

More and more voices took up the chant, "Renounce the throne, earth walker!"

Sahar's hand came to my arm in a public show of solidarity. "Don't listen, Your Majesty." I turned to look at her, and she dropped my hand like she'd burned herself.

I didn't care that she'd touched me. But she was wrong in her advice. "Of course I must listen to them. I am an outsider. They have no idea what to expect of me. It's natural they're upset." I kept my false smile and tried to appear calm, stay diplomatic. I didn't say that they were right to suspect me and my intentions, though they were. If only they realized that this little tournament was just chumming the water so that I could sink my teeth into one of the men.

Instead, I turned to my herald and extended my palm. Despite our "separate" balconies, he was only five feet to my right. "May I use your shell please?"

The man's eyes went wide, but he swam over and handed me the shell.

I took a deep breath to calm the nerves that were tangling up my stomach in knots. Then I spoke into the shell so that my voice was amplified. "Good afternoon. I appreciate those of you who came out today to protest. Unfortunately, this is not the proper forum for protests. I will hear grievances in the throne room each Tuesday and Thursday. Assassination attempts should also be completed on those days, because otherwise, my schedule is quite full."

That earned a chuckle as I'd hoped.

I glanced sideways to see Sahar stifling a smile before I continued, my voice a million times brighter and lighter than it had been just moments before. "As you may have noticed, I've got a lot of rebuilding to do since the battle with the undead army. And there's also the small matter of your fellow countrymen who have set out here to compete for my hand. I do ask that you restrain from any attempts to kill me that might inadvertently harm these poor gents. They are only guilty of making the poor decision to test their wit, will, strength, and heart with the possibility of public humiliation at being the first to be sent home. They certainly don't deserve a worse fate than that."

That earned me another chuckle.

Part of me wanted to keep going, but another part cautioned me to stop while I was ahead. I always listened to that cautious voice. My sister, Bloss, didn't. Sometimes I wondered if she even had one.

"Thank you all for coming." I handed the shell back to the stunned herald and patted his shoulder. The scales on the side of his neck changed from yellow to orange as I did. Was that a blush? I made a mental note to ask Sahar later.

Sahar smiled and gave me a tiny, nearly imperceptible nod of approval.

I tried not to collapse as my wings stopped hovering and my feet touched down on the glass again. I was exhausted but relieved I'd fooled the throng below. My smile turned real when my heart ratcheted up and began pumping normally again. Just a little longer. I needed it to hold on just a little longer.

The orchestra began a new song, this time about a mer and a maiden fair. The stain one of my maids had painted on my lips, a deep red like precious coral, curved upward in a smile as contestants began to weave through the crowd, each carrying the banner of his house on a pole, the flags swaying in the current. To me, each pole looked as ominous as a jousting lance. It signaled impending doom. I was locked into choosing men who were power-hungry and had little to nothing in common with me because I'd been raised by heathens who breathed air instead of water. I felt like a player in a traveling troupe, set up on stage, enacting a role. And while I was used to putting on a happy face at court, I'd grown up in Evaness with the illusion that as a second daughter, I would get a more romantic marriage than this.

Hopefully, there will be one kind soul among them.

To my left, Felipe took a small step closer once the crowd had diverted their attention from me to the orchestra and the parade of men. He cleared his throat quietly.

I tried to ignore him, but my guard wouldn't be ignored when he didn't want to be. He was overbearingly obnoxious in that way, sure of himself and his protective responsibilities.

His feet edged closer to mine again. My guard was merman by birth but had taken potions in order to have legs whenever he was near me—for my own comfort, I was told, though I'd tried to insist he forgo them—and he liked to walk less than a foot away from me, like a shadow. His presence was subtle most of the time; he'd perfected the art of remaining visible and invisible at the same time. His sword always gleamed threateningly, polished to a bright shine, but his face was always an impassive mask of calm. The nobles hardly took notice of him as he purposely made himself easy to forget ... unless he wanted to be noticed. Like now.

He cleared his throat, and I had to stop myself from glancing over. The merman was twice my age with a dull scruff on his chin and temples that was prematurely grey, but in a way that was somehow incredibly attractive. He was big and burly as guards should be, his biceps nearly as large as my entire face. But more important than his brawn was his mind. He was quick and observant, perhaps more than I liked, I hadn't decided yet. Felipe's mixed hair, the black and blue strands streaked through with grey, was always slicked back but curled at the base of his neck.

He reached out, careful to keep his arm below the railing of the balcony and the eyes of the crowd, to steady me. His fingers wrapped around the bare skin of my forearm, and my skin practically sizzled at his touch.

How unfair. He was warm despite the cold current, and I instantly grew jealous of the soldier's leather and tortoise-shell armor.

"Are you okay?" my guard asked softly.

I fought the urge to look up at his face and meet the chocolate eyes that I knew would be devouring me, tasting each tiny expression I made and finding the truth. He couldn't know the truth. No one outside my circle could. I grew quite warm in my fury at myself. *Dammit, Avia. Do better.* I hadn't fooled him. He'd noticed my weakness.

I chose not to acknowledge him, hoping the brush off would save me from awkward conversations later. Instead, I gazed out over the crowd that I was supposed to rule and pulled my arm away, raising it.

I gave a little wave, hand cupped and wrist twisting delicately, just as a queen should.

Queen.

I was queen of the sea. That reality still sunk me like a stone whenever I thought of it.

Sahar spoke through her teeth once more, as was her talent during public events. Despite my teasing, she'd refused to get herself a small puppet and become my court entertainer. "Are you ready for the next part of this fishing expedition?" She used the term wryly; for the sea people it was a dark-humored term.

"Not at all," I told her.

"Come on, you can do it, Your Majesty. Think of that damned gargoyle who scared the ink out of Tina this morning. I've never heard you laugh so hard. Bring up that joy and transform it into excitement here before you speak with all these dullards," she coached.

Her mention did set an instant smile on my face. Pony had bounded into my bedroom this morning—my sister's pet gargoyle had no restraint—and scared the living daylights out of my poor squi-maid, a girl who was half squid. Tina had ruined my morning dress and filled the entire dressing room with ink before collapsing into tears. She'd been overwrought about destroying my gown and had tried to fire herself at least a dozen times before I told Sahar to reassign her because she clearly needed to be away from me.

"Big smile, just like you're posing for a portrait." Sahar gave me a huge toothy grin.

"Portraits take hours," I retorted.

"So will this," Sahar rebuked me. "You wanted a tournament. Now we're going to be invaded by bubble-butted males who'll constantly try to bite each other because of mating aggression."

"You make it sound so appealing." Though I literally thought the same.

"It shouldn't be. It took me six years to get my three idiot husbands sorted out. You'd think a stingray shifter would understand he can't just stick his barb in anyone whenever he feels like it. But no."

My eyes widened slightly in alarm. "You better be telling me attack stories not naughty ones. That's all I can stomach right now."

Sahar gave a true laugh. The sound was lilting like a harp. It was musical and enchanting.

I heard Felipe grumble behind her, but he didn't voice his opinion loud enough for me to catch. My heart fumbled again, skipping a beat.

Stupid shite of a thing. I couldn't continue to live with it much longer, according to my undead healer. But as a part human, part sea sprite, I could live with my heart in someone else's uninjured body. I could find a host for my organ and keep them close enough to access my power but at arm's length emotionally should they ever need to be ... replaced.

So, while these boastful competitors paraded below me, flexing their muscles for the crowd, they didn't know that they weren't actually walking into the lap of luxury and a chance at true love. My tournament was a promise as empty as the shaft of sunlight that shone down on me.

These men were walking into the monster's den. One of them would be sacrificed. Because that's what queens did. They took what they needed.

Like it or not, I was a queen now.

And I needed something.

2

Patience is but a game, and those who have it will always win.

—Sultan Raj of Cheryn

FELIPE THREW OPEN the door to my chamber and entered in front of me, to clear it of danger, a formality he insisted upon that made me roll my eyes. But to my surprise, my guard lowered his spear and growled, his legs vanishing and his navy tail magically replacing them, whipping back and forth as he disappeared behind the door. I heard low murmurs, but Felipe didn't yell for other guards to join him. So the danger couldn't have been that great.

Curiosity got the best of me, and though I knew I'd get an earful for it later, I fluttered my wings and swam forward just enough to peer around the opaque edge of the glass door.

Sarding shite!

There, at the end of Felipe's spear, his arms raised and palms turned out to show he meant no harm, was my fool of a brother-in-law. His blond hair flickered slightly in the waves we'd created entering the room, but other than widening his ice-blue eyes, he didn't move. He was right to stay still; Felipe took his job seriously.

"Declan!" I exclaimed in a reprimanding tone. *Why the hell is he here?*

Felipe's head did a slow swivel. He glowered at me as I'd known he would, his jaw going tight and his hand clamping down even harder on his weapon as he pulled it back slightly from Declan's neck. "You know this fool?" he spat out.

"Unfortunately. He's married to my sister." Felipe had only been assigned to me after I booted my heroic sister and her husbands from the castle because Bloss was too domineering for her own good, like all big sisters.

I narrowed my eyes at Declan as Felipe yanked his spear back but came to stand protectively in front of me. I leaned around my guard's wide shoulders as I shook my head at my brother-in-law. They hadn't even been gone a fortnight. "You couldn't even give me—"

"Call the tournament off." Declan crossed his arms and glared at me, bossiness oozing from every pore. Gills were on Declan's neck, magicked there by the undead witch Lizza, no doubt, so he could make the journey here on a gargoyle, letting the stone beast tromp beneath the waves toward my palace.

Ugh.

Why was he back? The only conclusion I could come to was that Bloss didn't trust me to take care of myself, which nettled me. Especially now. All I'd wanted was a moment alone after the procession of idiots. A moment where I closed the door to my bedchamber and dramatically flopped onto my bed out of sight, wishing I'd never stabbed myself in the chest to begin with and this nightmare parade would just fade away.

But now I wouldn't get my little pout. My cry. I wouldn't get to purge myself of all the stupid emotions battering my stomach before facing a night full of strangers, because my interfering sister and her husbands couldn't leave well enough alone.

I narrowed my eyes at Declan, who hadn't seemed to realize he was addressing a queen. "That's quite the greeting for a foreign monarch," I told the man I'd once been sweet on, back when I was young and foolish—before I'd realized what an overbearing oaf he was. Annoyance—the type that was a result of years of fondness and familiarity and knowing far too much about one another—filled me.

"Oh. Excuse me. Call off the tournament, *Your Majesty*." Declan gave a half-assed bow, sarcasm apparent in his every move. His smile said he knew just how he rankled me.

My nostrils flared, and I glanced back at Sahar, who looked shocked to see Declan here. At least she was cleared of any malfeasance. Who had let him in?

"What happened to your face?" Declan's jaw dropped a bit when I turned and he caught a glance of the squid ink. His gaze turned accusingly toward my guard.

"Nothing!" I snapped, hating how my dress jingled when I walked toward my dressing room, hating how my cheeks flushed and my heart dipped, knowing people hated me so much.

"I can taste your despair over it, you know, so it's not nothing!" Declan retorted.

I'd already been close to the tipping point, but that comment made my fury build like an inferno. How dare he use his magic to invade my privacy! "Do you taste that? It's called anger! At you!" I yelled, forgoing propriety and all sense, not caring that downstairs, strangers were slowly being let into the castle for the opening dinner and ball, and my door was still open. How dare he? How dare he say that in front of Felipe and Sahar? "Privacy please," I growled at my guard and adviser.

Immediately, they bowed their heads and retreated, swimming out the door, Felipe giving me one last look before closing it carefully behind them. I could still see his shadow through the opaque glass, but the semblance of privacy was the best a queen ever got anyway.

"What the sard are you doing?" I hissed at Dec.

"Preventing you from doing something you'll regret," he replied, striding over to my tufted couch, a shipwreck find that had been brought in recently.

"I won't regret it!" I snarled and dug my nails into my palms. Part of me wished I had access to my magic so that I could blast him with a jet stream of water. But a sea sprite could only access magic if she sacrificed all emotions, her heart, her humanity. And mine still beat weakly in my chest.

"You will. Look at Bloss." He jerked his hand to the side, gesturing as if she were next to him. "She couldn't handle the pressure—"

"Well, I'm not her!" This was exactly why I'd kicked them out of my castle. Overbearing, arrogant—

Declan didn't listen to my retort, just stepped within slapping range as he continued, "And she *knew us*, Avia. Your sister knew her intended grooms, most of them anyway, and she wasn't ready. You're trying to find strangers to wed, in a kingdom you don't even know—"

"And whose fault is that?" I yanked the crown off my head and stomped around him to the dresser where I slammed it down. "Dead women's. It's theirs, and there's not a damned thing anyone can do about it. It is what it is." I grabbed a rag off the dresser and leaned into the mirror. *Ack!* My face was horrifying. Nearly half of it was a mottled blue-black, like a giant bruise. Splatters of darkness went across the bridge of my nose and speckled my other cheek. I peeled my teeth back and saw that they hadn't escaped the destruction. They looked like pale agate stones.

I looked worse than the undead flower sprite, Posey, who had joined my army. And that was saying something, because half the skin around her mouth had rotted away. Perfect. What a lovely way to start the tournament for husbands. At least it would sort the shallow ones out. I scrubbed furiously at my stained cheek, even as I tried to strangle Declan's reflection with my eyes. My eyes, which had turned violet when my magical nature had been revealed.

Until merely months ago, my reflection had shown brown eyes, brown hair, a human girl. Now, I had golden hair, violet eyes, and iridescent scales lining my cheekbones, the outsides of my arms and legs, and wings that were as wide and gorgeous as betta fish fins that I thought of as wings. Everything about my appearance had changed. Just as I felt I had. I'd grown harder in the caves where my birth mother had held me prisoner. Months ago, I might not have resisted Declan so strongly. Now, I felt no compunction to do as he wished.

"Exactly. You've been tossed about all your life, used as a pawn. I know what that's like." His voice grew soft and gentle. His parents had tossed him across the ocean as a treaty toy when he was young, so he spoke the truth.

I let my hard expression ease a bit as I said, "Yes, well, I'm not a pawn anymore. And you seem to be unable to comprehend that this is my choice. Mine." I jabbed a finger at my chest and nearly broke a nail on one of the coins sewn into the bodice. I ignored my throbbing finger, because what I was about to say was too important. "This kingdom has been all but forgotten. Wiped from the map. And I have the power and connections to change that." *If I live,* I thought wryly. But Declan hadn't brought up that little tidbit yet, so at least my overbearing sister seemed to have enough sense to respect my privacy to keep that secret. A little. A very little.

Actually, I didn't quite feel like forgiving her, but tapping into the longing I felt earlier, becoming wistful and wishing she were here, might make me cry. I couldn't afford to pout, much less cry, because I had to change and get downstairs, so I just swept that thought under the rug. I stuck with one thought: Bloss was an ass for sending him.

Declan sighed. "You're just as stubborn as she is, you know."

I laughed and turned to face him, spreading my wings to either side and then leaning back against the dresser. "How dare you! *I'm* the nice one." But I said it with a smile on my face.

He chuckled. "Sometimes, I think you might be the cleverer one. Definitely more astute about all the ridiculous elbow-rubbing."

"True. Bloss is more of an elbow-to-the-face kind of girl." We shared a conspiratorial laugh, and the tension in the room lowered a bit. "I understand your intentions. And I appreciate them. I really do. But I'm fine."

A knock at the door interrupted whatever Declan had been about to say. It swung open, and Sahar and Felipe drifted back in gracefully.

"I'm sorry, Your Majesty, but you have to get ready." Sahar tried to smooth over her interruption with a smile.

As if she'd been waiting for Sahar's voice as her cue to enter, one of my handmaids, a mermaid named Gita, swam out of a servant's door at the back of the room, her golden tail glimmering, her breasts free and unbound as was the custom under the sea. A silver necklace with a modified seahorse on it, the sign of the royal house, swung on her neck and smacked against her breasts when she stopped suddenly at the sight of me.

"Oh, Your Majesty!" She didn't soften the dismay in her tone at all as her eyes traveled over my stained face.

"Can I get something mint-flavored? Some of it got in my mouth." I grinned to show her my awful teeth, and she recoiled.

"Yes. I will fetch you something. And some cream to remove that, um ... *squid* ink?" she asked delicately, trying to verify the source of my humiliation.

I nodded before I turned back to Declan.

He just shook his head and sighed. "Bloss was right. We should have stayed longer. Helped you settle in."

"I'm doing just fine, thank you," I gritted out as I fluttered my wings and swam awkwardly over to the dressing partition, my dress clanking obnoxiously. My shoulders were ready to be rid of the thing, aching from the weight. As soon as I was hidden, I slid the straps down carefully, cracking my neck as soon as the bodice fell around my hips. The physical relief was counteracted by Declan's sharp words.

"Why are you so resistant to our help?"

Hidden, I didn't bother to answer. I focused on wiggling out of the tight coin monstrosity. By the time I got it off, I was panting and pretty certain that if I'd been on land, I would have wanted to burn the thing. I didn't know how they handled such things under the sea. Was there a volcanic cleft somewhere I could toss the torture device and watch it melt?

I wanted to kick it aside, but doing so would probably break my toe. Instead, I stood and listened as Sahar tried to smooth things over. "King Declan, please take a seat. Would you like something to drink? We've got a wonderful collection of fermented seaweed bubbles you could sip on while Her Majesty gets ready."

"No, thank you kindly. I'd rather just wait—"

"It might be an hour!" I called out, just to rankle him. I didn't expect changing to take that long, but it could if I needed it to …

"That's an hour where you can listen while I talk sense into you," he countered.

"Sahar, get the man a drink. Or five."

Declan's chuckle drifted over to me. "You're not getting out of this."

I rolled my eyes and reached for a robe that hung on a nearby hook. I tossed it on backward. It was easier to tie loosely at my waist and leave space for my fins. I didn't walk back out, because that would have been awkward.

Instead, I peered around the screen. "I don't need a nanny."

"How about a tutor?"

I glared at him and then glanced over at Felipe, who stood solemnly by the door, which was once again shut to maintain my privacy, because my guard, unlike my brother-in-law, was thoughtful. "Would it start a war if you stabbed him?"

"Definitely," Declan declared.

"Nope," Felipe's curt response came at the same time.

"Maybe," Sahar replied.

I laughed when Declan's head jerked back toward Felipe. "Excuse me!" he grumbled at the guard. "I'm a foreign king!"

Felipe shrugged nonchalantly despite his armor. "Underwater breathing spells wear off all the time."

"Ha ha!" I crowed. "See that, Dec? Better not mess with me! No more bossing."

Felipe gave me a smug grin, and I couldn't help the tiny little bubble that rose in my stomach before I ducked back behind the screen. I should have switched him out for an uglier guard. But he was good at his job and proud of it. I swallowed that bubble down and tried to pop it. I didn't have time for girlish crushes anymore. I was due to select my mates via an old Okeanos tradition. I was bound to choose only from men who completed the tournament. But then a thought occurred to me. I hadn't really been able to see the competitors in the parade. What if all my people hated me? What if they'd chosen the rejects of their families? What if they'd chosen the sons who wouldn't work or couldn't work? The ones who still lived in the hayloft in their parents' barn? Wait... I didn't know the underwater equivalent. But suddenly I was a bit nervous about what I'd signed myself up for.

"No hiding!" Declan demanded.

"I'm not hiding, I'm naked back here! I'm showing decorum."

"Ew. You just made it awkward," Declan chided.

"You're the one who barged in here after I told Bloss I didn't need any help."

"You know I can taste your fear?" Dec said softly after a moment.

Dammit. How dare he go and say something like that again! I regretted immediately that I hadn't used our time alone to threaten his life for doing it.

"Stop that at once!" I commanded.

Sahar swooped in with more courtesy chatter to break up our impending fight.

I focused on taking a calming breath so that Declan couldn't taste anything else. The bastard could magically taste emotions now, and that was nearly as annoying as his personality. I couldn't hide anything. I was relieved when Gita returned, and I concentrated on ignoring Declan and watching her. She bustled about, swimming here and there to set out rags and creams and makeup so that she could clean me up. Declan was drawn into conversation with Sahar about tradition and left me in peace as my maid bounced about getting me ready.

She slid a new gown over my head, this time a soft golden lace with only an under layer of silk running over my torso and thighs for modesty because I'd insisted upon it. I was not wearing lace alone without any kind of undergarment whatsoever. The seamstress and I had a very heated discussion over it. She'd won the color battle though. Gold again, because apparently, that was to be my royal color. I straightened the long lace sleeves and pulled a loop over each of my middle fingers to secure them.

"Oh no, the seamstress ruined it!" Gita straightened from where she'd been fixing my train and started tugging at my plunging neckline. "She's covered your breasts!"

I heard Declan have a coughing fit behind the screen. My maid tried to shove the neckline aside, forcing my breasts to fall out. I yelped and turned, covering myself.

As I wrestled my breasts back into the gown, I said softly, "No, she didn't. I asked for it," hoping with every fiber of my being that Felipe was not overhearing this conversation. Otherwise, I might just find one of those volcanic crevices and shove my own head in instead of melting that coin dress.

I heard Sahar rush to my rescue once more. "So, Declan, how was your journey here?"

"Uneventful. Rode a gargoyle."

"You have any saddle sores from it?" Sahar asked. "Her Majesty wants to ride that Pony character throughout the tournament, but as we'll be touring the kingdom, I worry about the stone rubbing against her—"

"STOP! No more talking. Nobody in this room gets to talk!" I shouted as I strode out from behind the dressing room, breasts thankfully covered. "By all that is or ever was, are you all attempting to drive me *mad*? No talk of my *areas*." I gestured wildly at my body.

Sahar, ever the stateswoman, maintained a calm face, but I noticed Felipe had to raise a hand to cover his snicker.

Wonderful. Great. Guess I'd be the talk of the guard room tonight. I needed a map. It looked like a trip to a volcanic crevice was in my near future. That would solve all the stupid heart problems and tournament worries in one.

Sahar cleared her throat and changed the subject, turning to Declan where he reclined on the couch. She moved to sit in a chair opposite him, a move she'd taught me about breaking difficult news. She believed it was more effective to remain on the same physical level as the other person, not to float above them when they were sitting or vice versa. She thought it important to be on the same physical wavelength, equal footing ... or was it finning? "Even if Her Majesty wanted your help, I'd have to advise her against it. Her position here under the sea is already tenuous. She needs to prove her loyalty to her people and our ways."

"By marrying strangers!"

"By selecting suitors who represent the interests of the various groups here. Marriage can be delayed ... for a time," she amended. Sahar glanced at me, looking gorgeous, having changed for the ball while I'd ranted at Declan. She had pink sea stars clinging to her chest, with a bright purple sarong floating down from her hips. As a siren, she was preternaturally beautiful, even with the streaks of silver in her hair, which she chose not to magic away. Unlike many of the sirens that I'd met thus far, Sahar didn't seem to revel in her looks or use them to her advantage. She was far more concerned with educating me on the politics of Okeanos. Sun up to well after moonrise, she was at my side, teaching me about the various towns. Reef City, a bright bustling metropolis full of fun but also a bit of violence. Navagio, a town composed entirely of the recycled bits from shipwrecks … and others. I couldn't wait to see them all.

In fact, the plan was for the tournament to visit each of the major towns under the ocean. One competition would be hosted at each. It was going to be my tour of the country, my introduction to the people. Letting them watch their hometown heroes compete for my hand would soften them toward me, or so Sahar had advised.

I didn't mind the competition, *except* for the part related to my hand …

I blew out a breath.

No wonder Bloss had run.

Declan smacked his lips, running his tongue over them. "Tastes of fear in here."

"It's going to taste of blood if you don't shut up."

A knock came at my door just then, and Felipe answered, allowing a page to swim inside. The boy, who couldn't have been more than twelve, had the red hair of a hermit shifter, and a small ornamental shield shell at his back. He was bright-eyed and brimming with excitement when he said, "The contestants are ready, Your Majesty."

I gave a nod and tried not to fist my hands or give any indication that my skin suddenly felt as chilled as if I'd been dropped onto an iceberg.

Declan stood and walked over to me. He held out an arm. "Don't worry. Bloss and I have already figured out a solution."

My fear melted as though by magic. Instead of taking Declan's arm, I strode past him and then used my wing-like fins to launch myself down the hall. Because no one was going to solve my problems but me.

3

Beauty is a trick of the eye, designed to fool the mind into complacency. It's been the start of many a great deception.

—Sultan Raj of Cheryn

I TOOK A DEEP, completely unhelpful breath that did absolutely nothing to calm my nerves as I stood outside the grand ballroom. I slid my hands nervously down the sides of the new gown I was wearing, which had been cut like kelp to flutter gracefully around my legs as I swam. I adjusted the necklace that Bloss had sent me as a gift, the thick gold chain studded every so often with an etched bead that pictured the seahorse that was the symbol of Okeanos. Etched on the back of the seahorse pendant that dangled from the front was the rose of Evaness. That shite Declan had only just given it to me when that should have been his first order of business. I was even angrier with him because the sight had brought tears to my eyes, and that longing for my sister that I'd been fighting pierced my hollow armor.

I'd punched Dec and then made him put the necklace on me.

"It's got a bit of elven chain in there," Declan had whispered when he'd closed the clasp. "That will protect you from a lot of spells."

I glared at him. "More protection?"

He shook his head seriously. "Raj is still out there. We'll find him. But until we do, it's best to be cautious. Besides, Bloss said you always admired your mother's necklaces." I didn't bother to correct him, didn't tell him I'd started to call the woman Gela in my head. That wouldn't do any good.

I tried to accept the gift for what it was, a symbol that Bloss still cared, still wanted to be there for me, still thought of me as a sister. And that bolstered me. It gave me the courage to face what came next, to be as fearless as the woman I still considered my sister, blood or no. I might not want her advice *at all*, but I needed her support.

My hand drifted up to my raw cheeks and then checked the arrangement of my hair, which Gita had changed slightly, piling my braids higher on top of my head in a scalloped shell pattern. Then I nodded to the servants, who opened the double doors. In sea kingdom formation, we swam rather than walked through, me in front, Felipe and another guard behind me. The entire room bowed their heads at my entrance, and for a second, I felt overwhelmed by the sheer volume of people I'd need to meet and entertain. My eyes sought Sahar, who had come ahead of me. I needed to focus on at least one friendly face.

I spotted her next to a few young men, not far from the glass throne I'd get to sit on for the evening's festivities. Luckily, someone had seen to my comfort and added a sea sponge to the seat so that I had a cushion. The throne, while beautiful and carved to resemble a perfectly symmetrical scallop shell, was not the most comfortable, as I'd discovered last week during my audience hours.

As the crowd rose out of their bows, I swam forward with a soft, hopefully confident smile. My wings fluttered behind me, pushing water back as though it were light as air. Though I never said it aloud, I still constantly marveled at the magic that made this undersea world feel light and weightless, at the fact that each breath didn't feel like a heavy swish of water in and out of my lungs.

Making eye contact here and there, I took in the ballroom, a room that looked like a bubble chopped in half. Glowing mother-of-pearl walls rose into a dome. Magical torches flickered along the walls in rows, set in elaborate blue glass sconces shaped like sea fan coral. The blue of the glass and the flickers of orange flame contrasted magically in a way that stole even my breath away.

I could only imagine what the sea men who had come here to compete thought of it. My eyes drifted over the crowd, making brief eye contact with several very attractive men. Heat flared up my neck when one of them, a tall, dark-haired stranger, stared up and down my figure deliberately. *Oh my.*

I quickly slid my eyes away from that dangerous distraction and focused on the older couples clustered around the room. Many of the competitors had made the journey to the castle with their families, and so, luckily, the ballroom wasn't filled only with men, otherwise I might have had a heart attack from muscle overdose. Most of the men were shirtless, as was Okeanos' custom.

I passed a man with arms the size of a tree. *He'd snap me in half!* It took a lot of effort not to let my eyes widen, and even more not to mentally cross him off the list just because he was gigantic. Perhaps he was part giant, like Ryan, another brother-in-law of mine. Perhaps he was kind like Ryan.

My eyes met Tina's, the squi-maid I'd transferred this morning, and she bobbed her head respectfully though her eyes darted away from me. She looked lovely in a bright orange skirt with bits of matching coral arranged in her hair. I'd requested, much to the scandalized dismay of Sahar and my castle steward, Brontes, that the maids be given dresses and attend tonight's ball.

Brontes, a shark shifter whose wrinkled face was nearly as lined as the rotting plank that served as his desk, had argued ferociously against my proposal. "Your Majesty! It's just not done!"

My argument was that I'd never be able to entertain thirty competitors at once, and they all needed dance partners.

And so, the castle dressmakers had gotten the commission of their lifetime. Of course, Okeanos' dresses were a bit less work than those made by the seamstresses in Evaness. The sea women mainly went topless, because the mer didn't have the same human views on modesty. It was something that took a bit of mental adjustment for me, and I had to work hard not to stare, particularly whenever the women swam quickly, their tails pumping back and forth and breasts bouncing. I wanted to face-palm on their behalf. But alas, I was the odd one out underneath the waves. No one else found it the least bit embarrassing, not even the maid when I was blown over by a current two days past and accidentally grabbed her breast. I felt my cheeks heat at the memory, embarrassment coloring them bright pink. I was lucky that she hadn't been one of the maids here who resented me, the ones who darted dirty looks in my direction when they thought I wasn't looking.

They thought they were clever, but I was no fool. I knew I was lucky to have a loyal guard and a ruthlessly efficient, undead half-sprite named Posey at my back. Without them, I'd have been a sitting duck, an easy target. I glanced around but didn't spot Posey, who hadn't wanted to attend the affair.

"One of those idiots is bound to rip my limbs off! And they're only hanging on by a thread as it is!" Posey had smoothed back the petals she had in place of hair—as she was part flower sprite—her rotting flesh adding credence to her words. It was no surprise the zombie hadn't come, but still a bit of a letdown. I enjoyed her company.

I tried to refocus my thoughts toward the women who *had* attended. Nearly every maid had accepted my offer—one Queen Gela would have called a bribe. Hopefully, it would endear me to the female population of the staff. Because, as I'd heard a thousand times throughout my childhood, "A castle rises or falls based on the happiness of those within its walls." While Gela didn't teach me to believe emotions were appropriate for a queen, she did believe in using them against others. I didn't prescribe to all of her theories. But some ... some rang true as a bell.

The happy faces of a few maids made me hope that I might have made the right decision. And their joy made me feel good. Because my favorite part of growing up in a castle had been feeling like my family was huge, full of hundreds, not just my parents and Bloss.

My gaze landed on Declan, who hadn't turned around and ridden off into the shoreline like I'd told him to do. The overbearing know-it-all stood near a punchbowl at the end of a table full of food along the far wall. Declan spoke with some man I didn't know in serious tones, his blond hair turned eerily blue by reflections from a nearby sconce.

Bloss had sealed his fate by sending him to me. I'd have to find some utterly obnoxious way to get rid of him now if he didn't sneak out soon.

What a shite she is, I thought fondly, touching my necklace again as I sat down on my throne and halfway cursed how well she knew me. She'd sent the one husband of hers she knew I was closest to, trying to manipulate this whole debacle. For all our faux hatred, Declan knew he held a prized place in my heart. And to him, I would always be a precious, precocious little sister. I knew exactly why he was here, even if Declan didn't. Bloss wanted me to call off this tournament, cede the crown, and focus all my energy on finding a cure for my heart.

As if it would be *so* simple. Bloss needed to step back.

"Bitch," I muttered, my ire overcoming me in a way Queen Gela would have found utterly disappointing.

Felipe leaned close. "Sorry, Your Majesty, I couldn't quite catch that."

I glanced quickly at him, then stared at the sigil on his chest. It was a seahorse that had been fashioned with metallic spikes like spears protruding from its back. A violent representation of Okeanos' historical sigil, fitting of my birth mother. A monster's sigil. Now mine.

Felipe cleared his throat, recalling me from my wandering thoughts and forcing my eyes back up to his. "I was cursing my sister." The honest truth spilled from my lips unbidden.

Felipe pressed his lips together in amusement. He could infer enough from this disastrous interaction with Declan to understand why, I was certain. "I see." He gave me a curt nod and went to take his place at my right side, a hand on his spear, his presence warm and comforting in a room that felt like it was full of curious and judgmental eyes.

A gong sounded and the conversation in the room came to a slow, faltering stop as everyone in the room turned to my throne. Though I'd just had all eyes on me on the balcony, that was different, more removed. This time the gaze of the crowd felt heavy, like a weight on my shoulders. I used my best calm and courtly face and gave a soft smile as I raised a hand. "Welcome all. I'm delighted to have you join the Syzygos Tournament. I look forward to meeting each and every competitor tonight. The best of luck to you all."

The crowd clapped politely in response to my announcement, and I did the single gracious head nod and smile I'd watched Gela perfect at functions like this when I crawled through the hallways and bribed the footmen with sweets so I could peer through the cracked door.

Not so long ago, that had been my greatest exposure to these "adult functions."

Now, I had to keep my eyes from widening as the music started up and the dancing began. Sahar stepped out in front of my dais to give me a moment to adjust and have a drink before I had to speak with all of my suitors.

I forced myself not to gulp the fermented kelp bubbles that a server brought to me. The taste was similar to ale but with a briny tinge. The important thing about tonight's bubble was that it was potent, intended to get everyone in the castle into a festive mood. I wanted to down the glass and ask for two more. Instead, I sipped at it delicately, eyes on the swim floor.

Watching a ball underwater was fascinating. Instead of being bound to the floor for a dance, the participants moved through space, weaving up and down, creating diagonal lines through the water. Whereas circles and squares were common dance formations back in Evaness, cubes and three-dimensional diamonds were the norm here. My eyes couldn't help but be drawn to the fluttering skirts of the women, the formal shell necklaces strung around each man's neck.

Laughter and conversation mixed and melded with the music as people began to relax and enjoy the occasion. But just as my guests began to make merry, my own torture began.

Sahar escorted the first suitor up the stairs.

I thought my heart had faltered on the balcony. That was nothing compared to the wild nosedive it did now.

The sea man's hair was as red as blood, it was parted in the middle, and soft tendrils drifted down either side of his face, ending near his eyes, eyes that were such a dark brown they were nearly black. He was thin, but his shoulders were at least three times as wide as his hips, so not unattractive. A flat black shell was strapped to his back like a shield; I could make out symbols carved onto the edges. The man bowed gracefully, twisting his wrist with flourish.

When he rose, I could tell the smile in his eyes was friendly, not judgmental.

"Why, hello there, Majesty." His accent spoke of far-off places, but it was also warm and inviting, a slow drawl to it.

"Call me Avia, please."

"Radford."

"Nice to meet you," I responded. I noted that while his skin was pale, he was covered in freckles that seemed thicker on the backs of his arms and neck. Up close, there were even two I could spot underneath his left eyes. He took my hand, and his touch made me hyper-aware since his palm was rough, the pads of his fingers thick and calloused.

His touch was proper but firm and called to some baser, instinctual part of my mind, a part that told me to step closer. I resisted it of course, suddenly grateful for the elven chain around my neck, but at the same time, a bit unnerved. Because he couldn't be enchanting me, though he was.

"Nicer for me, I should think." He gave me a wink, but it didn't feel sly, it felt playful. "I've got the better view." His cheeks grew pink. So did mine.

Did one compliment men on their looks? I wasn't sure.

I liked the way he playfully bit his lip, like he was almost embarrassed he'd said that. He glanced up at the dancers swirling above us before he cleared his throat and added, "This castle is a mite bigger than my shell back home, for sure."

"It is a bit big, isn't it?" I glanced around the ballroom, which could have housed a blue whale.

"Compensating for anything, Majesty?" There was a sparkle in his eye and a twitch at the corner of his lips, and suddenly I had the mad urge to make him laugh, to watch that twitch become a full-blown smile. I was willing to bet a smile would catapult him from striking to irresistible.

Radford was being playful. He was unafraid of me. Possibly even attracted, if his first statement were true. Not full of vitriol. If I were on land, I'd have called him a breath of fresh air. His playfulness was catching. I released his hand to tug thoughtfully at my hair as if I were considering his question seriously. "Well, size does matter, of course. In a castle."

He chuckled and the sound was just as husky and endearing as I'd imagined. "You're more fun than I expected."

"Yes, well, you're the lucky first. I expect I'll get more boring as the night goes on and I run out of things to say."

He looked back at the long line of sea men waiting to meet me, some of whom waited patiently, others less so. When his gaze swung back around, it was thoughtful. "Here's my trick. When I run outta things to say, I just say, 'Interesting.' Seems to work alright." He followed his advice with a dip of his head.

"Does it? Interesting." I couldn't help the smile that crossed my features at the look of sly approval he gave me. We held one another's gazes for a moment, and all the fear and anticipation I'd felt building up to tonight suddenly seemed foolish. This was easy. Radford made it easy.

But suddenly Radford's posture stiffened. The twinkle in his eyes changed. That little curl at the corner of his mouth flattened. And then he spoke, wiping away the ease he'd just handed me. "Majesty, you look as radiant as a volcanic eruption."

My eyes widened. *Was that an insult? Or a bad compliment?* Shite. What had just happened? Had I been too familiar? Had I done something to offend him? I'd prepared with Sahar, practiced conversations even, to understand the different greetings. The hermit crab shifters were supposed to be more informal, more relaxed. And he had been, but now … his entire posture had grown stiff. I must have done something wrong.

Sahar was busy, wrapped up in a conversation with the next man in line. I'd have to improvise.

"Yes, well, I'm certain everyone believes I'm as volatile as a volcano. Sadly, I'll disappoint you there. I'm pretty boring," I told him, trying to take what might have been an insult and turn it into an olive branch. Secretly though, I chanted in my head, *I hope it was a joke. Please let it be a joke. Please let this be one of those awkward moments when someone's made a joke that no one else gets and then they retract it.*

He didn't retract it. Instead, he made it worse. "I'm not so sure about that. Sure, sitting in a castle, eating food someone else has prepared for you all day long, sitting on a throne and listening to people drone on about their problems—I'm sure you do think that's plenty boring. But—"

"I'm so pleased to meet you. I hope you enjoy the ball." I tried to cut off whatever mad rant had suddenly taken over Radford, erasing the charming man who'd mounted the steps. My mind raced like a thoroughbred. Sahar had warned me that some of the shifters were a bit unstable, but she'd mentioned the predators, not the crabs! Was Radford mad? Did he have some sort of mania?

Please, Sahar, stop chatting and save me.

"Starting this husband hunt off with lies, huh? Seems like a good precedent." Radford's eyes widened suddenly, and he put his hand over his mouth. He shook his head as if he couldn't believe he'd had the audacity to say that.

Frankly, I couldn't either. I wasn't certain what was going on. I was sure that he didn't seem all there.

Felipe seemed to notice my distress and swam closer.

Radford stared at him in shock for a second before blurting out, "I'm sorry. I dunno what happened." Color rose on his neck and spread up to his cheeks and down toward his defined pecs as if he was blushing so furiously the color had stained his entire body.

"Foot-in-mouth disease?" I suggested, feeling a bit more confident and less adrift now that my guard was beside me.

"Blow to the head recently?" Felipe queried.

"Well..." Radford gave a sideways tilt of his head. "I didn't think it was that recent, but maybe you're right." He glanced out into the crowd. When he looked at me, his features hardened again, but he slid his eyes so quickly back to Felipe that I questioned what I'd seen.

"What do you do for work?" Felipe asked conversationally.

"I'm a whale breaker." Radford lifted a red brow and gave a grin, the sweet man from the start of our conversation emerging once more.

I just looked at Felipe, feeling as clueless and confused as I had during my first day in Okeanos' court.

My guard leaned sideways toward me, and a shock of grey hair that ran through his blue mane fell forward as he whispered, "I believe the land-based equivalent would be a man who trains hoses."

"Horses?" I questioned.

"Yes, those." Felipe nodded.

"Hmmm. Thank you." I'd seen Jace, the stable master in Evaness, suffer from a kick to the head more than once. Perhaps that's all this was. A crack to the skull had made Radford loopy. I'd send a castle mage his way to check on him later. How embarrassing. I tried to ignore the offense I'd taken and have a bit of compassion instead.

"Can those horses on land crush a trainer's spine with a flick of their tail?" Radford questioned, an insulted throb in his jaw. "I think it's a mite more dangerous down here in the deep," he told Felipe.

My guard just looked at me, eyes wide. "I've never seen a hose, horse. Aren't they covered in scales? Don't they breathe fire?"

I suppressed a giggle. It was completely unacceptable for a queen to laugh at another's ignorance. Another of Gela's lessons that had been smelted into my brain. "Horses are soft and covered in hair not scales. They run, don't fly, and while they're taller than a man, they're much smaller than a tree—" I realized by their blank looks that was a bad comparison. "I mean, they're about the size of a dolphin."

Both of them gave knowing nods, and my stomach fell when Radford's eyes darkened aggressively again, and he pressed on. "But could those beasts swallow a man whole? My whales could—"

"Your whales eat krill," Felipe countered, unable to help himself. "Tiny fish smaller than …" He held up two fingers and pinched them together.

I fought a smile as my guard and this stranger threw eye daggers at each other. While I would have liked to prolong the moment for my own amusement, I was here to make friends not enemies. Radford was wavering on the edge of the two, and while my ignorance about the sea kingdom was vast, my knowledge of politics was not.

When it all came down to it, countries were the same. People were the same. Whether they had scales or petals or skin ... they wanted three things: to belong, to be proud, and to be envied. I let false admiration light my expression.

"So you must be wonderful with animals, right, Radford?" I pretended an interest I didn't feel, throwing in his name to add a sense of familiarity. Animals had never been a passion of mine. I hadn't spent any great amount of time at the barn, unlike Bloss and Connor, her "childhood best friend turned husband number four of five." Although that didn't really matter. Especially not now.

But unfortunately for me, the insane Radford re-emerged. His mouth twisted cruelly as he looked at me. "The ignorant might call it good with animals. But really, what it is ... I'm quite good with a whip. I'll show you sometime." He let a dark, meaningful look accompany this statement, the kind that made goose bumps rise on my arms.

Blow to the head or not, I was done with tiptoeing around him. Anymore and I was likely to actually break a toe. He was too changeable. Too unpredictable. Until a mage saw him or a healer cleared him, I wanted little to do with him.

"Well, it's been very nice meeting you." *I hope I never have to speak with you again.* "This conversation was most enlightening." *It couldn't have been more awkward.* "Please, help yourself to some clams." *If you choke on them, you might save us both a lot of future misery.* I redacted that last thought because it was a smidge mean, though I couldn't help thinking it. That interaction had been painfully strange.

Radford gave a bow and quickly swam off without looking back. I wasn't certain if he or I was the more relieved. Felipe and I shared a subtle "can you believe that" look before he swam back to his post at the side of my throne, slightly behind me.

Sahar was at my side before I could even let out a deep, cleansing breath. "Your Majesty, may I present the next *fool* attempting to win your hand?" Her voice was harsh and completely void of the diplomatic sheen she normally spread on every word.

My eyes widened as I looked from Sahar, the one woman I'd come to trust here, to the very angry, very handsome young siren next to her. He looked younger than most of the other competitors. He was fit but lean, with golden skin typical of sirens, but he'd made his hair a bright white blond with a lightning bolt of green slashing down one shorn side. His chin dimple was pretty adorable even if he did have quite a baby face still. He actually looked close to my age, unlike the dozens of other competitors who looked more like they should be my tutors.

"Queen Avia, meet Keelan. My son." Her entire body was stiff and full of tension. She stayed, hovering in place for a moment before Keelan cleared his throat loudly and Sahar gave a shake of her head before she swam back to the line, which now wrapped around one side of the ballroom.

"Welcome."

"You're charmed, I'm sure," Keelan said as he scooped up my hand and gave it a kiss. "It's alright to admit it. I'm pretty amazing." He crossed his sparkling amber eyes and stuck out his tongue like a doof. He was lucky his dimples were the size of canyons and his voice was deep and resonant. I worked very hard not to notice the muscles on his pecs as he continued to be silly, because I'd just been burnt by a man being silly, one who'd turned out to be insane. Still, though I worked to tamp down on my natural attraction this time, his ridiculousness deserved to be answered in kind.

"Yes, that right there was *so* talented," I complimented. "Very few people can cross their eyes with such finesse."

"I know. I should use that pose for statues more often. But generally, they want these babies on display." He flexed and my throat most certainly did not dry out because of it. I just suddenly needed another sip of my fermented bubble.

I was torn between amusement and suspicion over Keelan. He seemed to be mocking himself, but I wasn't quite certain. And after Radford, I was hesitant. "And who buys these statues of you?"

"Fishwives everywhere." He winked again, and I began to wonder if that was his signature move. "Or, at least, they *would*. I've been trying to get mother to invest in them for years, if she would only commission a few thousand, they would sell instantly … alas, she has no business sense. She's a bit … feebleminded." He said the last loudly enough for Sahar to overhear.

To my surprise, she swam back over to us. Her eyes narrowed suspiciously on her son as she asked, "What are you saying?"

My eyes darted between them, her annoyance as tightly tuned as a harp.

"I was just lamenting how you won't invest in my statuary business."

She rolled her eyes, staring at me with an expression that said, "I'm sorry. I tried to prevent this." Aloud, she said, "There has to be a willing market, son. And no one wants to see your blobfish self sitting in their garden each morn—"

"You see? She's practically senile." He gestured at Sahar and shook his head, wearing a wide-eyed, completely innocent expression that I knew to be a complete lie.

He was poking the bear, as we would have said in Evaness. And he was enjoying the hell out of it. He turned to me and gestured at those pecs I was avoiding. "Is there any blob on this fish? Seriously. You can tell me. I won't cry. At least not in public."

Sahar shook her head fondly at him. "You obnoxious little sea monkey." She turned to me. "I told him he wasn't serious enough for court life, Your Majesty."

"Do you hear that madness?" Keelan put a shocked hand on his chest.

Sahar's fist tightened, and I realized this banter must be common between the two of them. "You've got barnacles for brains."

Given that Sahar was this man's mother, I thought I might be a bit safer jesting than I'd been last time. So I decided to play along, because this was literally the most amusing thing that had happened to me since I'd inked Bloss, but also because I felt secure enough in my relationship with Sahar to tease her a bit. After all, we were side by side day in and day out. I let my brow furrow as I stared at the siren woman in concern. "Oh dear. She does sound a bit off. Are you feeling okay?"

Sahar narrowed her eyes at me, and a crease appeared right between her brows. "Your Majesty?" Her tone grew suspicious.

I turned to Keelan, false concern written all over my expression. "Do you hear that? She's slurring her words. You're right. She must be going loony."

"Yes! You see! It's the only possible explanation for why she won't invest all her sand dollars in my risk-free, *return-guaranteed* statue scheme!"

"Well, you know, if you ever need to bypass her, I can send her wages directly to you, you know, so you can ensure she gets the care she needs." I let the years of practice at court make my tone drip with excessively false concern.

Keelan's shoulders shook as he laughed, and Sahar glared at me ferociously, though I could see she had to tamp down on a grin quite a few times. It was actually a quite delicious feeling to tease someone I liked, but without any true fury or malice—unlike Declan, whom I was still halfway mad at. One I'd missed. One I hadn't had since Bloss.

"Alright, you two. That's enough. You have a minute left before I send the next candidate over. And, Majesty? The next candidate is going to be a *solid-gold winner*." She let the threat linger in the water, her punishment for mockery would no doubt mean she'd send a half-wit booger-eater my way next. But I couldn't quite be sad about it. This was the highlight of my week. I nodded and she huffed before she turned and swam away.

"That was brilliant." Keelan grinned and cocked his head, bringing a hand up to brush his chin as he evaluated me. "Based on that interaction alone, if you asked for my hand, I'd say yes."

I laughed. "Those are low standards."

"Well, I mean, I'd definitely insist we commission at least forty statues of myself." He propped a hand on his hip and popped a ridiculous pose that made even Felipe snort.

"Oh, that's quite the picture." I pretended to be impressed, but mostly just tried not to ogle. *Stare at the green streak in his hair,* I commanded my wandering eyes.

"Oooh, look at mother glaring daggers at you. It's a great look on her, don't you think?" Keelan raised his brows before lowering them and then turning a bit more serious. "You'll have to excuse her though. She didn't want me competing. She's protective. Even a queen isn't a good enough match for me apparently." He ran a hand through his hair and pretended to toss it like a prima donna. "She *will* try to dissuade you with horrible stories about my childhood, but I have to let you know they're utter lies. I was an absolute angelfish." His wide-eyed, innocent expression reappeared.

I couldn't help chuckling. "Were you now?" I arched a brow.

He planted a hand on that chest I was trying to avoid staring at, and I couldn't keep my gaze from sliding downward just a bit. He definitely worked hard to get those muscles. They were definitely more defined than any man back home, any but Ryan or his men. Only they had abdominal muscles chiseled into stacked blocks like Keelan. Which made me wonder...

"So, Keelan, the angelfish, what do you do for work?" I queried.

"I'm a poet."

My jaw dropped, startled. I definitely had not pegged him for a poet.

"Just kidding." He waved his hand nonchalantly. "I was part of the royal guard, outer legions, assigned to Kremos, the cliff city. But I resigned."

"Resigned?" I tried to keep my face neutral.

"Yes, well, members of the royal guard aren't allowed to compete in the tournament, are they? If they lose, their loyalty falters."

My throat grew dry as I tried to recall whether or not Sahar had covered that bit of information with me during our planning sessions. Probably. But I clearly hadn't absorbed it. My gaze darted over to Felipe for half a second before I yanked it forcibly away. I didn't allow myself to check his reaction to this statement. He clearly relished his post. He didn't have an interest in a girl like me. He probably had no idea that I had a slight crush on him. A tiny, insignificant crush. I was good at hiding my feelings when I liked someone. Declan hadn't known I'd liked him, and I'd been merely a child then. Men only knew things when you hit them over the head with it. Mother ... Gela ... was right about that.

I focused back on the siren who clearly was interested in me, interested enough to give up his career path.

Keelan snagged my hand and kissed it. "I'm going to end my time with you with a horrid joke, Your Majesty. Why did the mermaid blush? ...Because she saw the ocean's *bottom*."

I girlishly giggled as he retreated back into the crowd. Relief. I felt like sagging in relief that everything with Keelan had ended so well after everything with Radford had capsized.

Once Keelan disappeared into the crowd, my eyes met Felipe's. He gave a curt nod, as if acknowledging that Keelan would be a good fit. He most definitely did not look at me with longing.

Sigh.

Well ... even a queen couldn't have everything.

4

Why kill with a sword when a word will do? Learn your enemies' secrets and then topple them with whispers.

—Sultan Raj of Cheryn

ALL AROUND, voices rose in yet another song I didn't know. People had gotten far into their cups and progressively louder. I thought we were on at least our third round of refreshments. I'd seen stewards bringing in new barrels of alcohol, and the songs had gotten rowdier. In this latest song, the orchestra sang every few lines and the entire room boomed with the two recurring lines. I'd never been more caught up in music before.

Off he went, for Nowhere bound

Watch the tides, you veeda vey

He swam 'til his tail cried foul

The air will suck your life away

The waves tugged him back and forth

Watch the tides, you veeda vey

He'd no strength to change his course

The air will suck your life away

Gold sand and bright old sun

Struck his eye and burnt his hand, oh!

Watch the tides, you veeda vey

The shore was rough, hard as stone

Poor old Cade couldn't get home

The air will suck your life away

Watch the tides, you veeda vey

Watch the tides, you veeda vey

I smiled and bobbed my head from side to side as yet another suitor approached.

"You like 'Fool Cade,' do you?" the tall squi-shifter asked. I tried not to eye the tentacles on the underside of his arms as if they were disgusting growths.

I focused on the scar on his chin as I nodded. "It's quite the catchy tune."

"Yes, it's a traveling ditty that soldiers sing. I prefer 'Amala.' Tune's better. Lyrics are a bit crude though. It's about the woman that traveled with the soldiers and, you know ... serviced them."

The smile froze on my face. "Oh." I stopped moving my head and bit my bottom lip awkwardly. *Thank you, Sahar. You sent over another winner.* After three awkward conversations in a row, I was nearly ready to call it a night.

The man with the scar said nothing else, just stared at me without a smile or any sort of expression on his face. It was awkward, but I'd learned silence could be far less awkward than words with some of these men.

Why couldn't I get a break this evening? Was every man in this line besides Keelan destined to have an awkward interaction with me? Or was Sahar deliberately punishing me? She'd promised me a bad egg after Keelan. And oh, had she delivered. The sexist pomposity of the bastard that had followed was like the stench of sulfur. I'd had a normal man or two after that. A rather sweet shy one. But she'd taken a brief break, and this was the fifth guy in a row to be deliberately idiotic.

I was beginning to hate my insistence on this tournament. I was a fool. My eyes darted over to Declan, who'd stood annoyingly close and no doubt had overheard all of these horrid conversations. I felt like a fighter in the ring, facing round after round of horrid, face-melting conversations. My brother-in-law smiled smugly and raised a glass toward me, toasting my downfall.

Sard it.

I wouldn't give him the satisfaction of believing he was right. I would salvage this conversation come hell or highwater. "Your name, sir?" I asked, blinking in a way I hoped was coquettish.

"Tavetti," he replied with a bow, reaching out to kiss my hand. "I must say, you're quite beautiful. I was worried that you'd look"—he leaned in sheepishly—"more human. Blech." He shuddered and reached out a finger to trail it over the iridescent scales that lined the outside of my right arm.

I tried not to stiffen when he said that or when his fingers drifted up toward my neck, but it was hard to fight my instincts to recoil.

"May I ask, do you have a third nipple? Lopsided breasts?"

Shock.

Utter shock pervaded my system, and I temporarily lost the ability to speak. Had he really just asked me that? In public?

I cleared my throat, giving myself time to answer. My eyes darted to the side. Declan was outright shaking with laughter, that turd. At least Felipe, my guard, had lowered his spear a bit threateningly, as if the question had offended him as well.

I turned my eyes back to Tavetti, who seemed to realize that he'd offended me.

"I apologize," he sputtered. "But why else would you cover them?"

Cultural differences, I chanted in my head. *Cultural differences.* I tried to keep my voice smooth and calm as I replied, "Where I was raised, a queen is valued for her mind first and foremost. Though I'm hosting a tournament for my hand, I wanted to emphasize that those who win will be joining their minds with mine." *Does that line of bullshite sound good?* I wondered after I'd spit it out. It sounded better than *I don't want to show my boobies in public because only trollops did that where I grew up.* Another solution came to me. *Could I just hit him for being rude? One little smack?*

I held still, studying Tavetti's giant black eyes, a feature that was prominent in most squi-shifters. He blinked a few times as if I'd surprised him, but then a smile lit his face. "Of course. That makes complete sense."

Finally.

"But you still didn't answer about the third nipple," he added. "So it's a yes, then?"

He was going straight to the bottom of the list. Back of the line. He could ride on the whale's tail for all I cared, and I hoped the damn thing went up for air and then flicked him off. My wrist flicked slightly as I imagined smacking him as hard as Bloss actually would.

Thankfully, Sahar came up and escorted him away with an apology in her eyes before I could find the nearest object and bash him over the head with it. Not that I'd really do that. It was more of a Bloss move. But I imagined it in detail, and would at least five more times tonight.

The next siren swam up, circumventing the line while Sahar dealt with the last ass. The new man's fingers interlaced with an attractive woman's. Was he just an attendee? Here to congratulate me? I smiled at the couple, who turned to one another, radiating excitement, and shared a quick peck on the lips before untangling their interlinked fingers.

The siren swam a bit closer. "Majesty, this is my mother Sabina. And I'm Saburo, her son."

Mother and son? I froze my facial features so that shock and disgust couldn't weave their way across my lips like they wanted to. Bloss had always complained about this part, the fakery. But damn. It was difficult.

"Ohh, stand together, let me look at the pair of you," Sabina squealed and clapped.

Saburo moved faster than a flash. One second he was in front of me, and the next second he was next to me, hand patting my ass as he posed by my side. I deftly moved to cover his hand with mine and slide it back to my waist.

Make that six assholes in a row. And I needed at least five husbands out of this damned competition.

This tournament idea of mine was very possibly *doomed*.

Would this night never end? I'd had the servants stop serving me fermented drinks long ago and asked Sahar if someone down here knew about coffee or how to make it. She'd shook her head.

As I fought to keep my eyes open, I vowed that coffee beans from Lored would be one of the first trade negotiations I'd embark on.

At the same time, I felt guilty as I met the men toward the back of the line. Either my exhaustion was making me more tolerant of stupidity, or the men at the back were more intelligent and capable.

A handsome siren with golden skin and pale green-colored hair, one of at least seven sirens who—unfortunately—all looked the same to me, came forward and bowed and kissed my hand.

I briefly hoped that none of these men had diseases; otherwise, the others were likely to get them, kissing the same spot.

When the siren rose, his smile was softer than the others. His long aquiline nose was a bit sharper than most. His frame might have been a bit thinner. Actually, his skin was more bronze than gold up close. And his eyes looked intelligent. So, perhaps he was a little different from the others. "You look glorious tonight, Your Majesty."

"Thank you." I inclined my head. And while I knew a siren's voice was intended to be seductive, I couldn't help the blush that stole across my cheeks, hoping that he was sincere. "Your name?"

"Julian, Majesty."

"You don't have to be formal with each address. What is it you do for work, Julian?"

To my surprise, Julian blushed and ducked his head. "I'm ... a scientist."

I furrowed my brow. "I'm sorry. I'm not quite certain what you said."

Julian's light brown eyes met mine. "I search for solutions to problems without using any magic." I leaned back, feeling a little blindsided. "What?"

Julian bit his lip. "Well, magical genes are diluted each generation they meld with human genes. More so on land than here, but it still happens here. Quite a few mermaids have to go on land to visit their children who cannot breathe underwater. My parents are only half sirens ... if my dad had been human, I probably would not have had enough magic to even breathe underwater. As it is, I can't change my hair like most sirens. But the point is, once the ratio of magic being to human dips below the threshold of one eighth magic being to human ratio ... well, there simply is no magic. Magic is declining. We need solutions to the world's problems that won't involve magic."

My head tilted to the side, watching as this shy siren became more animated. I studied his features. Like all sirens, he was a type of handsome that humans just couldn't match. It was part of his predatory heritage. But that wasn't the most attractive thing about him. Hearing him talk about this "science," which was clearly his passion, made his entire face light up. I doubted he even realized it, but he radiated energy. His aura became a magnet, and I felt drawn to him.

"—as of late, many surgical procedures," he concluded a sentence that I hadn't heard the start of, as lost in admiration as I had been.

"That sounds fascinating." I smiled up at him. "I'd love to learn more about it. Would you care to ride with me on the way to the first tournament in Reef City?"

Startled, he blinked a few times. "You mean it?"

"I wouldn't have asked if I didn't."

"I … of course. This is better than I ever imagined this going." He gestured between us. "Not many sea people are open to the discussion of science over magic. I'd hoped, but not really believed, that you might be an ally for the cause."

There it was.

I felt like I'd been doused in ice water. The connection that I'd felt brewing between us, the interest and excitement, vaporized. Julian hadn't come here interested in me. He wanted to use me. Just like every other mer, it seemed. Publicity was my greatest asset, the one they were all attracted to.

I wanted to sigh and lean on my arm, staring out a window in forlorn disappointment. Instead, I gave him a small encouraging smile and then signaled for Sahar to bring up the next candidate.

Another siren stepped closer. Unlike the others, who'd dressed all in bright blues and greens, which seemed to be the fashion, this man wore only black. All black, he even wore a shirt, though it was molded to his abs like a second skin. He was athletic looking and had that perfect balance of muscle, his waist tapering to narrow hips that strode forward with confidence. He walked toward me, which I appreciated. It made me feel a little more at ease, because I wasn't used to people swimming right at me just yet.

The most alluring siren yet gave me a slow bow, his pale pink hair falling forward, his hazel eyes locked onto mine the entire time. "Good evening, Your Majesty. Worn out by the pageantry yet?"

I laughed lightly. "It's what I signed up for, isn't it?"

He stared at me a long moment, causing fire to lick up my spine. Eventually, he responded, "True. But I have yet to see you dance tonight. Would you do me the honor?"

Shite.

He'd immediately gone for the chink in my armor. I didn't know all the undersea dances yet. And I definitely couldn't swim proficiently enough to keep up with those around me.

"I still have others—" I gestured at the line behind him, but he simply took my outstretched hand in his and led me confidently down the steps. His grip on my hand was firm and warm, and completely in control. I couldn't have slipped away if I'd wanted to.

"I took the liberty of learning one of the court dances from Evaness," he said smoothly.

I glanced up at him sideways, a little taken aback. Most sea people hated sky breather traditions. "You did?"

"Well, I do want you to be more comfortable around me," he murmured as he turned toward me and snuck a hand around my waist.

As if the orchestra had been waiting for this cue, they struck up a waltz, and the handsome siren, whose name I didn't even know, led me around the glass dance floor.

He didn't sing, but his eyes were just as enchanting as a siren song. Their hazel green color held me captive as he pulled me close and spun me out, reeled me back in and dipped me. My feet moved on autopilot, having had years of ballroom training. But my heart was hardly keeping pace with my feet. It was sprinting.

I felt light-headed and giddy.

I felt like I was floating.

As the music drifted through the water, it felt like it enveloped the two of us in our own private bubble. The rest of the world dissolved. There was only the grace of the dance, the fluidity of the movement, the slide of his hand over my arms, the grip of his thick hands on mine. There was only the warmth of his touch kindling an equally strong warmth inside my chest.

When he stopped moving, it took a moment before I realized the song had ended.

He released the hand that had held my waist, took a step backward. Then he bowed and raised my hand to his lips, pressing a soft kiss to my knuckles before turning and disappearing into the crowd.

I stared at the point where he'd disappeared for a long moment before I realized he hadn't even told me his name.

THE NEXT MAN THAT SWAM UP TO ME GAVE OFF THE VIBE of a cold-hearted predator as he approached me where I stood in front of my throne. The combination of the jagged scar on his bicep, the shock of white that ran through his otherwise black hair, and the shark fin on his back told me that he wasn't someone to mess around with. He was stacked with muscle, and his face looked far too young for his expression, which dripped sarcasm.

He didn't bow like the others, which immediately put me on high alert.

It only took me a second to realize why. "You're one of the rebels I invited, correct?"

His black eyes glimmered with amusement. "Not as stupid as you look."

Felipe turned, spear tip gleaming, but I held up a hand to slow my guard. "Well, now, I suppose I'm a bit brighter than you, protesting when you're surrounded by guards."

The rebel's eyes narrowed; apparently, he hadn't expected to be insulted. "We're standing up for ourselves. If someone had bothered to do it when Mayi first ascended, then maybe that entire debacle—"

I interrupted what I could tell was going to be an impassioned speech. "Mayi was deranged. I highly doubt she would have let you live."

"She only became that way after she got involved with that sky lover." The rebel's deep grey eyes gleamed with the fierce conviction that he was right.

"Ah." I nodded. "I see. Sky lovers can't be trusted."

"They only want to murder us for their own ends, dump their trash to pollute our home—"

"I can see your point," I acknowledged, realizing that this fellow was rather long-winded. Seeing as I'd been standing and receiving competitors all night, I decided that, if I was going to have the energy to listen to his theories, I needed to be seated. I gestured toward a nearby table, where my untouched plate of food sat. "Please sit with me and express your concerns for a moment."

The rebel raised a black brow, surprised by my offer. "Sit with you?"

"Yes. Please." I started to flutter my wings to swim the few feet to the table, assuming he'd follow. Immediately, I felt a swish of water as Felipe moved to protect my back, which I'd inadvertently shown the rebel.

Damn. I'd get a lecture later for that one, I was certain.

I sat and shoved aside my plate. I wasn't hungry, my body floated somewhere on the strange plane between tension and exhaustion. I took a deep breath, but that was the only break I allowed myself, because I was in public. I did lean and call to Sahar, "Can I get a pen and something to write on?"

Sahar smoothed out the surprise in her expression quickly and found a servant to swim off.

After a long moment, the rebel joined me at the table. "I've been instructed to keep my hands above the table at all times and my legs visible if I don't want them cut off. That normal protocol for talking to you?"

I turned to glare at Felipe. "Only when my guard really feels like he needs the exercise of mucking out the seahorse stable."

Felipe's expression remained neutral, and he didn't respond, the shite.

I turned back to the rebel, who'd tilted his head and was staring at me with something akin to curiosity.

"My apologies ... you haven't given me your name."

"Watkins." The shark shifter set his elbows deliberately on the table, fisting one hand and cupping that fist with the other as he studied me steadily.

There was something the tiniest bit unnerving about his gaze, perhaps because he was a shark shifter. My stomach gave a nervous little flop, and for a moment, I felt like prey. I was relieved when someone shoved some parchment and a quill and ink at me, all magicked so they wouldn't be ruined by the water.

I opened the ink and dipped the quill. Then I tried to hand it to him. "Why don't you go ahead and list your demands ..."

"Why? So you can write them down and laugh over them?" His voice grew so feral it was practically a growl. His eyes dipped to my quill, then lower before his nostrils flared and he gazed back up at me, twice as angry as before.

"So I can discuss them with my advisers." I tried to keep my tone even. Was he furious with himself for gazing at me? *Was he gazing at me?*

"You won't do that," he scoffed.

"Of course I will." *Why would he doubt me?* He didn't even know me.

"Royalty don't give a shite about—"

"Here I am, saying I give a shite, and you're the one refusing to take advantage of this opportunity." I gestured at the crowd, making a wide, sweeping arc with my arm. "You obviously were chosen out of your little group to approach me. How do you think they're going to feel when they know you wasted the opportunity?"

For some odd reason, a smug expression came over Watkins' face. His eyes took on a gleam that hadn't been there previously.

"What?" I snapped, a bit irritated and too tired to hide it at this point of the night.

Watkins' grin only grew, and it was the kind of grin that sliced one open, cut through flesh and made the heart pump frantically. It was the kind of grin I felt quite certain he gave a fish right before he caught it. "Oh, I wasn't the only one who approached you tonight."

I blamed exhaustion for the fact that it took me a second to process what he said, but once I realized, the implications were as loud as a gong in my head. I'd invited those protesters as a show of good faith, but clearly, they had absolutely no boundaries. They'd gone about distracting Sahar and impersonating actual competitors! Why? Just to humiliate me? That seemed likely, since they clearly didn't take my offer to discuss things seriously.

I set down the quill and carefully closed the ink bottle so as not to disclose my rage. But inside, I was smoldering.

I didn't think it was possible, but Watkins' smile spread even wider, like he knew what was going on inside my head.

Internally, I dissected every interaction of my evening. "Third nipple, that was one of yours." I didn't even phrase it as a question.

I saw surprise flicker across Watkins' face. Had he not expected me to discern what he meant so quickly?

"What about the man who groped me in front of his mother? That one yours too?" I fiercely hoped so, because I really never wanted to interact with that idiot again. He'd given me a serious case of disgusted shivers. If he was an actual competitor, I wanted to disqualify him.

Watkins gave the world's most frustrating, most infuriating shrug. As if this were all some game and not my future they were messing with.

I snapped. Later, I'd blame it on exhaustion, but I was honestly utterly livid in that moment. They'd warped my kind gesture and used it to torture me.

"You know what, I don't think I'll be writing that list after all." I folded my hands demurely on the table, my face stoic. I'd learned from years of playing cards with Declan not to tip my hand too soon.

Watkins' face twisted in fury. "I knew it—"

"It's going to take far too many conversations to understand exactly what you want. So…" I turned in my seat. "Sahar, come here for a moment, please!" I called loudly.

She swam quickly, confusion on her features. I don't think she'd ever heard me yell before. But I kept up my theatrical tone so that it carried throughout the room. Nearby, sea people had already turned to witness the commotion. "There's been a mistake. Watkins here wants to officially register for the tournament."

I enjoyed the shock that rippled across his features, dragging under that smug look like it had been caught in an undertow. I stood slowly so that I was above him, breaking one of Sahar's cardinal negotiation rules. But this wasn't negotiation. This was punishment.

"I do hope you aren't the first to lose." I put on a sickeningly innocent expression. "I wouldn't want you to be utterly humiliated."

Watkins had no words. I'd made a man speechless.

I turned to Sahar. "I trust you can arrange it."

After issuing those commands, I swam back to my throne, head held high, as if I knew exactly what I was doing. But as fury cooled and my chest was no longer a molten pit of anger, I wondered if I'd just made the biggest mistake of my life.

I'd just invited an enemy to compete for my hand.

5

Bravado is a bear trap that one day will snap and shred you.

—Sultan Raj of Cheryn

THE DULL BUSINESS of managing a country kept me occupied for the next two days, while my staff made arrangements for the travel to Reef City for the first round of tournament trials.

I sent my first royal letter to the country of Lored, reaching out to see if we could establish a trade agreement for some of their goods—particularly coffee—in exchange for some of our natural resources like pearls or whale blubber.

I met with the castle treasurer in my official meeting room, a chamber set with a long table taken from the wreckage of a downed ship and a mishmash of chairs that had been painted with gold leaf. The room was filled with fascinating books on the history of Okeanos, tales of its wars, the history and development of the different groups. I learned much from these books about the home I'd never known. While Reef City and Palati, the capital city that sat next to my castle, had become metropolitan mixes of all sea peoples, other regions were mainly comprised of one type of magical being. Places like Nowhere and Sky Stones didn't have nearly the same diversity. Nowhere was a desert to the south and was still mostly the realm of nomadic hermit crab shifters. To the north, a place called Sky Stones was made of the buildings from an entire sky breather village that had sunk beneath the sea, and it was still ninety percent inhabited by sirens.

I wanted to read those fascinating accounts all day, to curl up and add words and phrases to my vocabulary. Thus far, I'd learned that "Oh, go sing for your supper," was an insult to a mer or siren, a slur that meant they had no more talent than the magic the gods had given them. "Pokey" was a term used for the hermit crab shifters, both a reference to their claws and to the fact that they came from the podunk regions of the country. Shark shifters were never hammerhead sharks, and to call a shifter a "hammerhead" was basically to compare him to a base animal. It would, according to the historian in the lexicon book, be a sure way to get bitten. I loved those accounts, sneaking in reads here and there between the endless meetings, taking some of the books to bed with me.

Unfortunately, life wasn't all fascinating reading. There were also numbers to deal with, lots of them. Hence, I had quite a few meetings with Camden, my treasurer.

Two afternoons past the opening ceremony, he came in with a scroll of parchment under his arm that was twice as thick as his head. Camden was a puffer fish shifter and skinny as a rail, though the pants he wore, a deep wine-colored velvet, were quite baggy in case he puffed up. A smattering of tiny spikes dotted his chest like freckles, and he had the habit of worrying his shell collar as he pointed out credits and debits and other numerical items that were so dry and dull that I was surprised he didn't suck all the water out of the room.

We discussed finances ad nauseum, Declan perched next to me in my official meeting chambers, pulling the parchment over to himself and chiming in whenever he pleased as if this was his country to run. Part of me wanted to disagree with his suggestions just to be contrary, but I resisted the urge, because typically—annoyingly—he was correct.

"Look, if you minimize the glass work to repair the castle atrium, you can reassign those workers to—"

"The glassblower's guild won't be happy about that. They don't like to change mid-project when everything's been set up. They'll add on extra fees," the treasurer, Camden, argued.

Declan gave him a dull stare. "Turrets are still more important. The castle is vulnerable to attack from above, and we can't man shattered turrets."

I rubbed at my forehead. "Is there another guild, perhaps from another city, that we could contact for turret repair?"

Camden's naturally round eyes blinked at me. "That's just ... not done, Your Majesty."

"Well, tell the guild here then that we need both items done at once, and they can decide if they want to subcontract to another guild or not, but if they don't figure it out soon, I'll reach out to another guild myself."

Sahar stood and swam over to Camden, who seemed frozen in shock at the idea that he actually had to deliver unpleasant news other than a bill. "Camden, I'll come with you. You just create an estimate ... alright?" As usual, Sahar smoothed out the rough edges of my plan. I'd have been lost without her.

He shook his head slowly as he rolled up his parchment. "It will be expensive, Majesty."

"Yes, well, if we need it, I'm certain Evaness will extend me a line of credit." I raised my eyebrows and gave Declan a droll look.

He chuckled. "Well, perhaps. If our queen is over the whole ink-to-the-face business. She did mention that such an unprovoked attack could be considered an act of war." He steepled his fingers and gave me a fake serious look.

"When are you leaving again? Should I get your gargoyle saddled?" I poked at him fondly.

"As soon as things are *settled*." There was something smug in his tone that I didn't like, but before I could figure out what it was, Sahar swam over to me.

My siren adviser leaned down, a small smile making the crow's feet near her eyes wrinkle. "Your Majesty, I've arranged a little meeting for you with two of the competitors who got less attention at the ball."

"Ugh," Declan grunted his displeasure.

Sahar kept doing this, finding tiny holes in my schedule so that I could have awkward conversations with these men. I'd stopped asking the normal get-to-know-you questions, because if I heard blue was a man's favorite color one more time...

"Okay, thank you." I nodded.

Declan shoved back his chair and stood. "That's my cue to leave. Enjoy your stilted conversation."

I gritted my teeth and glanced over at Felipe, who'd been standing by the door, spear in hand, throughout our conversation. "We can send him home without a few fingers, can't we?" I asked my guard.

"Absolutely," he replied.

Maiming Declan had become a bit of an inside joke for us the past few days, and I had to physically tamp down the thrill that traveled up my spine when Felipe's eyes crinkled at the corners as he smiled. I really needed to stop the banter; it wasn't doing anything to quell my attraction to a man who wasn't interested, but I couldn't seem to help myself. If only I'd gotten to choose the competitors for the tournament.

"Har har," Declan replied, not fazed in the least, as he gathered up a parchment he'd filled with notes and tick marks. He stopped to cross this meeting off his list before turning to my siren adviser. "Sahar, do you think you could introduce me to the stable master? I'd like to discuss travel arrangements and security with him for this whole tournament fiasco that my little sister insists on having."

"Certainly." Sahar nodded.

Camden reached the door and pulled it open for all three of them. After they swam out, another siren swam hesitantly in, hands clutched in front of him. He must have been the man Sahar had arranged for me to meet.

I smiled as I tried to recall his face. He was blond haired and beautiful, like all sirens, but his aura was different from most of the others. They donned sexuality like it was a shirt to be worn in public. He did not. He felt more like a sculpture: beautiful and open to interpretation rather than instantly understood. I got the feeling he was not as shallow as the others. Of course, I'd met him for all of three seconds during the ball's introductions, so that was merely an impression. And it wasn't long enough for me to even remember his name. Dammit.

His shy smile was the only reason I remembered him at all. None of the other sirens had an ounce of shyness. He was less cocksure despite his beauty, which was impressive. His skin was golden, his perfectly formed chest bare, and his golden calves were sculpted beneath the short pants he wore for modesty. His liquid blue eyes dipped down to the floor, his lashes painting soft stripes on his cheeks. He was every bit as alluring as a siren was meant to be, but he did not use that allure on me.

It immediately made me soften toward him, a man who finally seemed as intimidated by this process as I was.

Behind the siren was a man who didn't fit in with all of the other competitors. His name I recalled, if only for its oddity. Humberto. He was a bit squatter, a bit round about his middle, not a strapping example of manhood. But his face was kind. Humberto had bright black stripes on his skin, on the outsides of his cheeks, across his chest and arms and legs, even in human form. He had black hair on top of his head that was tightly curled. I tried to recall what kind of shifter he was. He'd told me, but we'd been interrupted by some of the rebels getting rowdy and toasting Watkins as a sellout. Was it … a cardinal fish? Yes, that sounded right.

I nodded toward him.

Luckily, Sahar swam back into the doorway, announcing, "Your Majesty, thank you for granting an audience to Stavros and Humberto. I'll be back shortly." Thank goodness. She'd saved me from the embarrassment of having to ask. What would I ever do without her?

I nodded in gratitude, and she left, water wavering behind her as a guard pulled the door closed to provide us the semblance of privacy, even though he and Felipe remained inside the room.

I smiled with teeth, gesturing for the two suitors to sit, hoping that they couldn't sense my discomfort. Getting wooed by two or three men at once felt unnatural to me, even though I knew it had been done this way for centuries. I reminded myself that Mateo and I had been unusual. I'd met him when he'd accompanied his father, an ambassador from Macedon. It had been love at first sight, the kind that I'd only ever read about in fairy tales set before the curse that changed the kingdoms of Sedara forever, the curse that made it so incredibly difficult to bear female children. Mateo's brown eyes and dimples had been my undoing. But his playful nature and his willingness to help me in my shenanigans to set up Bloss with her husbands had cemented my affection. His deep kisses and dark touches had transformed affection into something more. Our love ... I'd thought it invincible. But that was before I'd realized I wasn't human, before I knew I was the daughter of a monster.

I attempted to focus on the present moment, because there was nothing I could do about the fact that a dragon and the truth had sent my life spiraling in an entirely different direction. "Welcome to our main meeting room. If you win the tournament, you'll get to spend so many hours in here that your seat will wear down to have a permanent impression of your ..." I trailed off.

Stavros chuckled, while Humberto glanced around at the tapestries hung from the walls, his brown eyes bouncing from one to the next. They depicted various sea animals: turtles, dolphins, and of course a seahorse tapestry hung behind my chair at the end of the table. The woven hangings added a bit of beauty to the space but also helped muffle the sounds so that meetings couldn't easily be overheard.

"So, this is basically an auditory torture chamber?" Stavros asked softly, surprising me with his wit.

I laughed lightly. "Exactly. Welcome."

We all sat, Humberto twiddling his thumbs. Stavros dug a nail into the arm of his chair before meeting my eyes and giving another shy grin. Neither spoke, waiting for me to take the lead.

"So, this is where we learn a bit about one another," I started. "But to be honest, if we stick with the normal questions, I'm never going to remember a thing. All the answers blur. Hometown. Favorite color. There are already twenty answers floating through my head for those. Would you mind if I ask some things that are a bit more unusual?"

Humberto's fingers clenched together, but he nodded quickly. "Of course."

I glanced over at Stavros, whose eyes were on a tapestry, but once he noticed my gaze, he quickly flickered his bright blue eyes to mine before sliding them away again and giving a silent nod of his head.

Both men seemed a bit reticent. They did not lead off with stories of their own exploits like some of the others. Did I need husbands like that? I could see the value of it...men who listened. My sister's husband Quinn never spoke, and he made an excellent spy. So perhaps there was potential, even if I didn't feel some grand attraction yet. I needed to draw them out a bit, so I decided on a question to test their mettle and their minds. "Great. If you could plan a murder, how would you do it?" I kept my tone conversational.

Humberto paled, even his black stripes dulled to grey.

Stavros narrowed his eyes and tilted his head, almost as if he were evaluating me, deciding what kind of answer I'd want to hear. Interesting. Maybe Quinn could work with him. Teach him a thing or two about spy work and the other, darker skills, the ones that required visits to the dungeon.

I tried to break the tension with a laugh. Clearly, both men thought me a bit unhinged to ask such a question. Then, to my own horror, I realized that it might sound to them like the kind of thing my birth mother would have asked. Her reputation for cruelty was only exceeded by Sultan Raj's in all the kingdoms. "This is all theoretical, of course. You will not be required to implement your theory." Part of me wanted to hide my face in my hands. I couldn't help a hot blush that stole up my neck. But queens didn't hide.

"Of course." Humberto nodded, but the smile he gave was still washed out. I wasn't certain he believed me.

Stavros used his thumb to trace the wood grain on the tabletop before he answered thoughtfully. "I'd feed them to the giant squid that supposedly lives near Nowhere."

"There is no giant squid, that's just a myth," Humberto grumped.

"It's just a theoretical murder, isn't it?" Stavros replied, raising a brow. "I mean, I suppose I could say that I'd do something worse, like tie them to a buoy above the water and let them slowly suffocate. Is that better?" He wrinkled his nose. "It's awfully mean. Or I guess I could say I'd get them stuck in a fisherman's net and let him do the dirty work for me. You like that more? Or you want worse? It might take me a minute." Stavros glared at Humberto.

"Giant squid is a fine answer; after all, this is theoretical," I replied, "but I am curious as to why you'd choose that. Since we are getting to know each other."

Stavros tilted his head as he looked at me. "Well, if they were eaten, there'd be less evidence. If I fed them to a mythical creature, fewer people would believe it. If the mythical creature isn't real, I could still shove their body into some nook in the cliff so it wouldn't be discovered."

His thorough explanation was so wrong and yet ... so right. I found myself moving Stavros up the ladder of contestants until his name hovered on a rung near the top. He could potentially be a spymaster, or at least he seemed a decent alternative to the squeamish Humberto. I wasn't certain which part of his answer I admired most, but I gave him a grin that spoke for me.

His eyes flickered back down to the table, but the small grin on his face told me he was pleased with himself. That was slightly adorable.

Humberto chimed in with a tap of his hand on the table. "Well, then, if we're doing whatever we want, I'd hire one of the mobile island people to squish them."

"Oh, good one." Stavros nodded his approval. "I've heard pressing is a painful way to go."

"Well, I mean, they're so huge, I can't imagine it would take long," Humberto replied, a bit smug. "But, like you said, it gets rid of the evidence. Though in all honesty, Your Majesty, you can publicly execute enemies whenever you feel like it, so I don't suppose you'll ever need these little tricks."

I nodded along, but for the millionth time that week, I was left feeling woefully ignorant, not about methods of execution—my supposed father had been the spymaster before Quinn—but about this strange new world I now inhabited. I'd never heard of the mobile islands. "Tell me more about the island people," I prompted.

"I mean, they're triple the size of giants. That's probably the one good thing that your mother did; early on, she got them all to move north of Kremos. Before that, it was a nightmare. Imagine a giant, so big that the tip of his head is an island, suddenly stomping about in your neck of the sea. When I was a kid, a friend of mine lost his house and parents to them. Dead awful."

Stavros started to chuckle, and both of us furrowed our brows to look at him. He quickly reddened and sputtered, "Oh, I thought you were exaggerating. Making a pun. *Dead awful?* I—I—" His eyes hit the table again.

"No puns."

I interrupted before the awkward tension could build more. "I honestly didn't know about the island people." Perhaps my own ignorance would be enough of a distraction. Men loved to be experts, right? "I've never seen one, though I'd love to." I blinked a few times, not quite enough to be considered batting my eyes but definitely more than necessary.

Humberto's lips thinned, but he took my conversational bait, swallowing it whole. "Oh, you think you want to, but their feet could crush all of Palati here, your castle and the surrounding area. Some people say they're responsible for that huge crevice near Nowhere, the one with his supposed squid in it." Humberto jerked his head toward Stavros.

Well, that hadn't quelled his bitterness as much as I wanted. I tried quickly to steer the conversation in a new direction, since the tension radiating from Humberto had become palpable. "I definitely think your answers to that question will firmly plant you both in my mind in comparison to the other tournament contestants. How about we follow up with something more typical? What were your parents like?" I looked at Humberto since Stavros had answered the prior question first.

He waved a striped arm dismissively. "My parents were alright. Bit thickheaded, but you get a lot of groupthink in cardinal fish."

"Can you tell me about your people?" I asked, trying not to let fascination creep into my tone.

Humberto launched into a tale. "Well, we didn't live in the reef that long. My parents moved us into a private conch, trying to get a bit of separation from all the other fish shifters, you know? As nocturnal people, we typically sleep during the day, and it gets awfully noisy in Reef City. Anyway …"

He continued speaking as a maid came in with some refreshments for the three of us. She had bowls of cooked shrimp and bright cups of bubbles flavored with mango, my new favorite drink.

Humberto continued, "School was my favorite, but it's also quite exhausting for shifters because you have to learn to swim in fish form with your school, and then you have to shift to human to go to school and learn all the things you need for a trade. Ten hours a day can get old quick."

"It sounds like an exhausting childhood," I told him.

He shrugged before snagging a shrimp and sucking it into his mouth. "When you're young, you don't know any better. You do as you're told."

"True enough. What did you decide on as your trade?" I asked as I lifted my teacup, a cup that had clearly been scavenged from a wreck. It was delicate china but had a small chip in the base. I smiled encouragingly at Humberto before taking a sip of my drink, but I wasn't sure he even noticed. He'd been given rein to talk about himself, and his shyness had clearly worn off.

"First, I thought I wanted to be a teacher. Signed up as an apprentice and everything. Then, I watched those little shits get drunk in front of me in class, not even caring, and I decided sard that!" He set his mango bubble down emphatically to emphasize his point. The poor little cup looked like it was ready to break as his thick striped fingers squeezed it aggressively.

"Yes, children can be quite awful," Stavros agreed.

Interesting. Two men had joined my tournament but had little interest in children. So fatherhood wasn't a priority. Were they interested in power? Wealth? Stavros fell a few rungs as I tried to puzzle them both out while maintaining conversation.

"Your parents?" I asked Stavros.

He smiled softly. "They've been gone so many years I hardly remember them."

"I'm sorry."

He shook his head. "It's not a problem. They were around long enough to teach me what was important."

"And that is?" I nudged aside my plate, more interested in our conversation than food.

His light blue eyes studied me for a moment before he answered, "Set a goal and work toward it."

For some reason, those words made me breathless. They shouldn't have. For all intents and purposes, he'd simply called me a goal. But it was the way that he said it, the rough scratch underlying his words, the fierce burn of his gaze scorching my stomach. The shy, reserved varnish had been scratched for a moment, and the determined predator beneath revealed ... Somehow that revelation made my heart skip.

Of course, my heart skipping turned into my heart stumbling, and I had to force a smile as my idiotic organ fumbled inside my chest.

The door swung open just then, and relief swept over me; Sahar had come to take these men away, and no one would witness my struggle to breathe.

But Sahar didn't step through the doorway.

The one man who could ruin all my plans did.

6

A clouded mind cannot see the sun. Those with clouded minds end up burnt.

—Sultan Raj of Cheryn

SHOCK MADE me forget to breathe as I stared across the room at one person I never thought I'd see again, the one person who could make me weak enough to change my course, to leave everything else behind.

Mateo.

Was I dreaming? The brown eyes that blinked back at me in shock as he took in my new sea sprite appearance told me I wasn't. I thrust my fins behind me, suddenly self-conscious, as nervous and uncertain as the first time I'd seen him.

Shite. I'd forgotten there were other people in the room. Witnesses.

"Excuse me, gentlemen." I cleared my throat as I stood, struggling not only with my shite heart but with the weak knees that were a side effect of seeing *him*.

Immediately, Stavros and Humberto stood and bowed, exiting the room with curious glances in Mateo's direction, which were to be expected because he'd arrived fully dressed as a sky breather. But neither man said a word, and I hoped their more reticent natures would assume that Mateo was merely a messenger from one of the "dirt-kicker" kingdoms, as Sahar told me people called them. I plastered a court-appropriate smile onto my face and waited until the doors had closed behind them before I turned back to Mateo and truly took the time to study him.

He was tall as he'd always been. Not slight but not quite muscular either, he had a scholar's build. He had on black pants that clung to his lean legs and black leather boots swallowed his calves. His white shirt was clean but clearly patched near the collar, which was unusual, because ambassadors were typically dressed by their queens in order to properly represent the status of their country. Macedon wasn't wealthy, but it was a proud nation.

Mateo's eyes scorched a trail down the scales that edged the outside of my arms, then down my calves below the hem of my knee-length skirt. I bit my lip when his eyes went to the betta fish fins erupting from my back, or wings, as I thought of them. Was I too changed? Too freakish? I hadn't inherited Mayi's black eyes; my own were violet, but I didn't look at all like the girl he'd once loved.

He, however, still tugged at every heartstring I had as his dark hair wavered, curls loosely swaying when he smiled brightly enough for his dimples to show. His pale skin was a sudden change from the striped people and colored tails that constantly surrounded me in the sea kingdom. A sudden but also very familiar change that set off a nostalgic ache in me.

At first, I thought he looked exactly as I remembered, but as I stared, I noticed little things that weren't there before. His jaw was lined with a light smattering of stubble. His hair was a bit unkempt, as though he'd gone too long without a trim. Back when I knew him in Evaness as the Macedonian ambassador's son, he was clean-cut and his grin was as bright as the morning sun. Had that really only been months ago? Everything before the dragon seemed a lifetime away.

Mateo smiled at me now, but there was a desperate edge of grief lining his expression. When he stepped closer, I was overwhelmed by feelings of relief, urgency, and regret so thick that it lined the inside of my ribs like a bad meal.

Oh, what could have been.

"Via?" he asked softly, using the nickname he gave me.

I nearly laughed—no, I nearly cried—to hear that name again, a name he had only used in secret when we were alone together. A few months might as well have been a decade for all that I had changed over that span.

"I sent a letter asking after you," I said. It was a poor greeting, but I was desperate to know why it hadn't been answered. I had sat at this very table and written a letter, sealed it with wax and love on one of the first days after I'd taken over the sea kingdom, hopeful that Mateo would be sent as an ambassador to me and that he might help me with all my issues, from this shite heart to matters of state. I'd still retained a bit of my girlish naivete, wishing my true love would swoop in and help me with all my problems. But the lack of response from Macedon had convinced me that the other country did not take my requests seriously. That, or Mateo had refused the call.

And what could I have done about either? Nothing but make alternative arrangements. Move forward as I cried into my pillow each night.

"I was up in the mountains of Macedon." Mateo cleared his throat, and his eyes scraped the floor. "I was still searching. For you and the dragon. I hadn't heard that you'd been … found."

I couldn't help myself. I moved slowly around the side of the table until I was in front of him, so close that the water between us grew warm with our shared heat. His eyes finally met mine, and they were devastated.

Oh my heart.

My fingers landed on his arm, gripping it tightly. "You were still searching for me?" My emotions were caught somewhere between elation and confusion. He'd gone up into the mountains of Macedon? The ice-coated cliffs? The horridly narrow paths etched into the rock, where a single wrong step could send a man plunging into the afterlife?

My fingers clutched at him as if he was currently in danger of falling. Or perhaps because I was. I was utterly in danger of falling in love with him all over again.

And that would be treacherous.

I had bound myself to this tournament. To this kingdom. Sahar had warned me that once the tournament began, there was no ending it. Not until I wore rings around my neck, one thick golden ring for each husband I took.

"Of course I looked for you, Via. How could you even ask that?" Mateo's tone held a bit of hurt that I wanted to soothe away. He turned over the arm I held so that his hand clasped my elbow as I held onto his forearm. He didn't flinch at the feel of my scales. When he stared into my eyes, it felt like he saw *me*. Not the princess or the sea sprite. Not the queen. Me.

I edged closer, my eyes tracing his face, and the urge to kiss him nearly overwhelmed me.

But I couldn't.

My eyes darted to the side. Felipe and the other guard were very pointedly not watching us. But the reminder that we were not alone was all that I needed to release his arm and take a step back. That step back created a chasm between us, and he knew it, if his wince was anything to go by.

My chest locked up tight, like a box, and it felt as though someone was trying to fit the wrong-sized key into it. Wrong. It felt so wrong to have taken that step back. Though my eyes apologized to him, my feet didn't move closer. The gap remained.

Sard it all.

"Why the mountains?" I tried to keep my tone light and curious when all I wanted was to throw my arms around him and clutch him to me.

"Dragons hid in the caves near Macedon after the last Fire War. There are so many cliffs and crags that are hard to get to … It was impossible for us to rout them out entirely. I thought the beast who'd taken you might've gone there. I *thought* it was a good bet. Of course, turns out I miscalculated horribly." He gave a laugh that was bitter and full of sorrow.

Pity smacked my cheeks and turned them pink. *My poor Mateo.*

He'd been on a fruitless quest to save the princess. All because his hunch had been good … but wrong. I briefly wondered how many people died without reaching their goals, perished without answers, simply because their intuition had taken them in the wrong direction. Picturing Mateo climbing the massive mountains of Macedon with cold wind ripping at his skin, the howl of the canyon beneath him, where he was one slip from his doom …

I had to shake that thought away because it wasn't productive and made my heart falter. Instead, I glanced up through my lashes and asked, "How'd you hear what had become of me?"

He gave me a half grin, one that let me know even before he spoke that I was not going to love his answer. "Declan figured out where I was. Your sister's husbands found me."

Declan's smug expression from earlier suddenly made sense.

But Mateo's presence made me feel like a brass scale, weighing two things, one against another, favor tipping in his direction when it shouldn't. It couldn't. I needed to sit down. A myriad of thoughts raced around my head like a school of fish. This was why Declan had come. This was why he had urged me to cancel the tournament. Why hadn't he simply said?

Unless he'd been uncertain Mateo was alive. Or uncertain he'd come. Had he been waiting to find out?

I pulled out a chair and sank into it, my mind a sloshy mess. I had cursed my brother-in-law for interfering. I'd been stubborn and determined. I'd been wrong.

But I'd chosen my path and declared this tournament because my heart was mere weeks from collapse. That dragon had delivered me to my birth mother, and I'd learned my heritage. But I'd also learned about sea sprite magic. When Bloss had come to rescue me, I'd learned my chest housed not only my own heart, but the heart of a monster. Because in order for a sea sprite to access magic, they had to sacrifice their humanity, their heart. They had to physically remove it from their own body and place it in someone else's for safekeeping. But then, their host had to stay near, had to remain true, couldn't put that heart at risk. My own mother had chosen to make me her marionette, thinking her daughter would do as told, that her own flesh and blood would never betray her. But she hadn't planned on her enemies kidnapping me and hiding me on land, raising me as their own, denying her powers. She hadn't planned on my own loyalties switching. When Bloss told me that Mayi's heart was in my chest, I'd taken a dagger to myself to dig the rotted thing out. But I'd damaged my own heart in the process, foolishly counting on others' magic to heal me. Now, Bloss's undead castle mage, Lizza, had given me a prognosis of merely a month to live unless I handed off this damaged heart of mine, placed it in someone else's body, and embraced my sea sprite heritage so that I could access my power. Then, maybe, possibly, Lizza's experimental spells could keep me from becoming a monster just like my birth mother had been when I accessed that power. I needed to find a puppet of my own.

Mateo pulled out a chair with a peacock-patterned cushion and sat down beside me, turning so our knees nearly touched, and I studied the planes of his face, memories flooding me. Our first kiss had been spontaneous and full of laughter. We'd snuck out of Bloss's ballroom with two glasses of wine, both of us caught in that pleasant floating sensation that lay somewhere between tipsy and drunk. Our hands had linked, and my belly had felt tickles, as though a hundred feathers whirled within it, teasing my insides. Our eyes had burned like twin fires, flames stoked by our mutual gaze. He'd pressed me into the wall of the castle, and my heart had pounded so loudly it thrummed in my ears as he'd leaned forward, his lips hovering just over mine until I'd shoved up onto my tiptoes and closed the gap between us, pressing our lips and souls into a precious kiss.

Mateo's eyes heated, as if he could sense my memories. Perhaps he could.

I knew, if I asked him, Mateo would gladly take on my injured heart, wear it inside his chest like a badge of honor. But I also knew that asking him would be a mistake.

I broke our gaze, and my head sank into my hands. I had learned many things from my birth mother, most of them terrible. I'd learned that the darkness that a sea sprite was capable of was infinite. But one of the things I did believe from her life's tale was that a heart wasn't a trifle to give away. A sea sprite couldn't give her heart to someone who couldn't protect it.

My Mateo, sweet as he was, was merely human. A few months ago, when I thought that *I* was merely human, we had been a perfect match. But now, I was something else. And I needed a host for this weak heart, a host with the magic to protect it, someone I had no compunction about controlling. I couldn't do that to the man in front of me. I'd never be able to force Mateo to do anything.

Which meant I couldn't leave. I couldn't run from this tournament or this kingdom or the doom I'd signed up for. I couldn't steal away, elope, and have *him*.

My heart gave a plaintive thump of longing.

It disagreed with my logic. But then it faltered, and all my reasoning simply gained more weight.

I should have sent him away. I knew it at that instant.

But I was weak.

Mayi would have laughed at me, harsh noises bubbling from her lips before she slashed at me with knives made of ice again and again, punishing me for foolish emotions. She'd been heartless down in the cave where she'd held me prisoner, so that I was close enough for her to access her magic, and I was secured enough that the brainwashing that Evaness had done to "ruin" me couldn't affect her.

I looked up and eyed Mateo with longing, and despite all the synapses in my brain telling me otherwise, I wanted him to stay. Besides, what would it hurt if he stayed as an ambassador? I recognized my emotions twisting my logic, warping it like a kaleidoscope warps the objects under its mirrors until their true shapes are so distorted that they're unrecognizable. I allowed it because a little part of me couldn't bear to part with Mateo again.

He'd searched for me.

He hadn't given up on me.

He was here. And he hadn't run at the sight of me.

My heart went *thu-thud*.

I wish... I swiped the thought away before it could topple my resolve, because I wasn't a magicless second princess anymore. I was an heir, with the potential for powerful magic—with the potential for powerful good. All my life I'd dreamt of the throne, of making some monumental difference in the world, jealous that such a fate belonged to Bloss and not me. Yet here I was in this forgotten kingdom with the ability to restore it, enrich it, improve the lives of those around me and make a difference—the very thing I'd sworn to myself that I'd do if I ever escaped that awful underwater cave.

I took a breath, wondering how I would be able to break the news of the tournament to him.

But another voice cleaved the silence in two, as sharp and quick as an axe.

"Your Majesty, it's time for your next appointment," Felipe announced.

"Can't we delay it a bit?" I turned, trying to wipe away the beseeching expression that wanted to cross my face. Queens didn't ask permission. Didn't beg ambassadors to stay.

Felipe's expression softened. "No, Majesty. You are due to inspect the whales for the journey to Reef City. And one of your contestants, Radford, I believe, is to meet you there."

It was a not-so-subtle hint.

I needed to take it.

I knew that I did. But still, I turned back to Mateo. "Can you join me for dinner tonight? We can discuss ... everything then."

Mateo gave a brief nod, and I stood, letting my fins unfurl fully for the first time since he'd walked into the room. His eyes widened a little, tracing them with his gaze. Part of me wanted to ask what he thought of this change, but I was nervous. He took a step back, respectfully putting space between us as I moved toward the hall.

To my surprise, when I reached the doorway, Felipe turned to the second guard, another merman with carrot red hair, a matching tail, and a disposition that was pleasantly sarcastic.

"Ugo, please escort Her Majesty. When you pass the second corridor, ask Walid to join you. I'll be there shortly."

Felipe probably needed a quick break; he had been on duty since the early morning hours. His stamina was endless. I tried to keep my thoughts focused on him instead of the fact that I was leaving behind the only man who might ever love me for myself as I swam with Ugo through the corridors, following each flick of his bright tail, trying not to turn back and look behind me.

Don't do it, Avia, I warned myself sternly. The guards had already seen my weakness. There was no need for anyone else to know. I hoped that I'd kept enough of a facade when Stavros and Humberto had been in the room, or else everyone would be sniffing around for information on Mateo. He didn't need notoriety, especially if he decided to stay on as an ambassador. Because apparently, I was a glutton for punishment. I wanted him near, even if I couldn't have *him*.

I tried to slide a placid mask across my features, but I feared I still looked upset. A maid, one of the many I'd invited to the ball, passed us. Her smile when she came out of her bow was as bright as a copper coin. At least my hope to pacify some of my staff seemed to have worked. The hallways were no longer filled with resentment and scathing glances. "Two dozen down, only a kingdom to go," I told myself under my breath.

I had to prove to them that I wasn't Mayi, the harsh sea sprite who'd ruled Okeanos through force and cruelty. But I also had to prove I wasn't a sky breather without a clue. *My life's as easy as a plankton's.*

We exited the castle and made a sharp right toward what the sea people called "stables." They weren't like the stables on land at all. Really, Okeanos' stables consisted of lines of animals, whales, sharks, and seahorses, tethered to the ocean floor with various anchors. There was no building at all.

Radford's red hair was easy to spot amongst the stable staff who swam about, leading seahorses and polishing saddles. The hermit crab shifter had a larger shell on his back today than he'd worn to the ball, though it looked more ornamental than inhabitable. It was gilded with gold along the spiral that protruded from his back. He stood in front of the largest whale, which was a dull grey monster with a tiny eye and greyish-pink gums that were as tall as my face.

Radford called out to the mer stable boy, who was using a broom to scrape some barnacles off the chin of the gentle giant. "More to the right! That's it!"

The whale gave a shudder and a moan, making the stable boy jump.

"Don't worry, lad, he's not interested in you." Radford swam up, grabbing the handle from the boy's limp hand and then scrubbing furiously at the monster.

My eyes widened and my fists clenched in terror when the whale began to thrash his tail back and forth.

"That's it, that's the spot! See that, kid? If you get their sweet spot, a whale will be yours for life!" Radford yelled as the beast let out a muted noise of contentment, its eyes closing.

Sweet spot? Like a dog when you scratched his belly just right and his leg kicked automatically? Was that possible with whales?

Radford pulled the broom back and started to stroke the side of the whale's face with his hand. "Good boy, Shadow."

There was a thump as the whale's tail hit the ground and made it shake, the sand shifting beneath my feet. The thing was nearly the size of my castle! What was he doing, treating it like it was a pup? That was dangerous!

I couldn't help the tiny yelp I gave when my wings flared and lifted me from the ocean floor to avoid the miniature earthquake.

"Your Majesty." Radford shoved the broom back toward the stable boy and swam over, his strong arm muscles contracting with each stroke.

I immediately tensed. I'd sent one of my four castle mages over to him to hopefully pour a potion over his cracked skull. But the mage had swum back to me and told me that nothing was physically wrong with Radford, there was no crack to mend. I could only conclude that he was mad. The fact that he liked to entice whales to create miniature earthquakes only added mortar to strengthen my conclusion and build a wall between us. His look when he saw me, a bright look that faded to stiff-jawed fury, added another stone.

When he reached me, he bowed stiffly. But then, instead of addressing me, he turned to Ugo. "I'm sorry. I didn't realize you were there, or I wouldn't have done that."

He was going to snub me? What kind of contestant did that? Why the sard had he joined this tournament?

Radford's eyes darted out to the sea, his expression relaxing. But as soon as it slid back to me, his face tightened. I'd never seen anything like it. I'd seen courtiers hate Queen Gela, peasants loathe her. But none ever acted like this. Radford visibly struggled. He closed his eyes and tensed his fists. And then he spoke.

"Sir, will you deliver a message for me?" he asked.

Ugo looked around, his gaze darting toward the stable boy before he asked, "You mean me?"

"Yes, sir. I'd respectfully like you to tell the queen …" He paused for a grimace. "I'd like to request some parchment and ink please. And I'd like to thank … you for the mage."

My brow furrowed as a chill crept up my spine. Something was happening here. The look on Radford's face was almost pained. I exchanged a glance with Ugo, who seemed confused.

"What mage?"

"I sent a mage, to check on him after our meeting at the ball." I licked my lips and stared at Ugo while Radford remained there with clenched eyes and fists, standing stiffly and refusing to look at me.

The mage had said there was no physical injury. But what if there'd been a magical one? Rebels had invaded the ball after all. What if some sort of spell had set Radford off?

I leaned around Ugo and called to the stable boy. "Excuse me."

He dropped the broom. "Y-yes?"

"Can you run up to the castle and get someone to fetch my new handmaid, Gita? Then, when she comes to you, please let her know I need the necklace my sister gave me."

The little mer boy nodded his silver hair and shot off as fast as an arrow.

Ugo just stared at me. Even Radford's eyes had popped open, though he glared. I tried to shuck off the uncomfortable feeling I always got when hatred was shoved in my direction like a bouquet of thorns. Instead, I tried to focus on the problem. "Radford, the night of the ball, did you feel anything unusual?"

"You mean like vomit in my throat at the sight of—" He cringed and turned half away from me.

Ugo's spear lowered, recognizing the insult, but I shook my head and waved my hand. "He's not a threat. I think he might be spelled. You ask him."

Ugo's skeptical expression told me that I was alone in my theory. "You really want me to ask about his feelings?"

"Yes, yes, I know. Men don't talk about those."

"Or ask."

I huffed. "Just do it."

Reluctantly, my orange-haired guard turned to Radford and asked flatly, "What did you feel at the ball?" His lip curled and he muttered under his breath, cursing me, no doubt.

But I only had eyes for Radford, who was carefully staring off into the ocean, his face no longer scrunched in anger. "Everything was wonderful. Then all of a sudden, I couldn't look at her without feeling ... this rage. Still can't."

Ugo's eyebrows shot up. "Is that normal? That rage?"

He asked about feelings a second time without even a grimace now that he was curious himself.

Radford shook his head as his teeth worried his bottom lip. His blood red hair got caught in the current and swept back, and I could see a smattering of red freckles near his hairline. His profile was quite striking, especially with that spiral shell on his back. I hoped I was right this time, though my stomach twisted nervously.

Soon, my new maid, Gita, returned with the stable boy. Her gold tail glinted in the sunlight as she swam forward with a smile, my necklace dangling from her hands. "Majesty, I'm sorry, I didn't realize you wanted to wear this today."

I took it from her with a smile. "Oh, I don't. I thought Radford might." At first, I swam toward him, but he immediately stiffened and his lip curled. His mouth opened as if he wanted to verbally punch me, but he snapped it shut before he could.

I handed the necklace to Ugo. "Can you please put this on him?"

Ugo gave me a respectful nod and turned to Radford with a gleam in his eye. "Come on, pretty lady. Let's get you dolled up."

Radford rolled his eyes before he grinned and let Ugo drape the necklace around his neck and clasp it. "Be careful what you wish for. I might think you have a crush on me."

Ugo barked out a laugh. "Nah, I like my men with soft hands, not those iron paws you've got. Now, what exactly is this supposed to do? Other than make this asshole look ridiculous, of course."

Gita giggled. The stable boy snickered.

"I think he looks lovely." I didn't bother to tell them that the necklace had elven chain in it and that elven chain counteracted nearly all magics. There was no need for more whispers in my castle. But I hoped it had worked. I took a deep breath, ready to face Radford's white-hot scorn, before I slowly swam in front of him.

His face didn't droop into a scowl. In fact, he offered me a friendly smile. "Well, hello again."

Relief and elation swooped through my belly, two birds flying high. "Hello."

Regret immediately crossed Radford's face, and he said, "I want to apologize—"

I spoke over him. "There's no need. Whatever happened to you, it was clearly an enchantment."

His brow furrowed and he looked troubled. "I suppose I should tell you ..." He sighed. "I'm sure you already know, but some of the elders of Nowhere don't want me here."

It felt like a jellyfish sting. I blinked hard. "Thank you, Gita. And you, young fellow." I dismissed the servants before they heard more. No need for everyone to know exactly how hated I was. I clearly didn't do a good job of hiding the disappointment on my face, because Radford swam forward and reached for my hand.

I let him have it, and he squeezed softly. "Would you like to see the rig they have set up for the ride to Reef City? It's the fanciest getup I've ever seen."

"Of course," I responded, letting his enthusiasm wash over me, hoping that it would keep me distracted from the fact that my heart was wilting. Not only had someone enchanted Radford into hating me, but I also now knew that the hermit crab shifters—at least some of them—hated me. I'd never wanted to run in the opposite direction more. I felt the urge to swim right back to the castle and into Mateo's arms. I tried to compensate for all my hurt with a manic grin. "Is it utterly ridiculous?"

"Not if you love golden tassels like the sirens sometimes wear on their ... never mind."

"They wear tassels on their 'neverminds'? Really?" I teased, trying to slip into a lighter headspace as we swam up the animal's side to the giant tent mounted on his back. I knew he was referring to sirens who worked in brothels here, covering things up in order to force customers to pay for the reveal. It made absolutely no sense to me, since most women went about topless, but perhaps it was the chance of touching the breasts after the reveal that piled the sand dollars at the sirens' feet. I added, "I might prefer tassels to nothing around the palace."

Radford chuckled.

"I know it's all the same to you, but I grew up differently." I shrugged. "I'm used to three different layers of clothing."

"Three layers! By the bubble, how do you even move?" Radford shook his head as he pulled open the flap to the white tent.

We both ducked inside as I deadpanned, "Slowly."

The tent was made of material similar to a ship's sails but embroidered with golden thread. And, as Radford had claimed, someone had decided that royalty needed tassels. Hundreds of them dripped from the seams on the ceiling, like tiny jellyfish suspended in space. At the base of the tent, set into neat rows, were seats. They had backs but no legs and stretched seven across on the broad whale's back. Each row was held down with a series of straps and buckles. I counted the rows. There were ten rows in all. Thirty for the men competing, another forty for the staff.

"Impressive is an understatement," I said, running my hand along the back of the first chair. I almost regretted that I would ride separately on a royal whale, with only a few guards, Sahar, and one or two of the competitors at a time in order to get better acquainted.

"I'd say so," Radford replied. But when I glanced up, his eyes weren't on the feat of engineering and planning. They were on me. "Now, look, I'm not a fancy guy like some of these …"

"You certainly can come across a bit abrasive when you're enchanted," I teased, eyes on him. "But before that, you were quite charming. I need to warn you though, court can be a merciless place. You'll have to learn to take vicious cuts smoothly if you decide you want to join."

"If I decide?" Radford swam closer, and I had to tilt my head back to look up at him. "I'm here, aren't I?"

I swallowed hard and gave a brief nod as my eyes studied his, their rich dark chocolate color nearly black when he leaned in. I pulled back slightly and then swam over to run my fingers over the back of a chair, not ready for his intensity.

"Maybe your court could use a bit of roughing up," he added. "Most folk in this kingdom aren't the kind who live in glass houses, if you get my drift."

I teased, trying to lighten the mood, "Is that why you gilded your shell?"

The red of his hair leaked into his cheeks, and he muttered, "My mother did that."

"Well, it matches your new necklace nicely."

He laughed, free and easy, as he hadn't laughed since that odd moment in the ballroom. I turned, swimming back to the tent entrance and flicking it open, only to find Ugo and the other guard hovering just outside.

"I'd better go," I told him.

Radford looked disappointed. "So soon?"

"I have a ton to prepare before we leave. There's a lot of paperwork to running a kingdom."

"I'm sure there's more to do than that."

I sighed. "I wish there was. Unfortunately, I've become more intimately familiar with the royal bookkeeper than anyone else here."

"Intimately, hmm? I'll have to ask him for tips."

A blush rose on my cheeks, and I couldn't help laughing. "That's not what I meant, and you know it!"

Radford grinned. "Do I?"

I shook my head as I swam outside, but I did turn back. "Keep that necklace on for now, but I'll send a mage again to see if they can find the proper potion to reverse whatever happened at the ball."

He gave a brisk nod of thanks. And then I swam off with Ugo and another guard, heading back toward the palace. While I could feel Radford's smile warming my back, I couldn't help the chill that ran through me. Someone had enchanted Radford. But who?

7

An apology is a bow, a verbal way to kneel and accept another's authority. It's the perfect time to slit a groveling man's throat.

—Sultan Raj of Cheryn

I FELT like an utter failure for not seeing it before. People didn't just change in a split second. I should have instantly suspected magic. But I'd always hated whenever anyone hated me. It had always been something that had made me feel desperate, mind blank, made me feel like curling up in a corner. Before I'd found out my true heritage, I hadn't been hated. I'd always been more of a peacemaker. Now ... What was happening? Was it because of Mayi? Because I'd been raised on land? They didn't even know me! I couldn't wring my hands in public, no, I had to flutter my wings a bit more to swim gracefully and give gentle nods of acknowledgment to the people around me as the guards and I swam back to the glowing green palace. No public agitation allowed.

I wanted to cry though. *Why do people hate me so?* All I wanted was to be in this kingdom, this place I was supposed to belong. Did I really not belong anywhere? I didn't belong on land, my wing-like fins and scales proved that. If I didn't find my place here ... if I made too many enemies ... what was I to do?

I could feel a panic whipping up in my insides, as quick as the castle cook beating an egg. I'd be scrambled if I let myself continue down that path, so I tried to focus on something else. I could see the repairs going on, the hot glow of magically-created lava bellows and trowels that the glassblowers used to melt sand into magnificent shapes as they rebuilt my damaged castle. But the shards of the wreckage from the battle were still strewn about the ocean floor. I had to remind myself that the repairs to this kingdom weren't only physical.

Mayi had shattered the people as well.

She'd broken their hopes, cowed them with the might of her magic, bent their wills and tangled them with her own until they hadn't known sand from sky.

I needed to keep that in the forefront of my mind regarding whomever had enchanted Radford. They were probably angry, lashing out.

I paused, my feet sinking to the ocean floor as I debated whether I should turn back and ask him if any others from Nowhere were at the ball. One of my guards swam on ahead as I chewed my lip. No, I should simply have Sahar look into it. I didn't know him well enough yet. And as much as I liked Radford, I wasn't certain I could trust him to tell me something negative about his own people, especially if it might later implicate them.

Ugo turned toward me, a crease appearing between his eyebrows. "Majesty?"

"Queenie!" a boisterous male voice shouted across the courtyard. I whirled, water swirling around me, to find Keelan swimming toward me. Today, his white blond hair caught the rays of sunlight that pierced the depths. He'd changed the bolt of color on the side of his head from green to a vibrant blue as his legs kicked through the water. A sea turtle swam beside him, circling him and then playfully nipping at his heels. The turtle was a mottled green and gold, and roughly the size of a shield, and he looked utterly enamored with the siren.

Keelan didn't slow to a stop when he reached me; to my shock, he barreled right into me full force and sent us spinning, head over feet, in the water. We rolled a few times until his arms grabbed onto me and pulled me to a stop before he spun around to face my guards.

"What kind of *protection* was that?" he scolded, voice irate, hand tossed to the side. "I could have had a weapon hidden on me."

Ugo's cheeks blotched. "You're a competitor."

"Doesn't mean my intentions are noble. In fact, my intentions are pretty damned naughty concerning her, and I'm pretty sure some of the other contestants have motives that are much worse."

Ugo's eyes flitted over to me. I wanted to reassure him, but at the same time, Keelan was right. I sighed and turned to Keelan. "I think you've just condemned me to adding an extra guard at all times."

"Why not two?" Keelan grinned, the shite. He wasn't at all remorseful.

I peered around him, pretending to search the shadowy water in the distance. "Did your mother send you?" Sahar had suggested I increase my royal guard as we started to travel. I'd refused. Had she manipulated this little show?

Keelan shrugged as his sea turtle swam up to him, and he captured it in both hands, exposing its belly as he gave the massive thing a hug. "Even senile old women can have lucid moments."

My eyes narrowed. "I think I liked you better the other night when you and I teamed up against her." Traitor.

He gave an exaggerated shrug and then looked down at his turtle. He adopted a posh accent as he said, "Mr. Whelk, I think Queenie might be mad at us." He paused and tilted his ear toward the turtle's mouth. The creature's pointed pink tongue snaked out to lick the shell of his ear, and he nodded. "Oh yes, I agree, she shouldn't be. We're just looking out for her best interests." Another lick. "But you're right. Women can be utterly irrational."

With a wicked grin at me, Keelan released his turtle, then jetted away so quickly that nothing but a stream of bubbles and laughter was left behind.

"That ass," I grumbled, half amused and half frustrated as I turned back to my guards. He'd made his point, or more specifically, Sahar's point, and then bounded off before I could verbally lash him for it. Brat.

He'd already been at the top of my list, but this interaction cemented his place more firmly. Because even if he was a shite, he talked in silly voices to animals.

Ugo cleared his throat. "Majesty, I want to apologize …"

I waved him off. "I'm sure you won't let it happen again, Ugo. Besides, that bastard was one of you until last week. I'm sure you give him more leniency than you would any other—"

My words were cut off as Ugo grabbed my arm. The thick-browed merman's face was contorted in panic. "Inside now!"

"What?"

My question was swept away as Ugo and the other guard grabbed my upper arms and hurtled toward the castle.

"Faster," Ugo muttered, and their tails began to lash so quickly that their scales scraped the sides of my calves.

A horn started blaring somewhere, like an alarm. All around us, people stopped what they were doing. Nobles swimming in small groups halted their chatter. The glass workers dropped their volcanic bellows. Maids turned, laundry baskets in hand. All of them stared behind and beyond me before they wheeled around and rushed inside.

My heart skipped as bubbles and tiny currents from their flight filled my vision.

What is it?

What's going on?

Panic sizzled inside my skull. My guards didn't drag me to the front door, but up, toward the balcony I'd stood on during the opening ceremony. The door there was a royal entrance, used by none but me. Permanently manned. The footmen had the doors open before we arrived and shut them with a reverberating clang as soon as we were through.

My guards dropped my arms, and I spun around to peer out the glass walls of the castle, determined to understand this threat. Was it one of those mobile islands that Humberto mentioned?

What I saw took my breath away.

There was not a giant island. Instead, a massive orange and pink cloud swept toward the castle as if some magic had grabbed the sky and shoved a bit of it under the sea. Backlit by the sun, the cloud reminded me of sunset, streaks of orange and rose in it. But the texture was wrong. Instead of the cottony softness of clouds, there was a smooth, silken texture to this cloud. Tendrils dripped from the bottom, dangling like ribbons. I squinted, trying to understand what I saw.

A smooth, deep voice resonated in my ear. "It's a bloom of jellyfish."

I turned to find Felipe right next to me, his deep brown eyes firmly placed on mine before they slid down my body, giving me a thrill as strong as if he'd touched me.

He came to check on me. When the alarm sounded, he came to find me and make sure I was alright.

I tried to tamp down my physical response to him, to remind my body that he was required to do so. But when his eyes met mine again, there was a flame in his gaze that hadn't been there before.

I took a deep, calming breath before I asked, "What's a jellyfish bloom?"

He shoved his hands behind his back, transformed his tail into feet so that he stood beside me. He resumed his pose as a guard, reminding himself and me who he was, and what his station was.

I swallowed and took my own tiny step backward, acknowledging the truth he'd stated without words.

His eyes left me as he peered out at the undulating mass that was just reaching the outskirts of the castle grounds. Felipe cleared his throat before he stated, "The mauve stingers swim and live in groups. Sometimes, the current blows them through."

I gazed back out at the mass, and now that I knew what it was, it became quite obvious that every little bump and reflective surface was a jelly. There must have been nearly a thousand. And though they were blown by the current, their bulbous bodies not straining to move themselves, the tendrils that dangled curled and released like hands reaching out and retracting, searching for something to latch onto.

"I assume they sting," I said dryly.

"Yes, you wouldn't want to be caught up in a bloom," he responded. "If you did ... you wouldn't come out."

I watched the colors shift as they moved overhead and the waves changed and my eyes saw them go from a bright pink to a gorgeous purple mass. Such a shame that something so beautiful was so deadly. But that was the way of the world, wasn't it? Sirens and mer people were bewitching predators. On land, dragons were the gorgeous apex predator. The tiger I'd spotted once on our travels to Lored was a good example of another, with its soft stripes and resemblance to a cuddly oversized house cat. If I examined myself too closely, I qualified as another apex predator. Or perhaps I'd be classified as a parasite, someone who lived off another.

My heart thumped in agreement. Stupid thing.

I turned to Felipe, suddenly ready to look at anything other than jellyfish that turned me philosophical. But the way he stared back made me nervous, like he knew what I was thinking.

"You know, there are many intimidating things about living under the ocean," he said. "I can only imagine how I'd feel if I suddenly had to live on land." I swallowed hard when his eyes met mine. "You're quite brave," he added.

He'd never know how much those words meant to me. I had to press my lips together to avoid blubbering. I turned instead and stared back out at the jellies, wondering if they found me as strange as I did them. When I had my emotions under control, I glanced quickly at Felipe but back again. "What's next on my schedule?"

He turned to me, and his posture grew a little stiffer than usual. "Well, Your Majesty, it appears that you—"

"Majesty!" Sahar's voice cut him off as she hurried down the hallway toward me. She swam so quickly that a few of the round magic lanterns bobbed and clinked against the glass walls, making the light dance. "I need your help!" She was somber as she gave a cursory nod of her head, not bothering with a full bow.

"Yes?" I asked, fluttering my wings and swimming to join her.

"That Watkins fellow you added to the tournament is stirring up trouble." Sahar *tsk*ed as she led me up a stairwell that wound around and around, though actually, it had no stairs. Since nearly everyone in the castle swam, the more practical servant walkways that I called stairwells, in my sky breather vocabulary, looked like tubes. They were merely glass tunnels for people to swim through.

Sahar led the way, and my guards and I followed through a maze of intersecting cylinders that boasted a surprising number of servants bustling about their days.

When we had a brief respite from the crowded tubes and some privacy, Sahar muttered, "The situation is contained for now, but I wanted you to see ... I really think it's untenable. His behavior is just ... Watkins shouldn't be here."

I didn't have time to ask her anything further, because she reached an opaque glass door and turned the knob, opening it. We came out in a wing of the castle that had been set up for the competitors. While the castle boasted sixteen guest rooms, we'd had to bring in extra beds in order to accommodate all the contestants. They were "bunking" two to a room with a common lounge that I'd had set up with couches, card tables, and billiards in order to keep them entertained. But apparently, billiards weren't entertaining enough.

My gaze swept across the long room, eyes catching on each of the lovely new "artworks" hanging from the wall. Someone had taken all the cue rods and forced them into the lantern sconces so that they stuck out like flag poles ... or fishing poles. Swinging from each pole was a strip of cloth like a rope and a male effigy made out of what looked like pillowcases and seaweed. The eyes of each effigy had been painted with black *X*s, very clearly dead men.

Etched into the glass wall on the far side of the room was the phrase: "The Queen Goes Fishing."

Internally, I cringed at how close to the truth this life-sized diorama might be. While I didn't plan on killing anyone, I did plan on stealing a man's freedom ... and how far apart were those two things, really? I swallowed hard before I gave a sarcastic smile and turned to look at Sahar, who was studying my expression. "We've quite the artist in our ranks, don't we?"

She didn't answer my question, merely supplied, "I've had a glass worker summoned to erase these etchings. I've also delayed the return of the other contestants so they don't witness this horrid little display, but a few maids are on their way to clean up the mess."

I nodded, swimming closer to examine one of the dummies. As I did, Watkins emerged from a bedchamber at the far side of the hall, leaning against a doorjamb, his black hair with the shock of white making him easy to recognize. I fluttered my fin-like wings and swam over, setting my feet down in front of him.

Once more, I was overcome by a chill that ran down my spine and pebbled my nipples under my dress. Watkins was a dangerous man. His black eyes roamed my face in amused silence. He was quite proud of his work, quite confident in his ability to goad me. For a second, I grew suspicious about his possible involvement in enchanting Radford. But, in order to pull off something like that, Watkins would have needed to plan. Magic took time. Potions took time. I'd only invited the rebels to the ball just before it started. And besides, if he'd pulled off the Radford enchantment, he and his cronies wouldn't have gotten such a thrill out of raising my ire.

He'd succeeded at the ball, that was true. But I wouldn't let him win again. What did he think? Did he believe he'd infuriate me enough to kick him out of the tournament? Or something more? Was he trying to turn the others against me as well?

So many possibilities.

Yes, I'd invited him spur of the moment, in a fit of pique. But I had wanted to ultimately use the opportunity to speak with him. I'd wanted to smooth the waters. Could that be salvaged?

I turned to the nearest effigy and gestured at it. The gruesome thing had a patch sewn onto its chest, a patch representing the rebels' grievances. Sahar had explained the symbol to me. There was a long shell shaped like a horn, an amplifier. They wanted a voice in the government.

I didn't necessarily disagree with that, though both Queen Gela and Mayi would have disowned me upon hearing it.

Defacing my castle wasn't a wonderful start to a conversation, however. It was quite immature. As was his hatred of me. It wasn't even for me; it was for my station. For my predecessor! A woman I probably hated more than he did. Gah! My ire built, stacked up like bricks, until there was a low wall of fury near my knees. Suddenly, I didn't care if he liked me. Not one bit. If Watkins wanted to be immature about it … perhaps I needed to speak to him on his own level.

"You seem quite good with a needle." I gestured up at the dummy's patch. "Must be all that practice touching your tiny cock."

Watkins' expression darkened, and he took a step closer until he loomed over me. While that sent a shiver through me, it wasn't exactly one of fear. There was a darker thrill there, one I had never experienced before. It was luscious like black silk. It caressed my spine as I stared up into the blackness of his eyes. It only grew stronger the more I fought it, the lure of his gaze more intense. I had to be careful not to let my breath catch.

Watkins looked like he wanted to shove me up against a wall and rut me as he strangled me.

Why was it that anyone else could look at me that way and I'd hate it? Why did his looking at me like that, like he wanted to break me into a thousand pieces, shatter me like a shipwreck … why was it so *tempting*?

Was it because somehow, I realized that he couldn't break me any further than I already was? I was on death's doorstep, the knocker had already fallen, all I was waiting on was a reaper to answer.

The tension built between us, breaths growing shallower, eyes locked without keys.

No. If it had been that, then I would have invited all the other rebels to stay, but I hadn't.

There was another reason.

I just wasn't sure what it was, which was bad, because my wall of ire had crumbled. I should have been livid at Watkins. I'd given him a chance, and he'd spit in my face. Competing in the tournament gave him the opportunity to have a serious conversation with me. But apparently, he wanted to squander that.

We held one another's gaze. I watched Watkins swallow hard as his eyes slipped once again and roamed over my figure. I felt his hunger.

Felipe moved to push Watkins back, but I waved my guard off. If the shark shifter wanted to kill me, he'd had plenty of opportunity to wring my neck at the ball. But he'd chosen to stay. I swam even closer to the tall, muscular man, drifting up so that we were eye to eye. "I am going to send a quill, ink, and parchment to you. The quill will be a little bit bigger than what you're used to gripping." I enjoyed the angry flash of his eyes and the gnash of his teeth as I continued, "But I expect you to adjust to its girth and come up with a serious list of your demands of me so we can discuss them on our two-day ride."

"Like you're going to discuss anything with me," he growled.

"I plan to discuss everything with you," I replied softly.

"Liar. You're just like her."

It was as though he'd poured a bucket of ice over my head. "I should hope not."

"If you aren't yet, you will be. You stupid crown heads are all the same."

"Are we?" I turned to Felipe and Sahar. "What would Mayi have done with this asshole?"

"Had him executed," Sahar replied smoothly.

Meanwhile, Felipe simultaneously said, "Rammed a pool stick up his ass and set him up on the wall as an example for the others."

The others. An evil bit of brilliance bloomed inside my head.

I turned back to Watkins. "What's your favorite thing to eat?"

"For a last meal?" he asked.

"For our last meal here before we leave."

He shook his head, refusing to answer.

Sahar volunteered, "Most shark shifters love squid."

"Perfect. Squid for dinner then, Sahar." I reached out and stroked Watkins' arm. He didn't move a muscle, but I felt how tense he was. He really truly thought that I was the enemy. "I'm going to have the cook make your favorite dinner, and then you're going to write me a list. If you don't"—I leaned closer—"I'm going to torture you. But not the way Mayi would have. I'm going to ensure that you get to experience the joys of unjustified hatred, just like you're giving me. I'll make all the others think you're my *favorite contestant of all*."

"They won't believe you," he snarled.

I lifted a hand and traced his jaw. "Don't be so sure." He opened his mouth, but I slid my finger over it. I wanted to know what the rebels wanted. I wanted to know where they thought Mayi had wronged them. I needed someone with the backbone to tell me. And ... I wanted to hear it from him. But if he wanted to stoop to an immature battle of wills before we got to negotiations, so be it.

I heard Sahar chuckle.

Felipe was quiet at my back, but I could feel his grin warming me like sunshine. Or perhaps that was my own mirth as I spotted a maid emerging from a door at the far end of the hall.

I tripled my volume and, in an obnoxiously girlish voice, said, "Watkins, a kiss already! You're so naughty!"

If Watkins had looked like he wanted to kill me before, it was nothing in comparison to his new glower.

I couldn't help a smug grin as I swam away.

8

Happiness is the delusional goal of weaker men, those too afraid to seek power.

—Sultan Raj of Cheryn

WHEN I STUMBLED toward my chamber late that night, the waves above me were laced with moonlight, and I thought foolishly that I was finished with troubles until morning. How wrong I was.

I stepped through the door of my sanctuary, intending to strip off my dress and fall face-first onto my pillow, but Felipe did his cursory check of my bedroom and then swam past me to my door just as I headed for my dressing chamber. The click of the lock made me turn back toward him. He'd locked us inside my sitting room.

The move should not have affected me; I'd been alone in my chambers waiting with him for my maids or Sahar often enough. He was my guard. I trusted him with my life. He never locked the door though. Not of his own accord. Not with just two of us present.

My stomach heated and clenched, and my throat felt lined in syrup too thick to let me speak.

I clasped my hands, unsure of what to do with them. I stared at the glowing orange lanterns, then glanced at him. Then back again.

Should I be hopeful?

There had been that one singular moment as jellyfish sailed overhead, an undulating mass of pain. He'd gazed at me the way a man looks at a woman, not the way a guard looks at his queen.

At least, I thought it had been a moment. I started to second-guess myself.

Perhaps he wanted to discuss the fact that he thought that *I thought* that it was a moment. Oh, all the stars in the sky, I didn't think that I could handle being rejected by my guard. Especially since it would be horribly unfair of me to fire him immediately afterward so I'd never have to face him again.

I swallowed hard as the silence stretched on, and I became more and more certain that Felipe was going to tell me he saw me as nothing more than a child. He was just searching for the words to let me down easily.

Ugh. My stomach transformed, becoming as cold and heavy as iron. Why did I do this to myself? Why did I grow attached to men I knew I could not have? Felipe … Mateo.

I risked another glance at my guard.

Felipe chewed his lip, revealing how nervous he was.

Anxiety started to squeeze my chest and make my cheeks flush with panicked heat. My heart started to sputter. If we didn't get this over with soon, I was in danger of collapse. So despite my utter terror in the face of Felipe's rejection, I spoke.

"When Mayi held me in her cave, she wouldn't come every day. She'd leave me for long stretches with the ghosts." My voice grew quieter and quieter as I recalled my time chained in the cave by my birth mother. "When I asked her why … do you know what she told me?"

Felipe shook his head, his blue and black hair glinting in the light of the lanterns.

"She told me that sometimes anticipation was just as bad as torture."

His throat bobbed as he swallowed hard. "Your Majesty, I hope you won't think that I'm overstepping my place, but …"

Overstepping his place? Did that mean …Was I wrong? Had I been right about our moment?

Was he trying to tell me he was interested?

I felt tugged in every direction, like a puppet on a string, at someone else's mercy. My eyes pled with him to explain, while my nails carved crescent moons into my palms.

His brown eyes bore into mine.

And I started to feel certain again that this, right now, was transforming into another moment.

But he broke the moment when he moved.

Felipe's navy-blue tail emerged in an instant, and with a flick, he was across the room.

I turned to watch, in shock as he knocked on the panel that typically admitted my handmaid.

Disappointment flooded me.

He'd decided not to admit his feelings.

We were going to have to pretend everything was the same as before … only it wasn't.

I stoically swallowed my sigh of disappointment until I realized that the person emerging from the servant's hallway wasn't my maid.

Mateo swam into my room clumsily. Because while he looked like himself from the waist up, he now had silver hair and an iridescent silver mer tail.

I WAS ONLY AWARE OF THE FACT THAT I FAINTED WHEN I woke, laid out on the couch in the sitting room of my private chambers. My windows showed the waves outside were black as ink, meaning it was still night. I glanced at the door that led to the hall. It was still locked. The rest of my room, the tapestries of seashells, the marble sculptures, were all in place, not bowled over as I had been.

As I pushed wearily up into a sitting position, I overheard Mateo's harsh tone coming from behind the couch.

"She's not ready for this. She probably wanted to send me away earlier today. Declan's wrong. You're wrong. Everything is changed—"

"Mateo?" I asked, surprised at how scratchy my voice had become. I gripped my throat lightly as I cleared it and turned my head.

Mateo lowered his finger from where he'd jabbed it accusingly at Felipe.

It did not look like they were getting along.

"Is everything alright?" I asked.

Felipe gave a curt nod, and the two men immediately parted.

Mateo hurried to my side. Of course, he wasn't used to swimming with a mer tail. He flicked it from the knee joint area several times but didn't use his arms for counterbalance so he ended up making himself somersault clumsily through the water, a surprised look crossing his face as he spun. He crashed into a side table, his now silver curls sliding wildly and ripples emanating from where he landed, making all the little knickknacks in the room waver in their places.

"Are you alright?" I stood up far too quickly, felt dizzy, and had to sit right back down. Shite heart.

Meanwhile, Mateo used his arms to push up from the ground.

Felipe called out, "You need to push from the hips. Put your arms out when you move."

Mateo tried again to swim to me, his hips jerking awkwardly back and forth. But he had no rhythm and couldn't get the motion going smoothly, so he ended up just reaching for the nearest chair and navigating it like an ape, using only his hands. He reached out and latched onto the couch arm, pulling himself over to sit next to me.

All the while, I watched in dumb stupefaction. Why had Mateo gotten a tail? Who'd given him one? Why would he need one? And his hair! What had happened to his beautiful hair?

Mateo's hands closed over mine, and he leaned in, contrition written all over his features. "I'm so sorry. I had no idea you'd faint. We should have asked you before. This was a stupid plan. So stupid."

"What plan? What are you talking about?"

Mateo just kept shaking his head, and I glanced over to Felipe for answers.

My guard pressed his lips together. "I noticed how ... attached you were, Your Majesty. And I didn't mean to overstep. I just thought you deserved some happiness despite all this business. I can see how much the other contestants frustrate you."

My brow furrowed as my bleary mind tried to process everything he'd just said. The other contestants ... *other* contestants ...

I turned toward Mateo, eyes widening in horror. "You didn't!"

"See?" Mateo dropped my hands and jerked up from his spot, though he couldn't keep himself from tilting forward. He turned toward Felipe and started to clench his fists. "She doesn't want me."

His fierce words ripped a hole in my chest. How could he say that? Ever? "Of course I want you! But I can't—"

"You can't marry anyone who doesn't complete the tournament tasks," Felipe finished smoothly. "Which is why, Mateo, idiot *cousin* of mine, was late to arrive for the tournament."

"He's not from Okeanos!"

Felipe's brow quirked, emphasizing a little scar there. "Yes, he is. My *cousin* was attacked by a hammerhead when he was younger. It's left him a little uncoordinated and a bit soft in the head," Felipe replied smoothly. "He forgets things. Like his parents, or the national anthem, or what his favorite type of eel is."

No. My eyes flitted from one to the other. They both were still and calm. Felipe even looked confident. Couldn't they see how foolish this idea was? "No one will ever believe it."

"I already introduced him to his bunkmate an hour ago. A man named Julian. He didn't seem to have any issues." Felipe gave a careless shrug.

"If anything, he was fascinated by me," Mateo muttered. "Asked me if I'd ever heard of blood-letting treatments. Some fool has decided that draining your blood is a better idea than allowing a healer to use magic on you."

"What?" I shook my head adamantly. "You can't possibly win this tournament! I didn't even design these challenges! I don't even get to score them. They're meant to test sea men's wit, will, strength, and heart. But you've only been here—"

"I'm coaching him," Felipe interrupted. "He'll be fine."

"He can hardly swim!"

Felipe's eyes narrowed and his voice took on a low, commanding growl that I'd never heard from him before. "He'll. Be. Fine."

It was official. I was going to pull my hair out. Two of the most honorable men I knew had decided that they were going to hoodwink an ancient tournament in order to ... what? Fail horribly ... or try to ensure my happiness?

Tears suddenly brimmed in my eyes, which was ridiculous because we were under the sea. They felt just as hot and salty as ever, though. I shook my head, not quite believing but at the same time realizing that these two foolish bastards had just done something so wonderfully and dangerously dumb; they'd restored my hope. And what could I do? They'd already introduced Mateo to the other competitors. It was already done. Removing him from the competition would only make the others suspicious of me. Perhaps I needed to just realize and accept this wildly ridiculous gesture for what it was. A gift. So that my life wouldn't have to be filled with only loveless marriage.

My eyes met Mateo's and softened, all the longing inside me streaming out in a singular look, wrapping around him.

His own chocolate gaze grew hooded, and he sat back down beside me, reaching out and taking my hands in his. "If you want me, I'll do my best to win."

A tear dripped from my eye, and his face blurred as my tears joined the ocean around me, just another drop of saltwater. My heart contracted. And I couldn't tell if I was light-headed because of him or because I was dying. I pretended to myself that it was all *him*.

I reached out and let my hand sweep gently over his jaw, feeling the end-of-day stubble there. He was here and I was here, and he still wanted me and I still wanted him, and now we had a chance.

It was perfect.

The most perfect moment I'd ever experienced.

"You'd better go," I whispered softly, caressing his cheek, longing for a kiss but not wanting an audience, even if it was our matchmaker. I slowly lowered my hand, and Mateo grabbed it and pulled my palm toward himself. He kissed the base of my palm softly, and my stomach exploded with joy.

We lingered for a moment. Part of me didn't want him to go, but the other part knew that the other men in the tournament would be expecting him. If I showed too much favoritism, they might get suspicious. I didn't even want to think of what might happen if they found out he wasn't from the sea.

Felipe cleared his throat.

Finally, Mateo pulled back from our stare with a sigh. "Well?" he looked up at Felipe. "Come on. Help a poor crippled merman out."

"Stop saying that, people will take you seriously," Felipe grumbled as he swam over to help Mateo. He pulled the younger man up and put an arm on his shoulder to guide him.

"Now gently with the tail," Felipe instructed.

Of course, Mateo's tail swung out wildly and whacked my guard. I wasn't quite sure if it was on purpose or not, but it still made me giggle.

I watched the pair bicker as they left my chambers through the servant's entrance, a fond smile settling on my lips and refusing to budge.

Until my heart gave an untimely lurch.

That just brought everything back to the stark reality. I had to select one of these men to become a sacrifice, because my life and Mateo's happiness now depended on it.

9

Fascination is one step in the direction of foolishness.

—Sultan Raj of Cheryn

THE SOUND of a whale moaning woke me with a start. I bolted upright in my bed, for a moment uncertain where I was and what was happening. I glanced at the window. Outside the castle, the water had lightened from pitch black to a deep turquoise that I knew signified it was morning. Outside, the hum of people moving and chattering drifted up and reminded me of birdsong. That memory made me temporarily nostalgic because I was unlikely to hear birdsong ever again.

The things I took for granted about my old life ... even the simplest ones, had begun to resonate.

I heard a shrill whistle, and the entire castle swayed as the giant whale bellowed again, moving closer. That's when I remembered. Today was the day. The whale was just outside the doors so that we could load up our traveling party with ease. Excitement and trepidation leapt inside my chest as I shoved back my silken sheets. Today we left the safety of my walls in the capital, Palati, and traveled to Reef City for the first competition. We'd even have to make camp for a night, just like a traveling band of musicians. For a princess who'd been stuck in a castle most of her life, *that* was an adventure.

I stretched and sighed, rolling my shoulders to ease their ache before climbing carefully off of my circular mattress and flexing my wings. Despite the fact that I'd hardly slept—knowing Mateo had joined the tournament had left me tossing and turning with a mixture of anticipation, longing, and dread—I felt energized.

I went through my morning ablutions quickly, allowing Gita to help me slide on a red traveling gown. The golden-tailed mermaid *ooh*ed and *aah*ed over it, despite the fact that it was still conservative. I agreed. My seamstress had outdone herself, thinking of both beauty and comfort. The dress was made of silk and embroidered with golden angel wing shells, and while it lacked the layers that I would have preferred for riding on a stone gargoyle or sitting on a hard bench inside a shell carriage, I was told extra skirts would only get tangled around my legs if I swam at all in the swift open ocean currents. Unlike Palati, which was buffered by the Systrofi Mountains and Kelp Forest on the east, the path to Reef City was through the plains. There was nothing to stop the currents from shoving wildly out there, which was why a whale and carriage had been chosen to transport us. Well, that and the sheer size of our traveling party.

I sat still as my honey-colored hair was put into a side braid, with bits of pink coral woven into it. A necklace of multi-colored sky breather coins was placed around my neck, and several armbands decorated with more beads shaped from pink coral enclosed my biceps. There were no shoes because I was expected to swim. Okeanos residents didn't need shoes. But I was used to walking, and it was a hard habit to break. I had no problems inside the glass palace, but outside, well, I'd just have to learn.

I jangled my necklace nervously. "Do you still think this is a good idea? Wearing coins? Quite a few people hate my heritage."

Gita smiled and pulled my hand from the necklace. "Some do, but others are ready for trade, ready to embrace the world again. Besides, you are what you are."

When my face had been made up, Gita leaned back and clapped. Her own golden puff of hair—artfully pulled into a giant poof on the top of her head and offset with a silver starfish clip—bobbed as she sighed wistfully. "You look so beautiful, Your Majesty. They'll all be falling over themselves to get to you."

"I should hope not. I'm clumsy enough myself. I don't need husbands who are as clumsy as me."

She tittered like a young girl at my lame attempt at humor, and swam off to get our things loaded for the journey.

I, on the other hand, cracked my neck and fingers as if preparing for a fight. Then I swam forward. I had hoped to leave the castle and look over the whale and my own carriage before everyone else arrived. But my door swung open before I could touch it, revealing a very smug Declan.

"Why *good morning*, little sister," he declared as he shut the hall door, unable to keep an arrogant grin off his face. The self-satisfied bastard.

I couldn't even truly be annoyed at him for his interference. I was thrilled that I was going to get to see Mateo later today. And tomorrow. And possibly forever.

I did bite down on my smile, though, when Declan brushed back his blond hair and cupped a hand to his ear dramatically, saying, "Well? I'm not hearing any gratitude."

I gritted my teeth, but I couldn't keep the smile away any longer. My mirth betrayed me as I replied, "You might get some thanks if you weren't so arrogant about it."

Declan huffed, turned, and marched back to the door, yanking it open. "Felipe," he called, "come in here a moment, would you?"

My guard entered quietly, taking up his post by the door. His brow furrowed, revealing that scar in his eyebrow I was so curious about. "Yes?"

"Tell me, did she squeal last night when she realized?" Declan asked as he shut the door again, sealing our conversation off from the mer people swimming in the hallway. "Did she cry?"

Felipe's lips pressed into a thin line. "Actually, she yelled at us and called us idiots."

Declan waved a hand at him dismissively. "Bah! Spoilsport! That's not true at all." Declan turned to wag a finger at me. "I'm not sure what you did to get this guard in your pocket, but keep him there. He's annoyingly loyal to you."

I physically restrained myself from glancing over at Felipe in that moment. Instead, I focused on my "oh so superior" brother-in-law. Reserved with everyone else in the world, Declan had always been more playful with me. I was glad it was he who'd come, and suddenly a bit wistful. Because I realized that he wouldn't stay forever. "Well, I suppose now that your grand scheme is complete, you'll be returning to Bloss and the others?"

Declan put a dramatic hand to his heart. "Sadly, yes. But one of us will be back periodically to check on you, have no fear."

"On the contrary, I'll have quite a bit of fun planning just how I should meddle in your life." I raised a sarcastic brow, but I didn't mean it, and a moment later I had swung forward in order to wrap my arms around Declan's waist. I squeezed him hard. "Thank you," I whispered into his chest. Of all the people in Evaness, Declan had always seen me. He'd always seen what I needed. Always helped.

His hand came to my hair, and he gently stroked it the way Queen Gela used to when I was but a child. "Always, Avia. We will always be here for you."

Three hours later, I was dreading the fact that I had let Sahar talk me out of riding a gargoyle astride. Posey, the only other part-sprite I knew, had gotten to ride my favorite mount, a stone beast I liked to call Harry because he was carved to look like a lion. Of course, Posey could do all sorts of things I couldn't do. She wasn't queen, and so she didn't have to have the same protections.

"I'm also undead," she'd said, raising a half-rotted brow at me when I'd grumbled about the carriage. "The cold won't affect me the way it would you." It was an unfortunate truth. Posey was the half flower sprite that had been part of the undead army that had marched here with my sister and defeated Mayi. She'd stayed on to be part of my guard, and I relied heavily on her, since she was as much an outsider as I was. She'd been gone the past few days, after the ball, coordinating things in Reef City. But she was back to accompany us, her purple petal hair slicked back, her once-even features sagging as rot and decay set in. "You'll like the carriage. It's very ... girlish."

That was Posey-speak for gaudy. I'd peered through the crowd and spotted several gleaming white seahorses, their spikes painted silver, pulling an enclosed cream carriage decorated with swirling gold edging around the windows, roof, and doors. The shape had to have been taken from the sky breather kingdoms, for it looked a lot like those from home, just

... a bit more ostentatious. The fact that it was surrounded by a dozen guards riding seahorses, tiger sharks, and gargoyles only added to the pageantry. Each guard wore full armor and carried a spear lit with magical orange streaks that danced from the tips like streamers.

"I don't suppose I can ride on the whale instead?" I'd asked half sarcastically.

"The people expect it," Sahar had argued. "The seahorses are the symbol of your house. It's ceremonial. And the carriage protects you ... from the current." She hadn't meant from the current.

Foolishly, I'd listened to her advice and let Posey ride my gargoyle. But with two extra competitors, there were no longer enough seats on the whale for all the men. So I had the constant *pleasure* of entertaining them, two at a time.

I was currently tucked in the middle of the scientist siren named Julian—Mateo's roommate—whose brown eyes glinted a bit manically. The light of the sole circular bobbing glass lantern that floated aimlessly throughout the carriage reflected in his irises. When it bumped the side of his head, he shoved the little floating glass sphere aside as he continued a rant about medicine without magic, a topic on which he'd been speaking for the past twenty minutes. "Can you believe they think that?"

He snorted in derision. "Mesmerization as a means of sedation before surgery?! Utter madness. I can't believe they wasted the ink and parchment to write that bullshite down. Of all the foolish things. Yes, let me wave my hand in front of you and speak a bit, that will ease the—"

Basil, the squi-shifter on my other side, interrupted Julian, leaning forward so that I was forced to recline completely in my seat. "What is surgery?" His large forehead creased in confusion, and I had to say, I secretly found him one of the most unattractive men in the competition. His mouth area was a little … beaky. It was almost as if his squid beak didn't fully transform when he changed shapes. But acknowledging that, even to myself, made me feel a little guilty. Before magic had made me into a sprite, I'd considered myself on the wrong side of pretty. Until Mateo at least.

Julian's face flushed, and his eyes widened for a moment as if he could not believe the utter ignorance of the man sitting on my left side. But he took a deep breath and then calmly explained, "It's the treatment of internal injuries without magic."

"Wait. What? How do you treat them?" Basil let his thick brows draw together so that they nearly touched. He'd clearly done an excellent job of following Julian's conversation, which had basically begun as soon as they'd both sat and Julian had folded up the parchment he'd received from a fellow "scientist" in the city of Sky Stones.

"With knives and stitching to repair the injury, sewing it up just like a hem."

Basil snorted. "That sounds *stupid*."

I heard Julian grind his teeth together, and my eyes darted between the two of them, semi-amused. How would the budding non-magical healer handle the derision his work was likely to receive?

"I'll have you know I've performed four operations myself," Julian responded primly.

"Four people let you cut on them? Four *live* people?"

Color rose on Julian's cheeks. "Of course *not live*. It would never do to practice one's techniques on the living until they were perfected."

"Oh. I understand now. You're more like a butcher. Or cannibal." The squi-shifter sat back in his seat, tossing an arm casually behind my shoulders. Smug satisfaction radiated from him as Julian clenched his fingers and began to shake in a fit of rage.

"That's not it at all and you know it!"

I debated internally whether I wanted to allow this banter to continue, if I should stand up for Julian,—but that would show favoritism—*or* if I should put us all out of our misery by sending both of them away.

While I wasn't necessarily attracted to Julian, I did find his ideas quite fascinating. As someone who'd had to live without magic for so many years, I did recognize there was a huge need for people without magic to find self-worth and for the world to have solutions that didn't involve magic. I was attracted to his ideas.

As far as I could tell, based on the small amount of information I'd been able to extract from Basil, he was a fisherman who spent his days tossing nets and collecting shrimp. A completely necessary vocation. Honorable even. But a bit on the boring side. And it seemed like the mind between his ears was as soft as a fried egg. A small part of me was tempted to kick him out of the carriage and keep Julian so that I could ask about all the macabre details of his "operations," but the speculation that would cause was not worth it. Not when I didn't intend to make Julian a favorite because it would just be too unkind to him.

My curiosity would have to remain unsatisfied.

I opted instead for my age-old standby, to break up the tension by changing the focus. "So, tell me what you know about Reef City. Any favorite haunts?"

There was an awkward moment where both the men stared at me, and my smile grew a bit stiff. But gradually, Basil cleared his throat and said, "Well, there's a pub—"

At the exact same moment, Julian replied, "Well, there's a library—"

They glared daggers at each other.

Luckily, Sahar opened the door at just that moment and stuck her head inside. "Gentlemen, I'm sorry to disturb you, but some other contestants need time with Her Majesty."

Once they'd exited, she told me, "You get thirty minutes reprieve before the next batch come. Use it wisely."

I could have kissed her. A moment alone was a rare and precious gem to a queen. Of course, I squandered my minutes with a nap.

CAMPING WAS NOT NEARLY THE FUN ADVENTURE IT WAS made out to be in stories. First of all, it was bitterly cold, and my seamstress, who'd never left Palati, had left me woefully unprepared for that. I rubbed the scales that lined the outsides of my arms, trying to warm myself, even debating if I should swim closer to the surface in order to warm up a bit, despite being told repeatedly that we were just beneath hammerhead territory, and it would be incredibly stupid of me to do so.

The plains were much lower in elevation than Palati, and the water was chilly and dense at this depth. Our tents couldn't touch the actual sea bed, because that would be far too cold for most of us to survive the night. So instead, our tents were floating cubes attached to anchors buried in the sea floor. I watched Felipe and several other soldiers construct my tent with metal poles, drop the anchor, and then stretch whale skin across the sides to enclose it. There was only a tiny narrow slit for me to squeeze through in order to enter, and the entire thing looked hardly large enough to fit me, though I supposed that meant my body heat would fill the space decently.

Around my tent, my guards set up their own, and though they slept two to a tent, their rigs were the same as mine. I looked outward and realized we had created a little village of bobbing cubes. A smile quirked my lips, and a little sliver of excitement crept back into my frozen bones at that novelty.

Once my guards were finished, Posey and Felipe came to fetch me. They led me upward, swimming to above the little maze of cubes to the spot where the servants prepared our meal. Four magical, smokeless, purple bonfires floated in the water, with no kindling or source other than that provided by the four castle mages. Each mage had a hand pointing at the fire as they muttered some spell or another.

I didn't know the up or down of it. As much as I'd tried to get a handle on spells when I was younger, as much as I'd dreamt of surprising Bloss and mother—Queen Gela—with my brilliance, I'd never had a single potion go right for me.

"They're good, aren't they?" Posey asked, nodding her head toward the flames that I watched.

"Quite," I agreed with a nod.

"See how they keep the fire steady, unaffected by the current, giving off bright white and violet streams of light? Means they're doing it right," Posey added.

"Well, it means Lizza is a good teacher," I responded. Bloss's mage, Lizza, had agreed to come down on occasion to coach the four mages that had come from various cities in the kingdom when I'd put out a call. Thus far, a whopping single meeting in, the lessons seemed to be going well. Part of me wanted to ask the mages about what they'd discovered with Radford. He'd been cheery all day, but he was still wearing my necklace. I rather wanted it back. But I thought that questions might possibly distract them.

I was right.

I saw Julian approach one of the mages and ask a question. The mage's fire flickered.

Posey gave a strange guttural sound of annoyance—sometimes it sounded as if part of her voice box was rotting—and swam off to scold him.

That left me alone with Felipe.

I glanced around surreptitiously before I asked, "How's your cousin today?"

Felipe took his time responding, letting his eyes casually scan for onlookers. Once he'd determined there were none, he replied, "Well, Your Majesty."

That was it? *Well?* I'd been worried all day about how Mateo would do being in close quarters with other competitors. Would he be found out? Would he pull off this charade? I wanted to kick Felipe in the tail for that answer. No, somewhere higher.

He glanced over, and I swear for a second, I thought I saw a smirk cross his features. But it was gone before it started. Instead, his eyes latched onto someone behind me, and he gave a quick nod. "I'll be back in an hour or two."

I turned to see Ugo and a yellow-tailed guard swim up and flank me.

I didn't get to ask one more question about Mateo before Felipe's navy-blue tail had flicked and he'd shot through the water.

Ass.

"Your Majesty, you look like you need to warm up," Ugo stated. He urged me to move a bit closer to the fire. I was immediately relieved by how much warmer I felt. My fingers tingled almost painfully as feeling was restored to them.

The scent of cooking salmon drifted to me on the current, and my stomach rumbled.

My gaze roamed over everyone as they gathered closer to the food, competitors and servants alike, mingling without distinction. The mood was jovial; people laughed and chattered happily as several people began distributing drinks. I spotted Radford even serving. I recognized several men from the competition and gave them all polite nods of acknowledgment. Thankfully, none approached my fire, and I was able to warm up in peace.

"Shouldn't you be rubbing elbows with some of your future husbands?" Sahar asked as she sidled up to me.

"Why don't you just talk to them and tell me which ones I should pick?" I deadpanned.

"Har har."

"Well, I could just pick Keelan and be done with it," I teased. Well, half teased. He was actually at the top of my list.

Sahar tossed a hand over her heart. "Do not steal my baby. He isn't ready for married life."

I studied her face, the slight creases near her eyes, trying to decide whether or not she was serious.

Her expression softened. "Part of me is glad you two seem to get along. But the other part is a little bit terrified. I'm not ready for this. I wanted at least another decade of him being *my* baby." She sighed. "One day, you'll understand the mother's dilemma. You want to both let your child roam free and keep them locked up tight forever. A mother's heart is a giant contradiction."

I gave a shrug. "I suppose I've only ever experienced the locked up tight part of that equation. Then again, anyone who mothered me wasn't quite ... *normal*." I stared into the fire, realizing how bitter that sounded. I hadn't meant to say it at all. Though it was true. It was clear that Sahar loved Keelan fiercely and he her. Growing up, I'd always thought Bloss, as the heir, had been mother's favorite by default, despite the fact that they constantly butted heads. I'd always been closer to Gorg, the man I'd thought was my birth father.

Now, I second-guessed every interaction I'd ever had with any of my so-called parents. I had no idea what was real and what had been an act.

The flames danced in front of me as memories of happy times warped and twisted like they were inside the fire.

Sahar floated closer and placed her hand gently on my elbow. Her eyes swam with pity. But she said nothing because there was nothing to be said. My birth mother had not loved me. Queen Gela?

I'd never know. She'd passed away before all of this happened.

I forced my wings to flutter, keeping me aloft near the fire so that I wouldn't sink like a stone. But my heart itself had settled on the ocean floor, cold, sad, and as hard as one of the rocks that lay there in the darkness.

I felt a smack on my elbow as Sahar jerked me out of my thoughts. "None of that," she scolded. "The past is the past, and there's nothing we can do about it except not repeat it. Come on, let's grab some fish."

We swam to the next fire over and were handed two metal bowls with a bit of fish in each. No utensils. Felipe appeared, back from wherever he'd been, and handed me a flask of fermented bubble, saying, "I tested it. It's good."

My inner self shot up from the depths of the ocean at that little fact. His lips had touched this flask. My lips were going to touch the same spot his once had, like the ghost of a kiss.

God. I was an idiot. Still, that didn't stop me from raising the flask to my lips as a giddy little shiver ran down my spine. I took a drink, and the alcohol burned the back of my throat. When I lowered the flask, I had to swallow hard a second time, because the expression on Felipe's face made some little part of me wonder if he had thought the exact same thing as me.

No. Wishful thinking.

"Come on and eat. As soon as we finish, the singing starts," Sahar admonished me, pulling me back toward what I realized was my own royal fire. No one else crowded around it.

I felt momentarily guilty about that, but after having been in the cramped carriage all day long, I wasn't about to lose my chance at a small reprieve.

The fish went down easily, warming my belly and helping improve my mood, not nearly as much as the flask did. After a few more swallows from it, I was feeling very merry indeed.

I watched as several of the servants, and at least one of the competitors, got out instruments and set up in a rough circle. They began to play a song that was quite different from any that I'd heard in the castle. It involved a lot of clapping by all the participants.

Though travel is folly, boy,

Don't be melancholy, boy,

Just drink and be jolly, boy,

'Cause there is a dolly, boy,

Waiting for you.

Every single member of our retinue joined in the song. Some linked elbows and swam in circles. Others swayed with their hands held high as the song spoke about seeking a better fortune and hope. By the time the last note faded, my heart bobbed like a buoy high on the crests of the ocean.

For one single evening, I forgot all my troubles.

10

Fools scream and yell in anger. Smart men smile and plan.

—Sultan Raj of Cheryn

THE NEXT MORNING, the fact that all my guards wielded their sparking magic spears should have put me on high alert. But my mind was as slow as a glacier. Around me, everyone but Posey and Felipe moved slowly; I had a feeling we had all over imbibed the night before.

I overheard one of my guards tell Ugo, "My head is pounding, there must be a pressure change."

"The only pressure change is the fact that you're dehydrated from taking in so much damn bubble," Ugo quipped as he pulled a set of poles out of his own tent simultaneously, making one side collapse.

"Sard you," the other guard grumbled as the tent poles clanked loudly, making him wince.

Ugo tossed a sarcastic hand over his heart. "If only I thought that offer was real."

I tried but couldn't stifle my giggle. Both guards whirled around, their eyes growing round when they saw me. I waved a hand dismissively before they could offer an apology. "Carry on."

Once the camp was packed up, and a breakfast of seaweed-wrapped shrimp was dispersed for everyone to eat on our ride, I settled into my carriage, resigned to another day of awkward conversation and the overpowering scent of testosterone. It was a smell that had a wide range, varying based on the male's species. Sirens simply made everything saltier, almost as if they were brining the ocean. They made up the greatest contingent of my competitors; there were nearly twenty of them. There were also six mermen, not including Mateo. Mermen gave off a musky scent that was very similar to human male sweat. The shifters, however, gave off a very pungent and spicy scent. Yesterday, my carriage had basically become an olfactory dump, scents piling up and mingling until I'd wanted to retch.

I was pleasantly surprised when I climbed into my carriage and the scents from yesterday had washed away. Bless that swift plains current. I was even more pleasantly surprised when I realized that the one man I'd danced with at the ball, and had not seen since, had been assigned to ride with me.

The silent siren, as I'd called him in my head, perched gently on the cushioned bench seat. His golden skin was a bit paler or pinker than the other sirens, a bit more luminous—something. The man was tall enough that he slouched a bit so his head wouldn't hit the ceiling of the carriage, though some of his pale pink hair still looked as if it touched the top. He wore all black, just as he had when he'd asked me to dance. Like that night, his hazel green eyes burned fiercely, though his lips were silent as he held a hand through the open doorway to help me in.

My hand was tiny in comparison to his, and suddenly, I was very aware of how his biceps flexed when he moved me onto the seat next to him with hardly any effort. Unlike that night, I noticed he wore jewelry today. There were two golden rings on the top of his left ear, another gold ring pierced the corner of his mouth. On another man, they might have looked feminine. Of course, on another man, pink hair might have looked that way, but not on him. Everything about him was entirely and utterly male.

When I was seated, he stared at me for a long moment before he softly said, "Hello." His voice was melodic, sweet to the ear the way honey was to the tongue.

When I glanced over, I noticed a stray lock of hair had fallen across his eyes, and I felt the strangest desire to brush it back. I didn't. Instead, I fussed with my skirts a bit, then found myself fidgeting with my breakfast roll.

What an idiot! I gave him a bright smile, trying to overcompensate for my nerves frothing unexpectedly, like seafoam. I was probably making him uncomfortable. "Good morning, I've been wondering when I would get to see you again. You never introduced yourself, though you made quite an impression."

He gave me a slow grin. "Good." And suddenly, I very much doubted I had the ability to make him uncomfortable. I doubted anyone did. His smile was smooth as silk, full of confidence. It was the smile of a man who was about to take exactly what he wanted. And I had the feeling that was exactly what he'd meant to do. This siren, whomever he was, was patient. Strategic.

"So, what's your name, siren?" I asked as I slid sideways along the bench to give myself more space to peruse him, not because my palms had grown slick and my nipples had pebbled and I was attempting to keep my wayward body under control.

I'd have lied about it if someone asked, but I'd had at least one naughty dream about this nameless man, one vision of him spinning me out of the ballroom and slamming me up against a tapestry hanging on the wall … I hoped my eyes didn't give away my thoughts, but I couldn't be sure, because his grin only grew.

"Valdez," he replied, shifting in his seat so he could face me fully. His movement made our knees brush together, and I was suddenly self-conscious of the fact that my traveling dress today, a deep purple number with slits in the skirt for swimming, was a bit more promiscuous than I was used to. Not to mention that I'd only quickly scrubbed at my teeth this morning. My tongue ran over them, though it was foolish—we weren't going to be kissing.

Where was that other competitor? We were two seats shy on the whale's back, with my two last-minute competitors. I needed a distraction; I needed the other one to be gross and douse the fire that lit between my legs as Valdez continued his silent stare. I glanced out the window, but the carriage jerked forward, seahorses grunting as they began to move.

I furrowed my brow and turned back to Valdez. "Yesterday, I always had two competitors at a time in here. Did someone get left behind?" I leaned forward to peer out the carriage window, reaching for the door handle. "Perhaps I should find Sahar—"

Valdez's hand closed over mine. "Don't go. I asked her for the chance to talk to you alone."

I turned back to look at him. And all the prior impressions I had of him being sweet, romantic, the type of knight-on-a-horse that every princess dreams about while she jills off in her tower bedroom, vanished. This gleam came into his eyes that made everything else in the carriage blur, his pupils blew out, and the scent in the carriage changed … It was different from anything I'd smelled before, almost floral. What did that mean?

"Alone. Is something the matter?"

"No, nothing."

He didn't expand.

I couldn't help but glance down at our hands. When I looked back up, the intensity of his gaze pressed me back against the seat, and I struggled to find some distraction. "Your rings, they're quite unusual."

A slow grin crept over Valdez's face. "Yes, well, in my line of work, there's an old tradition, you get a ring for each conquest."

"Conquest?"

His fingers slid up my hand and to the underside of my wrist. Sensation and vulnerability swam up my arm. My breath fled.

His eyes grew hooded. "Yes. I'm what some might call ... a pirate."

"A thief?"

"Some call it thievery. I call it commandeering. I take what I want. Ships—"

"Carriages?" I tried levity as a means of breaking the tension that had built between us. But it was too colossal. Like a forty-foot wave, I was caught up in it, no escape.

Valdez grinned and leaned closer until we were merely a breath apart. His breath caressed my lips as he whispered, "Queens."

A second later, his lips pressed to mine.

Blood pounded in my temples, and my vision swam. And my brain screamed a million things at once. *I don't even know you! Yes! No! Wait! Pull my hair!*

That wave of lust crashed down on me, and I was caught in a dangerous undertow for a minute, unsure what direction was up, certain I was drowning.

Valdez didn't pull my hair, but he did nip my bottom lip before he pulled back, eyes smug. "I knew it," he whispered.

"Knew what?" My voice was ragged.

Crash!

The carriage rocked to the side, and I fell into Valdez. My nose smashed into his pecs, and my wrist crumpled in pain as it hit the wall behind him. My skull screamed. But adrenaline hit at the same time.

The sound of shouting came to my ears. But it wasn't the panicked shout of men during an emergency. It was the angry sound of a mob awaiting a hanging.

Frost formed inside my chest as I realized that we were under attack.

"What the sard?" Valdez's eyes narrowed, and a dagger appeared in his hands out of nowhere.

I shoved off of him and went to look out the window, but his long arm shot out and pinned me down on the bench. "Don't, Avia." He pointed the knife at me like a tutor would a piece of chalk, scoldingly.

Fury embroidered my every thought, weaving through me as I stared at him. What was going on?

My anger was obvious, stitched across my face. Valdez's expression softened in response, and he put the knife down to his side. "Forgive me. I forget, you have magic to defend yourself." His hand slowly retreated, but as it did, I felt suddenly bereft. Not because of the loss of his touch. But because he was wrong.

In order to possess the power to control the waves, to create tsunamis and typhoons, a half-sprite had to pay a price: her humanity. I had to get rid of my heart. Physically.

I already planned to do that. But Posey had warned me that, if I ever accessed the inhuman magic, I might become what Mayi had become ... an emotionless monster. Literally and figuratively heartless.

An explosion sounded, and shockwaves shoved the carriage again. I was thrown to the floor, my knees smacking and pain lashing me like a whip. Valdez landed on top of me, and my ribs stabbed my innards. Black spots filled my vision as he pulled himself up. I blinked sluggishly when he rolled me over, unable to catch my breath because the stupid organ in my chest stuttered.

I should just have him cut it out right now with his dagger, the errant thought floated up like a bubble. I saw Valdez's hand come down. He reached for my face, but all I could do was watch dully—

The door of the carriage flew open, and Felipe burst inside. His arms were around me less than a second later, and then we went hurtling out of the carriage in a blur of bubbles as he yelled, "Get out!"

Just then, a huge boulder smashed into the side of the carriage, denting it with a screech that made the metal howl and the seahorses scream in fear.

"Who?" I could hardly get out the single word.

"Rebels," Felipe whispered in my ear, one of his hands curled possessively just above my ass, the other still clenched on his spear, though the bicep of his weapons arm wrapped around the back of my neck, pressing my face to his collarbone, my lips just a hair's breadth from his pulse, which thundered. He didn't stop swimming.

Where's he going? We were in the middle of the open ocean! There was nowhere to hide.

The wild war cries of the rebels reached my ears, and I craned my neck to look over his shoulder. Men who were half shifted, with shark tails but male torsos and heads, surrounded our traveling party. They'd painted their faces and arms with bands of yellow and carried golden tridents in their hands. Behind the shark shifters, who aggressively circled, getting closer with each pass, was an entire contingent of mermen. But instead of rainbow colors in their hair and tails, these mermen had covered their entire bodies in squid ink so that they were nothing more than dark shadows. Only the whites of their eyes and their teeth were visible as they screamed, "Down with the foreign queen!" and "Sand and water don't mix. They make mud!"

Cold gripped me, just as it had in the caves where Mayi had held me. For a split second, my mind went back there. To darkness. To the depths of despair. But I forced those thoughts down when one of my maids shrieked in fear. The tent on top of the whale collapsed on one side, fabric sagging then writhing as the people trapped beneath it tried desperately to escape.

No!

I didn't picture my maid's face or her fear. I didn't picture any of the others. My heart instantly sought Mateo. I knew he'd been seated near the back of the animal, and my chest thumped furiously at each figure that emerged from the tent, hoping he was alright, even as several of my guards engaged in fighting around the sides of the whale, squaring off against the rebels.

Iron clashed as spear met trident, and the clang of metal and fierce yells of the men on both sides filled the water. The whale moaned.

I saw Posey, my undead guard, join the fight, moving mercilessly after the rebels. I saw Gita's gold tail flicker as she came out of the broken tent, then backtracked to hover above the whale, away from the fighters. Sahar and Keelan came out.

Where the sard is Mateo?

Finally, his clumsy swimming and silver hair caught my eye, and the relief was like coming inside after trudging through the snow, like placing my hands before the fire. Thank goodness. Mateo's eyes didn't seek mine, because just then one of the rebels shoved aside my guard and swooped closer, trident in his hand pointed directly at Mateo's heart.

If that trident so much as nicked him ... I had to look away, I had no power to enforce any threat that rolled through my head. Disbelief clouded my other emotions for a moment. Desperation. *This can't be happening. Not now.* I blinked, wishing my eyelids could erase this view, that they'd come down like theater curtains and rise on a new scene. They didn't.

Instead, I watched several of my guards swim forward, their spears lighting with apricot-colored magic, and knock that rebel attacking Mateo back, then go after the others with a ferocity that shocked me. Apparently, they'd only been playing at defense before. I held my breath, rapt, as they engaged the trident-wielders in combat, weapons clanking and crashing together. Orange magic sparks shot from my guards' weapons, hitting their targets. Victory surged through me, and I opened my mouth to shout. But it was premature. And the yell shriveled in my throat. The magic didn't singe the shark-shifter rebels as intended. It simply bounced off them and fizzled in the water.

My hands tightened, nails digging into Felipe's back as fear gripped me. *Why are they immune to magic? How's that possible?*

Those spears were designed to shock and incapacitate. I'd listened to a very boring lecture from Felipe about it. The rebels should have been floating logs, limbs gone stiff and useless as boards. But still they fought. *How?*

My eyes peered past the knot of mermen and spotted *her*. A hedge witch floated at the very back of the rebels' formation. She had wild blue-grey hair that was knotted and twisted with spiny pieces of dead white coral that protruded like horns from her head. Her eyes were a milky blue, nearly white. Haunting. Her skin was such a deep blue that if it hadn't been reflective, I'd have thought it was black.

I realized the mer had painted themselves in order to hide her. Which meant they very much intended to use her. Were using her. As her fingers moved, I understood quite clearly why our spears had no effect.

Sard.

"Where are our mages?" I whispered frantically in Felipe's ear.

"They're on the whale, preparing in case they're needed. They know to stay back until summoned."

"In case! What do you mean in case? Summon them!" My fingernails dug into his sides, and my heart … I clutched at it when a tugging sensation started inside, and it felt stretched taut, then tighter, tighter. My heart was being pulled on both ends, twisted, wrung out.

Felipe's brow furrowed as he stared at me. "Mayi would have …"

"I'm not her!" I screeched, both from pain and irritation, unable to hide my wince as flame seared the inside of my ribs. My hand flew to the organ, and I curled inward, instinct bowing my body to protect it.

"Shite." Understanding crossed his face. An understanding that I wasn't certain I wanted him to have. But what was done was done. I glanced down as I tried to relax my limbs, trying not to think about what would happen if we didn't make it out of here—

Suddenly, with a *whoosh*, we blasted through the ocean at top speed. The only time I'd ever gone this fast was in the claws of a dragon as he'd flown through the sky. The sounds of the rebels' yells grew lower and lower pitched as we zoomed away.

I glanced back and realized with a start that the whale and carriage were far in the distance. The whale was no larger than my fist, the carriage a speck.

"You have speed magic?" I asked.

He shook his head. "I always keep a swiftness potion on me."

"But … the others." I looked over again at the whale, which was thrashing his tail. The tent whipped off of the animal and floated slowly down behind him as he bucked in an attempt to throw off the shark shifters who'd landed on him. A few of them had managed to breach my guards and were stabbing the beast with their tridents.

Behind him, my carriage had been completely flipped upside down. The seahorses arched and charged at random, trying to free themselves from their harnesses as black-painted mer people swarmed the rig. I watched the rebels pry the gold filigree decorations from the doors.

Was that what they were after? Money?

But then, one of the rebels punched Valdez as he tried to swim off. The two started grappling, and I watched Valdez get his arms around the mer's head before twisting. The rebel drifted limply down, but another swiftly took his place.

Toxic fear shot through me, and my brain sang out, *My fault!* I had to shove aside that thought because it wasn't helpful. Useless as I was, magicless as I was, I'd been trained to find a way through chaos, and I needed to do that. Queen Gela had been good for one thing, self-pity was not allowed for her daughters, be they real or kidnapped.

Felipe's arms tightened around me.

No. I'd turned away a moment ago and that was wrong, it was weak. I tried to channel the stubbornness Bloss always had, the steady mien of Gela's. I was the queen. And I was not going to stand by and watch while my household and suitors were cut down. They were innocents. And Mateo … the very thought of him getting hurt caused an ache to bloom like an ugly purple bruise. But how could I fight? What could I do? I had *no magic*. Frustration lashed at me.

Sard it. I'd do the only thing I *could* do. *Hand myself over.*

"Bring me back," I insisted, swallowing down the jolt of pain that came with talking, because my heart was already at its maximum capacity.

"Majesty." Felipe shook his head.

My grip on his arm became iron. "Bring. Me. Back. Now."

"But you're hur—"

"Doesn't matter."

Felipe's lips pressed into a thin line, and an expression flickered in his eyes, like a shadow beneath the surface of water. I couldn't tell what it was, that dark intensity in his gaze. It might have been fury at me, but I didn't care.

Felipe's hands tightened where they held me, and he dutifully started to swim back toward our party, but slowly, as the potion's effects had worn off.

I twisted my body and trained my eyes on our group as their hands all raised above their heads in surrender. *What the hell are my mages doing? Why aren't they—*

A weak blast of blue lightning zapped from the hands of one of the figures on the whale, streaking out and hitting a shark shifter.

The blast barely dazed the rebel.

Shite! I'd seen weak hedge witches in Evaness work more powerful magic. Was this the best Okeanos had to offer? I thought the undead Lizza was training them! *I shouldn't have let her go off to gather potion ingredients! She should be here training their useless asses!*

But as soon as I had that scoffing thought, a whirlpool erupted beneath the shadowy mermen swarming my carriage, and I could hear their yelps—even from this distance—as twisting water sucked them down toward the cold sea floor. The carriage itself remained untouched, floating placidly in place.

So one of them knew at least enough to be useful.

Another blast of blue lightning zapped one of the assholes wrestling with Valdez. This zap was followed by a scream, and the man's back arched before he shifted into a full-on shark. He'd already had a tail, but his skin wavered for a moment, growing a dark grey before it popped out into a fish shape twice as big as Valdez.

My heart shrunk to the size of a peanut, but the pirate didn't seem fazed at all when the beast opened his mouth, serrated teeth glinting orange in the blasts of magic, white daggers decorated with splotches of orange and gold light. Sharp. Gleaming. Deadly.

The beast lunged. Valdez shocked me when he dodged and shifted into a pink dolphin. *A pink dolphin?* My mind didn't even have time to process that pink dolphins were a thing of fairy tales. Valdez showed no fear, flipping and moving twice as quickly as the shark, getting underneath him and then attacking, his dolphin nose barreling right into the shark's belly, slamming the bigger animal upward.

Another slash of blue lightning flared from my mage, flying through the water. Valdez was quick to retreat—hyper aware of his surroundings and far more agile than the predator. The lightning encased the shark for a moment, jolting so brightly that for a moment, I thought I saw the beast's skull through his skin before he jerked his tail and swam swiftly away.

I breathed a sigh of relief, trying to push out of Felipe's arms, but he wouldn't let go. His strong arms pinned me in place, and I could feel the tension in his chest as he leaned forward and whispered, "It's not over." His head jerked in the direction of the sea witch.

The entirety of her eyes glowed a pale blue, and her fingernails grew to blue flames. Her dark lips moved.

And suddenly, the tail of the whale everyone rode turned to stone, sending the creature and everyone still strapped to him—nearly half the passengers—spiraling toward the depths. Screams erupted. Shouts. People fought to release the cords they'd used to tie themselves to their chairs so that the current couldn't knock them over. The very cords that were supposed to keep them steady kept them trapped as they fell into deeper, darker, colder water. They plunged toward that space in the water that stripped the heat from your bones, where pressure pinched your heart.

The people of Okeanos called it the ebony way. Stray too far down the ebony way and there was no coming back.

Fury surged through me as people screamed and panicked, swimming up, jostling each other. Tears rimmed my eyes, and my throat swelled. I wanted to fight. I wanted to stop her. I reached down and grabbed at Felipe's belt, searching for a potion. A knife. Something. Anything.

"What are you—"

"I need to help."

"Wait." His hands closed over mine. Pity dripped down his face like wax on a candlestick, unsightly.

Suddenly, one person shot up above tangle of the others, rising fast in a blur of bubbles. A slightly portly man, with stripes on his arms. Humberto.

A shark shifter in half-human form darted toward him, but in the blink of an eye, Humberto quadrupled in size, his fingers expanding, his head ballooning, his legs becoming as thick as tree trunks. My contestant grew as big as a great white shark. His massive hand reached out, and he flicked his middle finger … the attacking shark shifter flew backward, tumbling tail over head.

Humberto continued to grow. Bigger and bigger. His head became so massive it blocked out the sun. His hand was as big and flat as a wall as it swept out and knocked over a row of the half-shifted shark rebels, tumbling them and giving my guards the opportunity to rush forward and disarm them.

I watched in silent awe as Humberto reached out an arm as long as a ship, fingers extended like claws, and tried to pluck the hedge witch out from her gaggle of merguards. They raised their black arms, and a small magical shield arose—she must have been training some of them. The shield glowed green, but the weak magical dome cracked like a sugar sculpture under Humberto's huge fingers. He plunged right through.

My breath hitched as I watched his fingers create a dusky shadow on either side of the hedge witch's head. He was going to pinch her head, squish it like a grape! It was no worse than she deserved. The pads of his fingers brushed the edges of that wild blue-grey hair, touching the white coral horns.

Her milky eyes landed on mine, and my gut dropped. The threat on her face was easy to read.

Humberto's fingers pinched together.

She vanished the second before his fingers mashed her flat. When his massive pointer and thumb separated, the hedge witch was gone, nothing but a flash of blue light and bubbles left in her wake.

Her disappearance lifted the spell weighing down the whale. The giant creature moaned as he came thrashing quickly back up toward us, the passengers who hadn't been able to flee sat clutching the seats or one another during the wild ride. He breached the surface and took in a mighty breath, exposing all his riders to the sun for a moment. Then he ducked back beneath the waves, hovering far higher than before, reluctant to descend to where the rest of us waited. The beast had a sense of self-preservation.

Radford was the first of those passengers to swim off the whale and go around to his front. He put a hand on the beast's great snout and petted him, muttering things I couldn't hear. Comforting the creature.

My maids sobbed in relief as some of the guards swam over to unknot their straps, which had cinched tight in the fall. Half the male servants still aboard the whale were pale-faced and woozy. The other half simply stared out with thin lips and terrorized eyes. I couldn't even make eye contact with most of my contestants. I'd failed them.

They'd expected a protector.

I wasn't one.

Did that mean I wasn't good enough to be a queen?

11

Weaknesses should be guarded with doors and walls and moats. They should be hidden in the tallest room of the highest tower and never ever be seen.

—Sultan Raj of Cheryn

THREAT GONE, I swallowed hard and prepared to deal with the fallout. I wriggled out of Felipe's arms and swam up toward the whale, where everyone gathered, either crying or laughing in relief as shock wore off. The beast itself trembled under Radford's touch, making their seats shake as if even the whale realized what a close call we'd had. My fingertips did too; I had to clench them to stop their shaking as my wing-like fins fluttered and I moved closer to the others.

Of course, my gaze darted to Mateo first. Knowing he was alright loosened the band that had constricted around my torso. His dark eyes found mine, and for a second, nothing else existed. We stared at one another in mutual relief, in awed silence, a giant wave of grief still crashing through our systems despite the happy outcome. Almost.

We'd almost lost each other again.

I had to take a deep breath in order to stymie the tears that rose to my eyes. I had to look away first, though I wanted to swim into his arms and never look away again. But doing that would threaten his position here. It would make the others suspicious. I had to remain conscious of the long game. Of the fact that I wanted him by my side for decades to come. Which meant I had to wait just a bit longer. I gathered my emotions up in a tight ball and tied them off.

My gaze scanned the others as I swam closer, and landed on Keelan, who had those around him laughing. Of course he did. He wasn't the type of man who looked death in the face and shuddered. He'd been a soldier. He looked death in the face and mocked her directly.

"Why did they shift to have just shark tails? The teeth would have been intimidating. They shifted the wrong half." Keelan clucked in pity before his smile and dimples reappeared. "And I thought today was going to be another boring day of travel."

"Got your excitement, did you?" Radford grumbled, the redhead shaking his head as he rounded the side of the now-calm whale and joined the knot of others gathered near Sahar's son.

"Well, it's better than another round of Crown and Anchor with you," Keelan retorted jovially.

"You just didn't like losing—"

"Well, can't deny that!"

The two of them chuckled.

I turned my attention from the pair, who were clearly not traumatized, and searched the crowd for those who were as I swam closer. It was the women who shook and the men who were white and silent that I needed to address the most. Not the soldiers and whale tamers who loved adrenaline so much that they'd chosen careers that gave them that heady rush.

Sahar reached me before I got close enough to speak. She kicked out, feet rapidly paddling, crow's feet near her eyes prominent as she squinted in worry. When she reached me, she took my arm. "Your Majesty, are you alright? I know you took quite a hit to the head," she spoke loudly. Too loudly. She was covering for me. Creating the story that others needed to hear. An explanation for why I hadn't blasted the bastards back and saved the day. Why I hadn't been the queen they all expected.

I nodded, gratitude filling my eyes, if not my entire expression. I didn't deserve her help. Perhaps I didn't even deserve this crown I'd so carelessly donned. Mother—Gela—hadn't had magic in Evaness, but she'd surrounded herself with the most magical men the nation had possessed in order to protect it. Was that what I needed to do? Sort through these men and find those like Humberto, who could fight where I could not?

What about after I shed this stupid heart?

Lizza had mentioned she might have spells to help me fight against the cold cruelty that had overtaken my birth mother. But it had never been attempted, never tried. If I'd mentioned it to the self-proclaimed scientist, Julian, he probably would have mocked me for hoping it would work. He didn't believe in chance. He believed in study.

Thoughts smacked me like a child was throwing blocks at my head. *Clunk. Clunk. Clunk.* One after the other. None of them felt particularly right. I had no idea what path I should take. I knew what Mayi had become, but in the face of attacks like those we just faced, what choice did I have but to become the same? To accept that the undead mage might be wrong and I might have to take up this yoke, become a beast?

Sahar grabbed my elbow, her face reprimanding, as if she knew my thoughts. Her nostrils flared, like she was warning me. But suddenly, she completely morphed. Her smile became bright as she called out, "Oh, and the hero of the hour!" She gestured behind me before beginning to clap.

I turned.

Humberto was shrinking, no longer larger than the whale. For the first time, I realized that growing so large meant he was now *very* naked, clothing ripped by his expansion magic. *Eep.* I worked hard to keep my eyes firmly on the stripes of his neck, trying not to let the corners of my vision focus on any dangly bits. The quite intimidating, driftwood-tree-trunk-sized dangling bits. Quite rapidly, he shrank enough for me to look him in the face. He was still roughly the size of an apple tree but contracted a bit more every second.

"Three cheers for Humberto!" Sahar cried out.

Joyous shouts erupted behind us as Humberto dwindled to the size of the huts in the villages that dotted Evaness. I glanced back to see that every single person on the back of the whale had stood in order to applaud him. We all owed him. Myself especially.

My eyes quickly scanned the whale's back. All that remained of the tent were two sorry poles strapped to the creature's sides, sticking out like broken bones. All the seats, however, were still strapped in place. I looked over the rows for empty seats or missing silhouettes. Had we lost anyone? Had anyone been seriously hurt? It was impossible for me to tell at a glance, but none of the faces I saw were devastated. If no one was missing anyone else, it appeared our injuries were minor.

Sarding hell, thank goodness for that small mercy.

I turned back to Humberto, who was blushing underneath the weight of all that praise.

A sense of awed appreciation ran through me, a sad gratitude. The people had expected so much of me. And I'd failed them. I'd expected so little of him. I scolded myself for that. *Look what magic lies beneath a rather ordinary exterior. Look what bravery can be found in a fisherman's heart.*

My eyes watered with humble, grateful tears, and I swam forward to grasp Humberto's hands. A soft thank-you fell from my lips. And then I leaned up to place a chaste kiss near Humberto's lips.

He ripped away from me, swimming backward as if I'd tried to attack him.

I put my arms up in front of me, showing I meant no harm, though I was shocked by his reaction.

Humberto waved his hands frantically in an *X* in front of him and shook his head as he shrunk to the size of a normal man. "I'm not ready for that kind of commitment. I mean, we just met, Your Majesty."

My eyebrows shot up. My face grew red. My neck grew hot, and my hand flew to my mouth. Embarrassment painted my vision a bright white for half a second. I'd just tried to kiss him in thanks, not attraction. A simple peck, but still his public rejection stung like a whip. "I'm sorry."

Humberto scrambled off, legs thrashing as he swam away and shrunk down to my size, then smaller. He must have been half human. *The price for his giant magic must be shrinking,* I realized dully. A common theme in Evaness, where so many people were part human, part magical. But not as many part humans survived under the sea. The ability to breathe water was rarer.

Humberto kept going, morphing from my size to a small boy's. He couldn't get away fast enough. He was a smart one. The other competitors should have done the same.

I watched him go as all the gratitude I'd felt ebbed away like the tide, and reality, stark and nasty, smacked me across the face. Humberto, a man I'd judged to be one of the more basic, honest men here, wasn't in this tournament for me. He couldn't even stand a thank-you kiss. Which meant he was here competing for other reasons. Ones that I, in my wisdom, had clearly overlooked.

"Don't let your mind go there." Sahar swam calmly over to hover beside me as Humberto shrunk to the size of a house cat. She whistled harshly, and one of the guards sped over from the whale.

"Yes, my lady?" the merman asked.

She nodded in Humberto's direction, where the cardinal fish shifter had become approximately the size of my fist. "Go scoop him up before he gets eaten by something in his panic."

The guard nodded and shot off, tucking his spear into a strap on his back so he could have both hands free to catch the man I'd sent off in a horrified tizzy, who had just become the size of a mouse.

Wonderful.

I couldn't wait until this story reached Bloss's ears. She'd devise a million nicknames for me no doubt. Death's Kiss. Fish Lips. Dog Breath.

It shouldn't have mattered. I should have been comforted by the fact that Valdez had very much wanted to kiss me and had seemed to enjoy it before we were interrupted. My eyes scanned the crowd, looking for a pink dolphin. I didn't find one, but Valdez's pink hair was visible on the far side of the whale and my eyes latched on. Someone wanted to kiss me. Someone besides Mateo. An incredibly handsome someone. A pirate. Gah! The mad scribblings I'd done in my journal when I was younger, a secret little bit of embroidery I'd hidden under my bed—both came rushing up through my memories. I'd never been able to resist a pirate. I'd written about sailing away, sewn a secret little fantasy image of me and a swashbuckler on a ship. And Valdez … my entire body hummed at the thought of him. Our conversation. The way he'd just grabbed me and kissed me. His tongue had plundered my mouth and the world outside had ceased to exist for a moment.

Until we were attacked.

That kiss should have balanced things out. But my damn need to please everyone still roiled in my stomach, and the fact that Humberto hated me mutilated all the other good things I could stack up. My fingers clenched. *Dammit.*

I blew out a breath and gave myself a pep talk. I needed to turn and focus on the others, to make sure that everything was alright. I needed to give a little speech, calm them. But feeling stupidly blindsided by Humberto's motives, on top of feeling magically useless, cut me up inside.

"Don't look so brokenhearted." Sahar grabbed my elbow before breaking protocol and throwing an arm around my shoulders, pulling me into her side for a hug.

The gesture warmed me in a way nothing had for quite some time. Even Queen Gela had never been so casually affectionate with me. I let my arm drift around Sahar's waist as I rolled my eyes. "I'm not brokenhearted."

"You look like you just realized your favorite dinner was baited with a human's hook," Sahar challenged, her eyes glinting.

"No."

"Yes."

"That's not it, and you know it." I poked her ribs.

She chuckled. "I'll have to tell Keelan he's got fierce competition."

"Don't."

"I like this." An evil smile lit her face. "Humberto is number one. You desperately wanted that kiss. I'll make sure all the maids spread the word."

"I'm just upset I misjudged him," I finally admitted.

She sighed and the teasing stopped. "I know."

"I thought he was one of the more decent ones, you know? In this thing for the adventure, perhaps, but not in it for the power."

Sahar's hands moved to my shoulders, and she turned me around to face her, a questioning expression on her face. "You do know Humberto comes from a line of mouthbrooders, don't you?"

I quirked up a brow. "A what?"

She pressed her lips together, stifling a laugh, before she explained, "In his family, the women place the fertilized eggs in the men's mouths to carry until they're hatched."

"You're joking!" She had to be. There was no way.

She laughed but shook her head. "I wish I was. It's an old, nearly defunct tradition. Most mer simply resort to legs and have babies the 'sky breather' way … because at least one can function. Can you imagine having to hold eggs in your mouth for two weeks until they hatch?"

Sahar's know-it-all face collapsed in laughter as I mentally pictured what she'd described.

When she bulged her cheeks out and gave me a visual demonstration, my nose crinkled and my tongue popped out. I was horrified. "Disgusting!"

"So, now you know why he ran away so quickly," Sahar chortled.

"He thought I'd give him eggs? I hardly know him!"

She shrugged. "It was a pretty massive display of masculine prowess he put on back there. I mean, he saved everyone."

I sighed. "Let me guess ... for cardinal fish, that's all it takes."

"Ohh, if we'd been closer to the reef, you would have had to fight the ladies off tooth and fin," she told me, matter-of-factly. "They would have been tossing eggs at him left and right, hoping he inadvertently inhaled."

"That's a delightful mental image." *Cue puking.* "It's definitely less offensive that he swam off now that I know that." I squinted in thought. "He literally thought I was going to dump a cluster of fish eggs into his mouth?" I repeated the question. I just had to be sure.

"Yep."

I didn't even want to think about how those eggs would be fertilized if they were in his mouth. Nope. Not going to do it. Not going to think about him swallowing his own ... ew. I tried to erase that mental nightmare with conversation. "But ... I'm a sprite. Not a shifter."

"He's not the fastest fish in the school." Sahar extended a hand and gently cupped my shoulder. She rubbed there for a second, a little "there-there" and a hint of mockery in her gesture. "Don't be sad he fled your net. There are plenty of others to catch."

I grinned up at her, shaking my head before fanning my wings out behind me. I glanced up at the whale, where conversation had started up as everyone recovered. The silhouettes of all the competitors for my hand were backlit by the morning sun. I sighed. "Yes. Plenty of others. Too many."

12

A good lie is the basis of every alliance and every fight.

—Sultan Raj of Cheryn

ENTERING REEF CITY, I realized, not for the first time, how truly foreign I was. But in this new city, that knowledge didn't come in fits and spurts, it smacked me across the face.

We had to leave the whale and battered carriage outside the city limits because there simply was no room for them. We'd disembarked, and my royal guards had spoken with the city patrol before leading a parade of men and servants through the winding street that was the entrance to this massive city. I was the last to enter, swimming with Sahar and Felipe on either side of me, and Ugo along with three others taking a defensive position at my back.

We ducked under a giant wall of sunshine yellow fan coral that surrounded the outer edge of the city. The coral was so tall and thick that I could hardly see shapes moving behind it. It must have grown over centuries. "Is it magically enhanced?" I asked Felipe.

Behind me Ugo snorted.

I glanced backward, and the orange-tailed merman stuttered. "Sorry, Majesty."

"Is there a story there?"

Felipe instantly said, "No."

Ugo said, "Not one I can tell and live."

I glanced between my guards curiously, and Felipe shot Ugo a withering stare. "Nothing important, Your Majesty. Just a little issue with my first leg potion."

Ugo snorted again, unable to contain himself. "They weren't 'big' enough for him, so he went back—"

My guard darted backward as Felipe reached for him.

I pressed my lips together and suppressed my own laugh. "Well, after all, if you're paying for a spell …"

"*Exactly.*" Felipe's hand shot out in agreement as he sent a disapproving look to Ugo. "He can't take anything seriously if it sounds the least bit dirty."

"I have a brother-in-law who's like that," I murmured. "And it's even worse because he speaks through thoughts and can plant images in your mind. Did you know he made my sister imagine all the courtiers naked once?"

Both the guards swooped closer, interest piqued. I told them about Quinn as we swam past the fan coral and into the city.

Our entrance wasn't filled with fanfare and a parade, because Sahar, in her wisdom, had realized we'd be travel weary. She might not have calculated exactly how much, given the surprise attack from the rebels, but I still felt grateful that I didn't have to keep a constant smile on my face. The parade to open the first competition of the tournament would happen this evening. And while we weren't exactly anonymous—I saw little mermaids and schools of bright magenta fish stop short at the sight of us— there still wasn't the pressure of a parade. I was free to look around and let a bit of awe slip over my face at the completely magical nature of Reef City.

The town of Palati and the castle hadn't been that different from home. With the number of sirens there, I almost imagined I was walking amongst humans. Golden-skinned, half-naked, incredibly beautiful humans. But it allowed me a degree of comfort and familiarity.

Reef City was a different story. The buildings weren't … well, they weren't actual buildings. They were rocks, piled and arranged along twisting paths. The rocks themselves weren't the smooth walls of houses and shops like I'd come to expect from the glass-blown capital city, but this dull, colorless rock was simply a base for corals of all shapes and sizes arranged in wild patterns.

There were yellow corals that looked like mums covering every rock wall in bright puffs of color. Sometimes, the yellow was broken by small three-dimensional fan corals in bright orange arranged into spirals that wove through the yellow. Other times, Antipathes, corals that looked like soft ferns, bloomed on the roofs in stunning shades of green, orange, and red. Roof lines were non-existent. The entire city was otherworldly. It very much felt like entering a field of flowers, only the flowers were larger than I was, and instead of plucking them, our troop ducked underneath their petals.

Purple corals that looked like hyacinth flowers to my sky breather eyes, were planted in containers that resembled flower boxes, set underneath what I assumed were windows, which were merely the gaps between rocks. I assumed that until I saw several fish swim in and out of these windows and realized that there were, in fact, no doors. No one walked. The paths between buildings were for swimming; even the roads had their own set of rough tan corals growing at their base, where colorful fish no larger than my finger darted in and out constantly, a miniature town right beneath our feet, a microcosm of the bustling marketplace we entered.

As we came to it, Sahar swam back until she was at my side—to play guide, I assumed, as she so often did. I nodded gratefully at her as I took in the heart of the town.

The market was a hollowed-out circle in the middle of all this chaotic color. It had evenly spaced patches of sand surrounding its edges, and I realized those bits of sand served as market stalls. Fishwives rested baskets of goods in the dirt as they held up samples of their wares and plied customers with tempting sales pitches like, "Get over here! If you wanna find a mate, you'll need this cream! Guaranteed genuine pheromones from an alpha shark shifter, magically collected."

I watched the highly attractive mermaid flip her pale pink hair and flutter her fin suggestively. It only took seconds before she had two or three male customers surrounding her, asking questions that seemed as much about flirting as they were about the product.

"Where do you put it?"

"Can you put it on for me?"

"You have a sample I can try?"

My eyes flitted away as that merwoman smartly answered or deflected each question, and I realized, to my surprise, that the entire marketplace was filled with female salespersons. I leaned toward Sahar and asked, "Why are they all women?"

She arched a brow. "What better way to get men to drop sand dollars? Not only do women run the markets here, but I've heard they try to send out fishwives during their fertile time of the month." She raised a brow, and I couldn't quite tell if she was skeptical or impressed. I was a bit of both.

I glanced around again, realizing that a good number of the shoppers were male. I hadn't noticed that before because the ratio of males to females was always off. There were always far more men. But it was fascinating, and a bit shocking, how different Reef City was from Evaness. There, women ran their households, and while men did most of the shopping, men also did most of the selling. The women were too busy with items like bookkeeping or trade deals, planning the next harvest ... My eyes made the rounds again but got caught on Radford's. For some reason, the redheaded hermit crab shifter was staring at me instead of the scenery.

I needed to thank him for calming the whale and thereby all the people still stuck on the creature, so I gestured for him to swim over.

Unlike a lot of sirens, who swam with quick flicks of their entire legs, Radford preferred a breaststroke. I wondered briefly if that was part of his hermit crab heritage or if it was a regionalization. I tucked that question away for some other time and doubled my smile. "Thank you for all you did with that whale."

A blush painted his cheeks a dull pink, and he reached back, clearing his throat as he fiddled with the shell strapped to his back.

"It's not a big deal," he replied.

Sahar tutted her disagreement from where she floated nearby, showing me exactly how private our conversation was.

I narrowed my eyes in her direction. "This is a private thanking."

"I'm sorry, did you say spanking?" a gregarious voice asked from the side. I turned. Of course, Keelan floated there. He turned his head sideways, gesturing at the streak in his hair, changing the subject before my shocked face could slip back to normal. "Like it? I made it black and white in honor of Humberto."

"It's very nice," I complimented the siren.

"Not as nice as a spanking. So, what were you two talking about again over here?"

I shook my head fondly and stared at Radford. "You'll have to excuse him; I think his mother might have popped his head above the surface a few too many times when he was a child. Addled his wits."

Radford gave me an easy grin. "You haven't been stuck with him on a whale for two days."

"One and a half," Keelan scoffed. "And it wasn't that bad."

"Not that bad? You asked me four times what color pants you should wear the first day of the tournament! That's eye-gougingly bad in my book."

"The people like a show! I just wanted to know if you thought magically reflective material was too much."

I watched the two of them banter with a smile—Keelan's arguments growing more and more ludicrous. Eventually, I noticed several other competitors drifting closer. I gave them all friendly smiles and settled into silence as they began to tease one another, goaded on by Keelan, of course. That made me feel a bit lighter. Perhaps, even those who came out of this with nothing would have a friendship or two after this tournament.

A few flasks of bubble were passed around, and when one made it to Radford, he held it aloft. "To Humberto the hero!" he shouted.

"Humberto!" the others chorused.

I didn't see the cardinal fish shifter, but the others were quite excessive in their praise of him. I smiled and, when a flask reached me, I too raised it on his behalf. I drank, swallowing down a bubble that was far more potent than any I'd tried previously. It burned my throat and warmed it as it slid down. I grimaced as I handed it to the man beside me, stopping when his hand gently slid over mine.

I looked up into the liquid blue eyes of Stavros. The siren studied me intensely for a second before taking the flask and removing his hand. He glanced shyly down and back up again. "I … I have something for you," he blurted almost clumsily.

"Oh?"

He held the flask in one hand as he slid his other into the pocket of his pants. He pulled out a small blue flower on a stem.

I stared at it, enchanted, as he handed the beautiful little thing to me.

"The saleswoman called it a Forget-Me-Not." Stavros touched one of the tiny petals, which was smaller than his thumb. "It's been enchanted so that it won't die. Won't wither under the water."

I inhaled sharply. When I'd found out my heritage, I realized all of the huge things I was giving up. But the knowledge that I'd never see flowers again was traumatic. It hurt in a way I'd never realized something could hurt. A small but pointed ache pierced my stomach. While my seamstress wanted to showcase the monetary benefits of my heritage, most of the rest of it was swept under the rug. I was forced to adapt.

Yet here was one of the competitors, acknowledging who I was. What I was. Giving me something so thoughtful ... My hand reached out and squeezed Stavros'. "Thank you."

There was a happy gleam in his eye as he nodded. But the others started up an impromptu song for Humberto and jostled him. Someone's arm came around my shoulders, and I was spun in another direction. I looked up to see Valdez staring down at me as his bicep flexed along the back of my neck and his hand traveled down my arm possessively.

Everything around me faded for a split second before I remembered myself, gave him a wink, and slinked carefully out of his hold to go chat with the other contestants. But I felt the pirate's eyes caress me even as I spoke with other men. And I couldn't lie to myself. I liked it.

13

Suspicion is a survival mechanism that must be honed, strengthened, cherished.

—Sultan Raj of Cheryn

AFTER THE BONDING I saw between the men in the marketplace, I was determined to ensure that the rest of the Reef City event went just as swimmingly. But of course, the best laid plans always end in disaster.

Sahar led our procession through the city toward the mayor's palace where we were to stay for the first competition's duration: a grueling pair of twelve-hour days. Grueling for the competitors at least. I still wasn't privy to the type of contest that would be held first, those preparations were Sahar's most closely guarded secret. I stared at her hair, which she'd magically turned a burnished deep orange today, while we swam.

As we approached the palace from above, my earth walker eyes had trouble discerning where the palace ended and the rest of the reef began. The only distinction between the palace and the homes beside it was the fact that the rainbow-colored corals growing on the palace were so massive that I felt no larger than a tiny fish myself as we descended into the entrance of the mayor's home, a gap between two rocks that looked as dark and inviting as the open maw of some great beast. I'd thought Mayi's glass palace had an awe and intimidation factor, but this place felt eerily ominous. I tried to shove the thought away, but the tiniest part of me was reminded of Mayi's caves and the torture I'd endured in them.

We swam into the gloom, and my mages lit the magical glass orbs that lined the grand entrance one by one, creating little circles of psychedelic color from the bits of reef that emerged from within the shadows. Even with the small lights, the darkness loomed overhead the further we descended into the tunnel. I bit down on a screech of shock and surprise when part of the wall near a light detached itself and swam forward.

I ducked behind Felipe, who just turned and raised, not his spear, but a skeptical brow in my direction. The burly merman scoffed at me.

Dammit.

I peered over Felipe's large shoulder. The bit of floating coral in front of me blinked his eyes and—too late—I recalled that Mayor Deacon was a painted frogfish shifter. Sahar's coaching had fled my head in my stupid flight of nerves. The mayor's magic gave him the ability to mimic his surroundings. And even though he was in human form when he bowed his head to me, his skin was still as patterned and wild as the corals around us. If he had been a sky breather, his entire body, eyelids included, would have been covered in tattoos. But the wild blotches of color faded a bit as he hovered in front of me, and the blush that overtook my cheeks was as hot as the sun. I blamed the attack earlier for the fact that I was so jumpy.

"Mayor Deacon." I nodded at his bow and let him kiss my hand. There was a strange little suction at the end of his kiss, and I didn't know whether to attribute that to fish lips or not. I wrote it off. Because after my little display, the least I could do was cut the man a break. "My apologies. You startled me."

"Oh no, Your Majesty, it's I who must apologize. I should have met you at the entrance, but I was delayed. There's been a bit of a timber shortage lately and it's been causing—"

I grasped onto this immediately. It was exactly the sort of thing I could help with. "I can write to Evaness and set up a delivery if you need."

Deacon clapped his hands together, delighted. "Well, that would be wonderful! Just wonderful!" He took my arm and swam next to me into a large, open cavern. He let go of my arm and swam in front of me, giving a grand bow and gesturing wide. "Your Majesty, I'd like to welcome you to the palace of Reef City." At his words, a thousand jellyfish-shaped crystal chandeliers magically illuminated the grand cavern. The room filled with their soft blue light, and I gasped in awe as the crystals clinked gently together in the waves created by our entrance. Bands of blue light radiated out from all of the chandeliers, landing on stone sculptures of mermaids that served as the base for crimson-padded seats or were topped by stone tables.

"It's beautiful." The cavern walls themselves were made of intricate orange corals that had clearly been trained to grow in symmetrical patterns, creating a vaulted ceiling and intricate scrollwork that would rival any sculptor's. I turned to look back at the mayor and had to blink several times before my eyes separated his figure from the peach-toned walls. His skin adapted rapidly. Too bad I had no frogfish competitors. His trick would be rather handy for an assassin. In fact, it made me wonder how he'd become mayor…

Assassin or not, Deacon was a charmer. He had me laughing when he took my arm once more and led us on a tour of the main rooms. It seemed every piece of furniture came with a story, and nearly every story featured his personal humiliation. True or not, the man wove great tales.

Eventually, he led us out to a massive arena, a gap in the coral city where the sea bed was actually visible and the water shallow enough that the sunlight penetrated, lightening and warming the space. The dirt oval was surrounded by color coded stands made of coral. Each of the ten floors for the stands was a different color: green, orange, blue, purple, and so on. I noted a canopy at the far end of the oval, several ship masts set upright with billowing white sails turned into an open-sided tent canopy. A throne and several chairs were visible just beneath it.

My eyes scanned the oval for any hint of what the tournament competition might be, but I saw no weapons, not even any footprints that might hint at sword battles or some such. My gaze drifted over to the competitors, and they were all studying the space just as intently as I was, possibly with a bit of trepidation from some of them, enthusiasm from others.

Mateo swallowed hard, his throat bobbing as he clumsily circled the space. His curls bobbed, and his expression was grave.

I had to force myself not to go to him and not to look immediately over at Felipe for reassurance. I didn't want to give up their ruse. I made my eyes find someone else.

Watkins merely crossed his arms and narrowed his eyes, making me wonder what exactly he was thinking. The rebellious shark shifter seemed angry more than intimidated. Perhaps he was angry at me for forcing him to compete. For some reason, the thought of him being angry at me turned my insides molten. That was nearly as dangerous a train of thought as the one I'd had with Mateo. I fluttered my wings and did another quarter turn so that I faced some others.

Humberto and the shy siren, Stavros, spoke in hushed tones to one another. I wondered what their theories were. Humberto gestured widely, while Stavros' eyes merely traveled the length of the sand and back as he chewed his lip. He gave a quick one-word statement to Humberto, making the portly man's eyes grow to the size of saucers.

Curiosity burned. But it wouldn't be right of me to join their conversation. I couldn't appear to give tips to anyone, though I was as clueless as they were. No doubt, assholes like Watkins would fail to believe I was ignorant. He'd accuse me of favoritism.

My eyes bounced over the redheaded man and to Julian. The self-proclaimed scientist looked about with open interest, his clever eyes measuring and calculating. For some reason, I hoped he did well. I hardly knew him, wasn't as drawn to him as I was to some of the others, but I did find him interesting. And apparently, some part of me wanted to learn more about him. Or from him. I wasn't sure.

Keelan, of course, was surrounded by a wide circle of the other competitors, laughing and joking. The golden siren didn't appear intimidated by the arena in the slightest. He wasn't smug about it though, just enthusiastically unafraid. Which was damn charming, and I couldn't help the little smile it brought to my face. On the edge of his circle, not laughing or talking, simply staring at me, hovered Valdez. His intense gaze made me tense.

Sahar, being her usual perceptive self, decided it was time to move on. "Alright, everyone! Time to freshen up and prepare for the parade. You have three hours!"

Mayor Deacon gave a nod, and several buxom mermaids emerged from archways on the sides of the arena in order to lead the competitors away. The mayor himself escorted me and my guards to my room. It was a grand, bright purple room with a tall ceiling. A small bubble fountain sat in the entryway, streams of tiny white bubbles emerging from a stone sculpture of a shell. They floated toward the ceiling and disappeared with soft, peaceful little pops. A bed with a thin white fishnet canopy sat against the far wall, draped in tufted silk covers that were the same bright purple as the wall.

Gita waited near a small dressing table and mirror, the tufted chair already pulled out and waiting for me. "Your Majesty." She gave a bow and then lifted her head with a saucy grin, gesturing toward the chair. "Your torture chamber awaits."

I sighed dramatically and turned to the mayor with faux fear. "Please, Mayor Deacon, help me escape this fate."

The mayor's eyebrows shot up in surprise, or at least, I thought they did. He'd turned nearly as purple as the room, though it seemed his pigmentation had met its match. He couldn't quite achieve the bright shade of the walls. Surprise soon gave way to a chuckle, and Deacon patted my hand. "I'm most happy to host you, Your Majesty."

"And I'm glad to be here. If I emerge alive from all this paint, that is. If I drown in it, please note, I'll leave the glass palace to you, and Gita is to receive her own statue engraved with the following: Here lies the monster who killed the queen with hours of boredom. Beware."

"Majesty!" Gita scolded.

"Only the truth," I told her as the mayor left, chuckling, and I swam forward to sit on her tufted pouf. "I only speak the truth."

"Majesty, forgive me, but you're a royal. We all know you lie."

"Never!" I mocked her with a gasp and a hand over my heart, my mood suddenly lifted. Despite the fact that I did indeed dread sitting for the next three hours straight, Gita was a good soul, and she'd grown comfortable enough to banter with me, which made everything all the more pleasant. "Love your hair today," I complimented her.

Her hair was a mess from traveling. She'd put it in a simple braid, and more than a few strands floated loose around her face. Her eyes narrowed on mine. "You've just earned yourself an incredibly elaborate hairstyle. Lots of tiny braids, I think."

"Evil."

Her face split into a smile. "Just wait, Majesty. Evil is yet to come."

I SIGHED AND SAT PERFECTLY STILL AS GITA PAINTED sparkling blue swirls around my eyes and then added dots of green paint to accent them. It looked like stylized ocean waves cresting on the sides of my face. We were only two hours into the three-hour span of torture. "Isn't this a little over-the-top?" I asked.

"It's a parade, Your Majesty, there's no such thing as over-the-top." Gita gave me a wink as she grabbed a new paintbrush and started adding pink stars on my forehead near my hairline.

The pink paint pot made me think about the pink-haired man competing for my hand. My mind drifted to the man who'd been inside my carriage when it was attacked. His kiss and his self-assured public touch made me wonder. I struggled not to bring my hands up to touch my lips as I recalled that possessive look he'd gotten right before he'd pulled me into him. I hardly knew him, but damn ... he'd made quite the impression. I realized, to my own embarrassment, that I hardly knew more about him than his name, or the fact that he was a rogue pirate. Did that mean he captured ships?

"What do you know about pink dolphin shifters?" I asked casually.

"Ohhh ..." Gita's smirk plumped her cheeks like apples. "Well, I hope you haven't seen one." A naughty smile crossed her face before she added another star.

"Why?" I tried not to wrinkle my brow and ruin her painting. But her comment and grin made me immensely curious.

"Well, first of all, they're so rare that they're legendary. They are supposed to be terribly seductive, more so than sirens or mermen. Dangerous even to those under the sea."

Hmmm. That certainly felt in line with my interactions with Valdez. He created a sense of longing and curiosity that were quite intense. It was almost a relief to realize they were magical.

Not a disappointment, a relief, I chided the tiny bit of my head that disagreed. The tiny romantic part of me that still wished that a single man in this competition was here for me, rather than riches or glory.

That was a fool's wish. And I wasn't a fool. At least, not most days.

"Pink dolphins are also supposed to give you nightmares. Lurid nightmares. And ... they've been blamed for more than one unmarried maid showing up with a swollen belly." Gita paused in her painting, chewing her thick bottom lip in thought as she both studied her work and let her thoughts wander to legendary creatures.

"Oh." I pressed my lips together.

Gita paused her painting and went back to my hair. She had twisted it up into a series of seven golden spikes that looked like conical shells and began adding tiny bright pink sea stars into my spikes in spirals.

My dress itself was a very thin, light pink silk that had been sewn with pleats so that the wide skirt resembled a shell as it fanned out around my mid thighs. It was far shorter than anything I'd ever worn, but still more modest than Gita wanted.

I wore no shoes. Instead, when Gita finished with my hair, I stared at my reflection in the mirror, noting how the blue paint made my violet eyes look even lighter than normal as my maid bent down and used the same paint she'd put on my face to decorate my legs with wild waves. I couldn't help but bark out a laugh when her paintbrush swept over the bottoms of my feet, tickling them.

"I can't believe people paint their feet! Who can stand it?" I asked, gritting my teeth and grabbing my small makeup table as she continued her work, unbothered by my twitching.

"Discipline, Your Majesty," Gita scolded teasingly. "You must be able to bite down on your discomfort, just as you do a million times a day at court or watching these two." Her head gestured toward Ugo and Felipe, who'd just finished a thorough search of my chamber, which involved tapping on every wall and pouring at least two potions across the doorway. "Those idiots would ensure my tongue had constant bite marks." Ugo bit his thumb at her in an obscene gesture, and she just giggled. "Paranoia is often the first sign of madness," she warned him.

He rolled his eyes and continued.

Meanwhile, I conceded that Gita had a point—I did need to practice focusing on something else. I sucked in a breath when her brush circled over the middle of my foot, and my eyes darted around for a target before they landed on Felipe.

That was a mistake. He's just begun preparing himself for the parade, painting bronze swirls onto his pecs. I'd never been more jealous of a paintbrush. His muscles tensed and swelled as he made the brush move precisely where he wanted it. After he painted his left nipple, he looked up—probably to get more paint—and met my eyes.

His expression remained as impassive as ever, but his eyes darkened. My breath caught, and suddenly, the tickle at my feet faded, and an entirely different sort of tickle captured my senses. The kind that made my belly clench and butterflies flutter from my chest up into my throat. It wasn't the magic intensity of Valdez. This was far more vulnerable.

"Doesn't she look beautiful?" Gita asked as she backed up and examined her work critically.

Felipe's eyes roamed down my figure, and his look was as scorching as any touch. He nodded slowly, and a warm heat spread between my thighs.

When his voice came out a rough scratch, I had to hide the tremble it sent down my spine. I looked down and rubbed my hands on the scales that lined the outsides of my arms, feigning a chill I didn't feel. In fact, I felt the opposite. I was on fire.

"Your Majesty…" I felt certain the soft familiarity in his tone was only my overactive imagination, until he asked, "Can I have a moment?"

My breath caught, and for a single second, my eyes flashed to his in stunned silence. Then I remembered myself, and the million practical reasons he'd want a word, and the million reasons related to Mateo he might want a word. I nodded.

Gita silently packed away her things and swam out with Ugo, the two of them chatting softly as they closed the door behind them.

I ended up knotting my fingers as anticipation coated my brain in oil and made my thoughts into slippery, blundering fools.

Felipe swam closer. My heart rate sped up, and I had to press my lips together so that I didn't gape foolishly at those massive pecs as he approached.

"I think we need to question Watkins."

Inside, I deflated at those words. But I smacked my mind. Felipe hadn't muttered what I wanted in my wild imaginings. But he'd said what I needed to hear, addressed a practical matter I needed to think about. "The attack?" I asked, though I knew his intentions.

Felipe nodded. "The route was secret. Only I and a few guards knew. The stable master. Very few people. But if Watkins allowed the rebels to place some sort of tracking spell on him, it would have been easy enough for them to find us."

The press of my lips increased to a nearly painful degree. "Yes. Bring him in. Better to get it over with now, before the parade. Before something else can happen."

Felipe gave a brisk nod and swam to the door, waiting until Ugo slipped back inside before my blue-haired guard disappeared with a flick of his mer tail.

When Watkins appeared at the door, I stiffened my posture and made my gaze cold.

Watkins saw my wrath, but it only made him grin. "You know, Your Majesty, fury becomes you."

14

Painted faces are the truest representation of the human soul. We paint ourselves in a good light so that we hide our hideous true natures, for we are but beasts.

—Sultan Raj of Cheryn

"You know what would become you? A set of shackles." I eyed the rebel I'd *invited* to join the tournament as I wondered if I'd made a horrid mistake.

Watkins' eyes drifted lazily to my bed; he turned his head, revealing that shock of white that ran through the side of his pitch black hair. His gaze flickered back to me, and his intensity was like a blow that knocked my knees out from under me. It made me breathless as he asked, "Did you already attach them to your headboard for me?"

Felipe immediately lowered his spear so it pointed threateningly at Watkins' torso. The taller man didn't even flinch. Instead, he kept his dark eyes on me.

Sarding hell, I'm in trouble. All of these men, all at once. Sahar had warned me that they'd be a mess of mating aggression. She hadn't warned me that I'd be under constant assault from my own hormones, in danger of making some very bad choices. Right now, I was torn between smacking Watkins across the mouth and indulging his sarcastic whim by chaining him to the bed and then ... well, I hardly had enough experience to pull off anything that happened after *then*—Mateo was my only experience—but my imaginary self would torture Watkins with teasing looks and touches until he begged for mercy.

The tension between the shark shifter and me built while I studied him in silence, wondering if the big man's defensive posture was created by guilt. Did he know that hedge witch? Some of those men had been shark shifters.

But then he swam closer, ignoring Felipe entirely, and I saw the anger that radiated off him. This delicious, dangerous unbridled anger that called to me the way siren song called to sailors. For some reason, Watkins' anger was captivating. He growled, "What are you doing today? Leaving lipstick stains on my skin before this parade? Your charade is pathetic."

His anger told a different story than his words. "If my favoritism isn't working, then you wouldn't be so angry. You'd be smug. So that means some people believe it?" I couldn't help my grin, couldn't help but let him sidetrack the conversation, because as much as he liked the look of fury on me, I was certain that I liked the look on him much, much more.

His arms corded when his hands tightened to fists, and I had to remind myself not to stare. I was already half mad from gaping at Felipe, I couldn't allow this shifter rebel to drive me over the edge.

"You know, when a woman sards me over, I at least like to come first." Watkins drew even closer, and I could feel the heat from his body.

I had to lock my knees to keep them from trembling as his eyes scanned my skimpy dress with clear interest despite his anger, or maybe fueled by it. If only his eyes trailing up my thighs felt as good as his fingers would.

No. No. I scolded myself for letting the predator in him dazzle me. I shook off the stupor that always seemed to come over me when Watkins was around. "Do you have any pink dolphin relatives?" I asked as I fluttered my wings and swam backward, giving myself some much needed space as I wondered if a dolphin shifter grandfather could account for the fact that Watkins' very presence made me dumb with lust.

"No. Of course not." His lip curled as if disgusted that I'd compared a predator like himself to a smiling mammal.

I shrugged and switched topics, though I already doubted Watkins' involvement with the attack. He might have been furious and disdainful. But he wasn't smug. If the attack from the road wasn't top of his mind when it came to dealing with me, then perhaps he didn't have a guilty conscience after all. Perhaps he wasn't involved.

I didn't acknowledge that the line of reasoning might have been wishful thinking on my part, because my thighs clenched together even as he stared at me in derision. Part of me wanted to do exactly as he had suggested with the lipstick, lean forward and drag my stained lips across his collarbone, marking him. I'd enjoy the fact that it pissed him off just as much as I'd enjoy seeing my mark on his skin. But indulgences weren't for queens. So I stuck to the matter at hand.

"What do you know about the rebel attack? Were you aware it was going to happen?" I tossed my hands behind my back, like many of the military men I'd seen in Queen Gela's court.

He snorted. "If I knew it was going to happen, do you think I would have kept to my seat?"

He had a point. I stared past him to Felipe, who merely glared. Apparently, my guard wasn't going to help in the interrogation that had been his idea. Wonderful.

"You might have kept that seat if you wanted both to attack me and to maintain your position to get insider information—"

"I'm going to stop you right there before I end up fighting that guard of yours because I can't hit a woman. Not all rebels are the same, that's the exact problem with you crown heads. You lump us all together and think us all fools."

His audacity set my head ablaze. I swam a tiny bit toward him before I clenched my hand and stopped myself. "I gave you the opportunity to speak your needs. You shunned it."

"Because it was a fake offer."

"It was not!" Gah! I wanted to stomp my foot in fury.

"You only made it because you were angry with me."

"I made it because you're blinded by who my birth mother was and you paint me with the same brush. I am not heartless." *Yet.* I left that last word off, bit it back.

After a long moment of silence, Watkins asked, "You are aware that group who attacked us had Sorcha with them?"

"Who?"

"The witch. After sea sprites, Sorcha is the most powerful damn creature in the sea. Do you really not know anything about this kingdom you've taken over?"

I narrowed my eyes and swam closer, floating higher so that we were eye to eye as I glared at him. "You might want to watch your tone."

"I might not."

The water around me felt like it was on the cusp of steam. Or perhaps that was just me—the combination of fury and attraction that Watkins stirred up in me churning my blood until it boiled. "Felipe, please take Watkins' arms," I commanded as I stared at the shark shifter. He'd given me information, but his derision had pushed me. He'd overstepped. Just like in the ballroom, he'd driven me to a height logic couldn't reach, even if it stretched up tall and stood on tiptoe.

Felipe swam up behind Watkins and pinned the shark shifter's arms back. If Watkins had chosen to fight, I'm certain the brawl would have destroyed my room. But he didn't. Instead, he sneered, "So what is it? The rack? Going to frame me for that attack? Execute me to make a point?"

The craving inside my chest grew as I swam closer. "No. I'm simply going to take your suggestion."

Watkins' sharp intake of breath as I bent forward and dragged my lips across his neck was the most delightful sound in the world. When I straightened, the beautiful red stain on his skin made my pulse thud possessively. I smiled demurely up at him. "Can't wait to have you swim through the parade at my side, *darling*."

I'D EXPERIENCED PARADES, AND I'D EXPERIENCED MAGIC, but nothing was as magical as the parade that signaled our official entrance into Reef City.

The parade was held above the reef itself so that citizens gathered at the very top edges of the reef and stared up at us where we swam through open water. On land, a human parade would have meant I sat in a carriage, waving demurely at the crowds. But in the sea, there was no carriage.

Instead, a school of clownfish swarmed around me, encompassing me like a cocoon. They swam in circles so that I couldn't see the crowd and the crowd couldn't see me. They waited until the orchestra started up in front of us, playing the national anthem of Okeanos. On a cue that I was not privy to, all the clownfish parted and swam away. I wasn't certain who was more enchanted, the crowd or I. It was amazing to look down upon thousands of people waving ribbons and cheering, little mer girls squealing in delight with little phrases like, "Mama, look at her hair! I want that!"

My soldiers flanked my competitors and me, performing acrobatic tricks and trident twirls to impress the children. Ugo was a crowd favorite, able to do at least ten consecutive backflips without making himself sick. Felipe, of course, took his job seriously, not straying far from me, his face always alert. I wasn't certain if it was because I was flanked by Humberto, the hero of the day, and Watkins, who—to my shock—hadn't washed away my lip stain. But neither appeared to be a threat. Both of the men smiled proudly at the crowd, though they were very careful—for very different reasons—not to touch me.

I didn't focus on the distance they kept; I was as caught up as the children below in the sights and sounds of a sea parade.

Even Mateo seemed to be enjoying himself. He'd been given a seahorse to ride and so was riding sidesaddle, a common technique for mer with their tails, as he waved at the crowd and smiled. The sight of him made my heart skip happily before my attention was pulled in a thousand different directions.

My mages might have been rotten in battle, but they knew how to enchant with the best of them. They shot out rainbow-colored bubbles all around us. When the bubbles popped, small bits of confetti rained down on the cheering mer children below.

Up ahead, one of the competitors—I couldn't tell who from this distance—started up a nonsense song that had the men and crowd singing and clapping.

Ray, Ray, Roll and go,

Roll and go with the wave.

Moon up, Roll and go,

Roll and go with the wave.

Mayor Deacon swam past, giving me a wink before he turned his skin a bright yellow, then a bright green. Children started shouting colors at him. "Orange! Turn orange!"

"Blue! I love blue!"

"He can't turn blue, stupid! He'll blend in with the water!"

Watkins and I both laughed, making eye contact inadvertently. He froze when he realized that he'd looked at me with something other than disdain. I merely raised a brow and turned back to the crowd, but inside, I was reeling. Because I liked an angry Watkins, but a smiling one?

It was a good thing we were in the ocean so that no one could tell exactly how damp my panties had gotten.

I squeezed my thighs together, wondering if sea sprites emitted mating scents when Keelan and his turtle darted past. Keelan wore an unusual jacket, one that was velvet with brass buttons and matched his breeches. It was a sky breather outfit. More particularly, a sailor outfit. It appeared Sahar's son had donned a costume. I grinned. He did have a bit of flair for the dramatic.

"Get back here, thief!" Keelan waved a furious fist at the turtle, who had something in his mouth. I stifled a giggle as Keelan and the turtle darted in and out of the crowd. The children joined the battle enthusiastically, joining together to form a little wall and block him from getting to his mischievous pet.

"Has anyone seen a Mr. Whelk?" Keelan demanded. "The thief has stolen my hat! Without my magic hat, I'll never get the queen to marry me!"

Most of the children shook their heads. "Nope. Never seen him!"

"Are you sure?" Keelan raked a hand dramatically through his hair, which was still striped black and white on the side for Humberto. "I mean, have you seen our Queenie?"

A dozen eyes darted in my direction, and someone in the crowd whistled.

Keelan snapped his fingers and pointed. "Exactly. So I need that hat back!"

A little mer girl whose tail was as striped and vibrant as a rainbow, took pity on Keelan and opened a gap in the barrier. "You promise you'll be nice?"

Keelan stuffed his hand over his heart. "I promise—ahh!" He shrieked and darted forward to seize the hat, but the turtle was too quick. He rose up high, and Keelan swam after him, stretching so he could finally get his hands on a corner of the misshapen hat.

Mr. Whelk and the siren climbed above all of us as a very elaborate game of tug-of-war began. It was clearly a game they played often because Mr. Whelk knew exactly when to turn his head in order to tug the hat out of Keelan's golden grip. He also teased the poor siren by popping his head into his shell, dropping the hat and letting Keelan dive for it, only to pop out at the very last moment and scoop the hat up, to the shrieking delight of everyone in the crowd.

Keelan was better than a court jester.

I watched every eye in the crowd and in the parade itself turn toward him. He simply redoubled his efforts, growing more ridiculous. Eventually, the two ended up rolling through the water in a series of flips even Ugo couldn't have managed. Keelan's hand emerged with the hat—victorious. Then, my suitor stumble-swam toward me, dizzier than the day he was born.

He gave me a lopsided grin, and I couldn't help but laugh as he swept his chewed-up, bedraggled hat down in front of him when he gave me a bow.

"Queenie."

I smiled as I reached out my hand, and he grabbed it and kissed it, to the grand delight of the crowd. "You've certainly made yourself a fan favorite," I whispered.

"Well, if I can't be yours, at least I'm theirs." Keelan's eyes drifted to Watkins and Humberto. Watkins gave an annoyed groan.

I leaned in and gave Keelan a wink. "Don't be so sure you aren't." I let my fingers squeeze his, enjoying the jolt that went through me when his fingertips caressed my palm in return. As I watched his face light up and his breath catch, I wondered if I might finally have found what I'd been hoping for from the start, a man who'd compete, not for the crown, but for *me*.

15

A sharp wit can cut deep enough to kill a spirit.

—Sultan Raj of Cheryn

THE PARADE WAS FOLLOWED by a torture session. Mayor Deacon had arranged a dinner at his palace, and he had invited the head of every guild in the city.

"Trade me places," I teased Gita as I sat in my guest room and she changed out my gown from the parade masterpiece to a top made only of lace—my attempt at a compromise between the sea's topless styles and my sense of modesty—and a skirt of bunched purple tulle that puffed out like a storm cloud around my hips.

"I'll trade you dresses," the mermaid offered with a grin as she swiped away the parade makeup and replaced it with dark charcoal for my eyelids.

"Dresses and places," I bartered.

Sahar clucked her tongue at me. "You'll be fine."

I made a silly face in her direction, but the truth was I was incredibly nervous. This was to be my first appearance, besides the tournament ball, where members of the public had direct access to me in an informal situation. Royal appeals in the palace were one thing. Queen Gela had taught me how to run a court. But mingling? That was the one area of ruling I'd been too young to learn from her. Balls, dinners, small talk preceding business. The art of saying what you wanted while your words remained inane and inoffensive.

I knew how to compliment these guild masters. I didn't know how to please them. I still felt far too ignorant of the sea and its functions to face them. Despite myself, I bit my lip, giving away my nerves.

Sahar swam forward and put a gentle finger to my chin, raising my gaze to hers. "Remember, treaties will benefit them. Trade will give them larger groups of consumers—well, for some things anyway," she acknowledged with the tilt of her head. "Swim lightly around those algae bloomers. They've got gold coins gleaming in their eyes but a product that tastes worse than …"

"An octopus's backside?" Gita supplied before opening one of my many trunks and grabbing some gold cuffs to decorate the tips of my wings.

"Does an octopus have a backside?" I asked.

"Bottom side?" Sahar offered.

"Any side, really," Gita replied as she wrinkled her nose. "They taste like …"

"Boots?" I supplied.

"Saw boiled boots for sale in a tavern once. Never tried them. Now, I never will," Gita replied as she clipped the ornate cuffs onto the fins that my earth walker mind couldn't help but call wings. "If they taste like octopus, they're trash."

Sahar laughed thoroughly as I spread my wings and swam to the looking glass to gaze at the filigree. My wing tips looked like they'd been dipped in golden scrollwork. And the cuffs themselves weren't heavy at all. I hardly felt them as I fluttered my wings, testing them out.

"Your mages spelled them for me," Gita explained before I could even ask.

"I love them." I smiled at her. "Thank you, that was clever." It was wonderful to know they wouldn't throw me off balance as I swam tonight.

Gita gave a brisk nod, but her eyes darted to Sahar, silently letting me know there was more to the story. I turned to my dearest advisor with a sigh. "What other spells did you request?" Suddenly, the pretty ornamentation felt a bit more like a chain.

Sahar gave a shrug that was far too casual as she swam closer and stared into the looking glass while she altered her hair from orange to a crimson red. "Nothing, Your Majesty." She waited until Gita bowed and swam out of my room. "Just a few little repulsion spells for attacks and the like."

"You think there will be more?" I asked, my stomach clenching at the thought. I'd been foolishly hoping that sea witch wouldn't dare come here to a populated city.

"Probably not," Sahar said, without a bit of confidence. "But I can't take full responsibility for the idea..." Her gaze drifted to my door, which was flanked by Felipe and Ugo. Ugo stared off to the side, watching the servant's door Gita had disappeared through. But Felipe's eyes met mine. His expression was unapologetic and fierce.

I narrowed my eyes at him, both annoyed and a tiny bit thrilled that he'd been part of this plan for me. I dismissed the fact that my safety was his entire job, because, well, because I wanted to dismiss it. My cheeks flushed at the idea that he'd helped craft my cuffs, his hands shaping them as he imagined fitting them on me...

Sahar's hand came to my shoulder and pulled my attention back from the whirlpool of imagination that had nearly dragged me under.

"Now... we should discuss a few things about tonight. First of all, Humberto's reward. I'll have the plaque ready for you just before dinner. There are also several key figures you'll meet tonight. This is about gathering allies..."

I blew out a breath and expelled all lingering thoughts of Felipe. I put all my attention on Sahar and nodded. Because, after a human sacrifice, allies were number two on my list of royal needs.

The pre-dinner cocktail hour stretched into two because the line of people to meet me seemed endless. Unfortunately, my glass of bubble was not bottomless —or perhaps fortunately, or I'd never have been able to answer questions like the following seriously:

"Why do humans always hide from water? Is rain painful for them?"

"Why do some humans wrinkle their nose when they stare out at the ocean?"

"Is fruit addictive? I've heard the sugars in it are addictive."

"Do human feet fall off and regrow like teeth? Don't they get worn out from all that walking?"

I attempted to explain walking with a smile on my face, equating it to swimming.

"But all that rubbing! Surely their skin falls off?"

Mateo was swimming clumsily by, brushing back his silver hair, when that question was asked, and his head turned. His eyes met mine over the shoulder of the squi-shifter who'd asked the question, and the sparkle of amusement in his gaze nearly broke me. I had to look away first and then use every single ounce of self-control to refrain from mentioning that some things could be rubbed quite vigorously without falling off. In fact, rubbing was highly recommended. Especially if it was done by Mateo's hand.

Mateo's loud snort told me he was thinking exactly the same thing. He attempted to swim off when the man in front of me was startled by the noise and turned to look at him, but Mateo ended up bumping into a mermaid and knocking over her cup of fermented bubble. He still didn't have full control of his tail.

I ended up repeating awkwardly hilarious conversations like that several times because it turned out quite a few citizens of Reef City had never been on land. Between their prejudices against sky breathers, fear, and Mayi's strict decrees, travel had been discouraged. The only time many of them had ventured to shore was when a mermaid or siren woman who'd lured a sailor into playing in the water gave birth to a half-human child. Often, these infants weren't born with the magic to breathe underwater. Orphans were placed on the shores of Rasle where the princess there assigned them to a human family. There was an ache in nearly every eye when I asked about their visits topside. I could only imagine what it would be like, to have a child and then be forced to part with them forever.

But I shoved down any sympathy that arose for Mayi. If she'd been heartbroken over me, it had been long ago. And she'd destroyed whatever humanity she'd had left before she met me. My mother wasn't like these sea people. She'd been a monster.

When I suggested to several people that it might be beneficial for them to venture to Evaness when we set up trade agreements with other guilds, several of them seemed delighted. However, those people fascinated by sky breathers, full of questions about life on land or eager to trade with humans, were few and far between in comparison with those who were skeptical, hostile, suspicious.

Their questions were far more pointed.

"Will you restrict those idiotic ships from travel and force humans to pay to rent a seat on our whales?" I had to explain that humans couldn't stand long durations underwater without underwater breathing spells. That led to a subtopic about humans potentially not wanting to be wet for the duration of their travels, ruining their clothing, and the preposterous human fear of shark attacks. That painful experience was followed by:

"Are we only going to be able to trade at seaport markets? What about inland? How will we trust that our goods will fetch a fair price if some human takes them?"

"How are you going to keep fruit from rotting down here so quickly? Magic? Doesn't ingesting magic rot your teeth?" Ironically, this question came from the same person who'd wondered if fruit was addictive.

"What should a bushel of algae go for on the market open to the sky breathers?" Sahar's warning had come full circle with that question. The answer: nothing. Humans wouldn't eat algae. Not even if you paid *them*. But I smiled and simply asked about the going rates under the water, giving polite ambiguities in response.

"Why should those dirt trotters get to fish if we can't spear their cattle and drag the lowing beasts under the sea?"

That there was a question I had been pondering but did not have answers for … other questions like that were items I had been researching. But I hadn't been prepared for an onslaught of this nature. Of course, Palati, the capital, was in deep water, and those in Reef City sat on the continental shelf, much closer to land, so they were quite concerned about interaction and trade with humans.

Ajax, the representative for Reef City's jewelry makers, was incredibly concerned about the imposition of tariffs in order to protect the miners and jewels under the sea. An octopus shifter—of course, after Gita's comments, he had to be an octopus shifter, fate wouldn't have it any other way—Ajax chose to keep extra hands even in his human form, which meant that his forceful gestures were all the more intimidating. His shell necklace bobbed on his chest as he slammed three of his right fists into three of his left. His skin darkened from pink to a dull purple, and fury overtook his features when he tried to make his point. "We spent all this time growing beds of oysters, and then those assholes try to rob us of our pearls!"

I knew better than to defend the actions of those on land, but I was at a loss for how to solve the problem.

I'd discussed the matter with Sahar twice, but we had yet to come to a solution that we thought Okeanos' residents would find palatable.

I needed Ajax as an ally; it was clear from the way he commanded the attention of the group that all ears were delicately tuned in to our conversation. A good impression was paramount. For a moment, I wished Declan had never left so that he could handle this man, but then I erased that thought as I realized how interfering my brother-in-law might have been. Bloss would've directly snapped back at Ajax that he should tell his guild mistress to hire guards.

I opened my mouth to ask what sort of protection he had set up for his pearl fields when Stavros swam up beside me. The shy siren gave me a gentle nod, and his beauty stunned me for a moment. Were his eyes a more liquid blue tonight? Did his golden skin gleam more? Always reserved and shy, in a land where those around him were more prone to sing and dance as they went about their day, I hadn't really thought he'd make a useful husband, not one who could stand the barrage of court life. That was until Stavros turned to Ajax and asked, "What percentage of your pearls do you grow? And what percentage do you simply wish into existence?"

I didn't let surprise show on my face but turned and waited expectantly for the guild master's response.

Ajax's face simply turned more purple. Dark spots appeared on his cheeks like freckles. Was he embarrassed? Had he been trying to use my ignorance to his advantage?

"Why ... I don't—"

"Doesn't your guild have an agreement with the nation of Cheryn?" Stavros lifted his hand to scratch his chin. "I could have sworn I heard—"

I narrowed my eyes at Ajax, who quickly threw up all six of his hands defensively and barely restrained from stomping a foot. "Not with that sultan! He'd never have agreed!"

But Ajax's wording was so specific. He hadn't outright denied having an agreement—only not having one with Sultan Raj. But Cheryn was a land full of djinn, any of whom could grant a wish.

"Oh, my mistake then. My cousin said ... I suppose—"

I cut off Stavros before he could finish his apology, and I reached for his hand before he could swim away in embarrassment. His eyes widened in shock and he nearly pulled away, but I merely tightened my grip and pulled him close to my side as I asked Ajax, "If not with that bastard of a sultan, then who?"

Ajax pressed his lips tightly together as Stavros turned his eyes on me. I rather liked the way his admiring glance made me grow warm inside. Particularly when he glanced down and his cheeks reddened, but his fingers tightened a bit on mine.

He wasn't a fighter, Stavros. Not really. But he wasn't a coward either. And the flower had been thoughtful. Maybe he could be an ally. He certainly seemed studied enough. Perhaps he fit more into a scholar's role. When Stavros' eyes lifted and he gave me a hooded look, I wondered if perhaps he could be even more than that.

Reality interrupted my musing when Ajax answered, "The youngest prince. We had an agreement with him a few years back. Not for a while though. Your information is outdated."

"My apologies." Stavros inclined his head.

"Well, that's for the better," I responded primly. "I don't believe in using wish magic." I stared directly at Ajax, ensuring the octopus shifter knew exactly how serious I was. "It deprives hardworking men and women the pride of a job well done."

Both Stavros and Ajax looked a bit shocked. But this was one area in which I agreed wholeheartedly with my dearest kidnapper, Queen Gela. "A hard day's work is good for the soul. Once this competition has ended, please come to the palace with your proposition for tariffs and your reasoning written out. If it is reasonable and fair to both parties, I shall use it. If it is not reasonable and fair, then I shall reverse the terms of the agreement and whatever you wished upon the sky breathers shall be put upon you." I let my look grow hard as the silence spread around us like ripples. "Am I clear?"

"As water." Ajax inclined his head before swimming off.

After he'd swum off, I turned to Stavros, staring up into his bright blue eyes. "Thank you for your help."

"Thank you for letting me stay," he responded quietly, his thumb stroking my hand where our fingers were still joined.

I reveled in his soft touch for a moment. He wasn't aggressive like the others, wasn't demanding. He seemed happy just to be beside me, content with this small moment, this light touch. A memory from when I was eight years old floated to the surface. I'd been hiding behind the tapestry in my room, crying my eyes out after Josh, a servant boy I'd girlishly admired, had betrayed me in our game of hide-and-seek so he wouldn't lose, and then, on top of that, he'd called me a smelly old poop stick when I complained.

My supposed father, Gorg, had found me, using all of his skill as a spymaster and spotting the lump in the tapestry. He'd gently pulled me from my hiding place and pried the story from my lips with sweets. "You know, true love is really mostly about friendship and loyalty," he'd told me. "So I don't think Josh is the one for you. Your true love wouldn't betray you or leave you behind. He'd stay by your side. Help you. Always."

I stared up at Stavros and wondered what Gorg would think of him. My chest gave a funny tug because I thought, perhaps, he'd approve.

A longing expression seemed to cross Stavros' face, and for a split second, I considered asking him exactly what he was thinking. I wanted to know if his thoughts were the same as mine. But we were in the midst of the huge ballroom in the mayor's palace, jellyfish-fashioned chandeliers tinkling above us, gossips tittering all around us. It was not the right time for such confessions. So instead I asked, "How did you like today's parade?"

He shrugged. "I'd rather eat boots."

I burst out laughing. "How many boots do people eat around here?" I waved a hand at his startled face. "I'm sorry. It's a conversation I had with my maid earlier. She doesn't want to try boots, but apparently they're a delicacy or something."

"Yes, you apparently can only get them after a shipwreck. They're quite popular here." Stavros pointed to a long table set with rows of shrimp and clams and …

an entire pile of boiled leather strips. Floating next to that pile, hand on his gut, was Humberto, who slurped the end of a bit of leather into his mouth.

Ugh.

And he was going to carry his children in that mouth? Didn't he care what he put into it?

I noticed Sahar next to him and realized that, around us, people were floating closer to the dinner tables. It was time to acknowledge Humberto's heroics publicly. Sahar took his arm, and he snatched up one last leather strip, biting a piece off as they came closer.

I reluctantly released Stavros' hand. "I have to go give a speech and thank Humberto."

Stavros' lips tightened in disappointment, but he gave a swift nod and a bow of his head. I turned my attention to the hero, who stuffed the last of his leather strip into his mouth so that his cheek protruded like a squirrel's. He swallowed some boot, making his cheek shrink a little; I swallowed my disgust. And then I took his arm so I could escort him toward the head table where Mayor Deacon stood, awaiting our arrival.

We passed several tables with competitors from the tournament, and I gave them all a huge smile. Valdez sat alone at one table, his black clothing drawing my eye. Then his eyes. Then his sultry grin. I nearly swam into a table, I was so caught up in his gaze. I had to swim sideways quickly to avoid it.

And that was when a strange gasp erupted from Humberto. I turned, only to watch the cardinal fish shifter grab his throat as his eyes bulged—he was choking.

16

The competition can only beat you if they're alive to win.

—Sultan Raj of Cheryn

I WATCHED in horror as one of the men seeking my hand began to turn blue. My gut churned with panic, and my hand flew to my mouth. Behind me, Felipe moved closer to me, his hand closed on my shoulder, and I nearly reached for it, nearly clutched at him in public to quell my fear. But he just leaned forward and whispered, "Back up. Leave room for the healers—"

"I've got it! I can handle this!" A familiar voice burst the panicked bubble between my ears. Julian swam forward. The tall, pale green-haired scientist's face was serious as he grabbed Humberto's face, squishing the man's pudgy cheeks and popping his mouth open.

"If someone's choking, you need to try to clear the throat—" Julian rammed two fingers down Humberto's throat, and my stomach jumped as if the siren were choking me.

Gasps erupted from the crowd as Julian slammed his fingers side to side in Humberto's mouth like he'd hooked the fish. I think all of us were so utterly shocked by the siren's actions that we couldn't move.

"No, too deep. I can't get it," Julian said matter-of-factly as his fingers and a trail of brown boot-colored spittle emerged from Humberto's mouth. He wiped his fingers nonchalantly on his short pants as he swam behind Humberto. He raised his voice and spoke in a tone my tutor had often used. "If you can't clear the passageway with your fingers, the next step is back blows." He grabbed Humberto's shoulder and slammed his hand into the man's spine so hard that Humberto jerked forward like a puppet on a string. Blow after blow made his portly body jiggle, but he didn't speak. Nothing came out of his mouth.

A healer swam up beside me, potion bottle in hand. "Majesty, do you want me to—"

"The final step, if the other two don't work, is to induce vomiting with this maneuver," Julian cut the healer off as he wrapped his arms around Humberto's wide, striped middle from behind and then forcefully punched into the cardinal fish shifter's stomach.

With a loud pop, a balled-up strip of boot emerged from Humberto's mouth and floated in front of me. Felipe used his spear to bat the nasty thing away as Humberto gasped and coughed. Julian grabbed a bottle of bubble off someone's table and handed it to Humberto, who took it and swigged down a few gulps before muttering a scratchy, "Thanks."

All around us, applause erupted.

Julian gave a shy wave of acknowledgement before he turned to swim back to his seat. But I swam forward and latched onto his wrist, carefully avoiding his hand and the fingers that had just been down another man's throat.

"Ladies and gentleman," I said loudly, in my best royal voice, the voice I'd practiced in the mirror for so many years. I glanced around the room, waiting until every eye was upon me, feeling their attention feed me, empowering me to say what needed to be said. "I want to thank you all for coming tonight. Mayor Deacon has been an absolutely amazing host. Your city is quite lucky to have him. And I wanted to tell you how utterly impressed I am by you, the residents of Okeanos. I've never met so many men who are selflessly heroic. Twice, today, I've witnessed these competitors protect and help one another." I lifted the hand of Julian's that I held and used my free hand to gesture toward Humberto.

I let the tide of applause rise and fall before I continued, "While I was told to stand up here and give an account of what happened, I'm certain your maids will tell you much more exciting versions than I would, and why should I deprive these men of the legends they undoubtedly deserve to become?" That earned a solid chuckle from everyone, even Ajax, the jewelry maker. With a grin, I borrowed a glass from the person sitting closest to me and held it aloft. "So, without further ado, please raise your glass in honor of two Okeanos men today: Humberto and Julian."

A cheer ripped through the room.

And after that, dinner wasn't nearly so awkward or awful. I sat the heroes down on either side of me, and congratulations to them seemed to deflect the pointed questions that had been lobbed my way before the meal. I was able to enjoy my stuffed lobster in peace.

When, inevitably, music started to play and those around me started to sing, several people floated toward the ceiling to dance. I'd intended to go look for Sahar, but when I turned in my seat, I found a hand extended in my direction.

My eyes traveled up an arm that was taut with muscle beneath a black shirt, over a deliciously thick neck that tempted me to bite it, up toward the mischievous eyes of Valdez. His rings were missing though, a fact that I found made me the tiniest bit disappointed.

"A dance, Your Majesty?" He grabbed my hand before I could answer the question and pulled me up toward the chandeliers. Several couples swayed in circles around the blue lights. He brought us to an empty space under the coral ceiling where the only things I could see were blue-white crystals.

"You're beautiful," he whispered as his hands wrapped around my waist, his touch flowing and soft as silk, leaving me trembling.

"You too," my idiot mouth replied without waiting for my mind. I stared up at his hazel green eyes and felt myself falling into that lusty trance that I'd come to associate with him. My awareness of the room around us faded. Even my self-consciousness about Felipe and Ugo swimming just a few paces behind me seemed to disappear. Only Valdez existed.

"You didn't wear your rings tonight," I noted.

"I didn't wear the visible ones," he replied.

That sent my thoughts into a churning whirlpool. Where else could he possibly have rings?

His naughty grin told me he knew exactly what I was thinking, and when he went to spin me, he grabbed my hand and deliberately dragged the outer edge of it across one of his nipples, the hard edge of a metal ring pressing against my hand.

Damnation.

I closed my eyes and bit my tongue, trying to force reality back to the forefront. The pain jolted a tiny sliver of sense into me, or at least the upper half of me. The lower half was ablaze, utterly consumed by lust. When I glared up at him, Valdez simply looked amused.

"I asked around about pink dolphin shifters," I grumbled. "I know what you're doing."

"Did you? Do you?" Valdez cocked a brow, and the arrogant expression on his face made me want to smack him and then kiss him. Then maybe smack him again. Or maybe have him smack my ass while we kissed.

"Stop."

"Stop what?" He leaned down, and his lips brushed my forehead, sending delighted tingles dancing like ribbons down my entire body.

My breathing quickened. My heart skipped. And not because it was faulty this time. Because his hands teased my hip bones as he pulled me closer. His thumbs stroked them, and I felt like a puppet. My entire body followed his touch, yearned for it, like I needed it, like his touch turned me from a wooden girl into a live one. Everything inside me pulsed.

I bit down on my tongue until I drew blood. "Stop. This." I mustered all my strength to push back slightly. Apparently, all my strength only gave me the ability to back away an inch. "It isn't real."

"Of course it is," Valdez replied smoothly. His head tilted, and his eyes hooked me, reeling me back in. "Haven't you ever met someone you were immediately drawn to, someone you wanted above all others?"

My mind drifted to the first moment I'd seen Mateo. There'd been a flash of attraction. Interest. But nothing this intense. The moment I'd seen Valdez and he'd asked me to dance...

I shook my head. "This is magic." This was too intense, too much. People didn't feel this. It was impossible. They'd combust.

Valdez raised a hand to my lips, gently tracing them with the pad of his thumb. "No, it isn't. What we feel for each other? It's pure, unbridled lust." He pulled his finger away just as I was about to suck it between my lips like a heathen, like a trollop, in front of everyone present.

He scooped my hand up into his and pressed a kiss to my knuckles. "Thank you for the dance, Avia."

It wasn't until he'd swum away and I was left floating alone amongst crystal chandeliers that shone brighter than the stars, that I realized the music had stopped.

What the hell was he doing to me? And was it real? Or not?

17

Confidence is a hammer. It can be both a tool and a weapon.

—Sultan Raj of Cheryn

MIDNIGHT FOUND me awake with nerves. The tournament's first competition would start at dawn and continue until dusk. Dreams of Valdez trapping me in a cave with his lust magic swirling a deep pink around me alternated with dreams of giant tentacled sea monsters swallowing Mateo up. I awoke panting, dreading the idea of closing my eyes again. So I didn't.

Mateo's face filled my mind. *How could he do this?* He'd survived the day's parade only because Felipe had found him a mount. He could hardly swim! But what would he face tomorrow? What if he had to wrestle an octopus? Steal something from a snapping turtle? What kind of tasks did they even perform under the sea? On land, it was shooting with arrows, sword fighting. What if he had to face off against another contestant with a trident?

No! It was too dangerous. It was foolish of him to do this. Foolish of me to allow it. I had to find Felipe and tell him that Mateo needed to withdraw. I couldn't risk it. I couldn't stand the thought of Mateo getting hurt because of me. He was too precious.

A memory of the two of us dancing in the ballroom came to my mind. Bloss had just publicly professed her love for her husbands—due to my devious machinations—and the entire ballroom had filled with the kind of joy that stuck to the skin like glitter. Sparkling. Impossible to avoid or remove. Everything had felt absolutely perfect. My own chest had been as bright as the sun, my smile so strong that I knew my cheeks would ache later.

Mateo had stared down at me, his dark curls framing his handsome face, his arms properly touching my waist but his fingers digging in, signaling his lusty intentions in a way that no one else could observe but had made me gasp in anticipation. He'd worn a deep blue vest and a white shirt that had been crisp to the touch. We'd spun and danced and laughed until I found

—to my surprise—that we were clear across the ballroom, near the arches that led off into long dark halls and rooms with doors that weren't strong enough to block out the moans of pleasure taking place within them. Mateo's deep brown eyes had sparkled mischievously as he'd glanced around the dance floor, then taken my hand and led me out into that corridor, the one that had always been forbidden to me.

My heart had still been whole then, and it had thudded so hard it felt like it might break my ribs. I'd been alight with nerves and excitement, utterly captivated by Mateo's smile when he'd glanced back at me before pushing open a door that wasn't yet shut at the end of the hall. I'd eagerly followed him inside.

I couldn't bear to remember what had happened next. It was too intimate, too sweet, and I was currently tainted with worry.

I sat up, kicking back my sheets. To my surprise, Ugo and another guard were in my room on either side of the door. Felipe was nowhere to be found. It shouldn't have mattered, he probably needed a break, but his absence left me feeling unsettled, so in my nightdress, I swam over to Ugo where he hovered by the door.

"Yes, Your Majesty?" His orange eyebrows shot up in surprise to see me awake, but I could see the dark circles under his eyes. He needed to sleep soon.

"Is Felipe off-duty?"

He gave a brief nod. "For another hour, Majesty."

"I need to speak with him now, please." An hour was more anxiety than I could handle. I needed someone to tell me what this competition was, to reassure me that Mateo could handle it, that he'd come out unharmed.

I tried to recall if Mateo had been there all night after dinner, but I couldn't. Too many citizens and suitors had kept me up into the wee hours. I hoped he had snuck away to practice … Did he even know what to practice?

I stared at my guard and tried not to wring my hands. Ugo, to his credit, didn't look at me curiously, though I was certain he wondered at my request, at why I couldn't wait a single hour to see Felipe. I didn't give him too long to ponder, however. "Take me to him, and then find someone to relieve you. Get some rest so you can enjoy the competition tomorrow." Someone should.

That did the trick. Ugo gave me a grin and said, "Always thoughtful, Majesty."

I smiled back at him. "Well, I have to be. You and Felipe work so hard. Someone needs to mother you both."

He belly laughed at that. "If you were mer, you'd hardly have gotten your final tail color. Can't think of you as motherly."

I shrugged as he held open the door for me and led me down the hall. The other guard followed behind silently and respectfully. I'd have to ask his name later. "So, where are they housing the guards?"

"Oh, he's not sleeping, Majesty." Ugo shook his head. "Not if I know him."

Curious, I opened my mouth to ask more, but Ugo shook his head, and I heeded his warning. I followed him through the mayor's grand house silently until we emerged at the arena. Moonlight interrupted by irregular clouds filtered down through the waves, coloring patches of the alabaster sand a pale blue. Three dark figures were on the far side of the arena, floating near the green row of the audience stands. Felipe's dark blue tail was just visible, Mateo's silver tail far more so. Between them was a fish of some sort, tail toward me, thrashing as they held onto it from either side. While the sea didn't carry the scent of sweat quite the way the air did, I could still sense tension and exhaustion from the way Mateo's neck drooped and Felipe's posture had lost its rigidity. Clearly, they'd been in this ring for hours. Were hours enough? Was he prepared? Would Mateo survive the first challenge?

I held up a hand to Ugo and the other guard, signaling them to stop where they swam. "Thank you. You may go."

"But, Majesty, two guards—" the new man protested.

"Felipe's cousin won't harm me," I replied calmly. I waited gazing firmly at them until the two slowly and reluctantly swam off. Then I turned and swam around the edge of the arena to give myself more time to watch Mateo and Felipe before they spotted me. I wanted to see how they got along, gauge their progress, because I was certain they'd both lie to me with utter confidence.

As I got closer, though, my concern about the competition turned to downright dread. Because that fish that they were wrangling was roughly the size of a horse. And it wasn't some fat tuna or bloated sunfish. It was a swordfish, with a long sleek body that faded from black on top to silver at its belly. Its dorsal fin was fitted with some kind of straps. I watched in horror as Mateo wrapped those straps around his hands and then mounted the bucking fish, turning it toward the center of the arena.

The clouds in the sky shifted, and the beast's massive nose slipped from shadows into light. I gasped in horror. The creature's pointed nose had been covered with a mer-made, double-sided, serrated metallic blade that looked sharp enough to slice through the rocks that formed the arena wall.

My gasp had both mermen craning their heads to look at me. But for Mateo, that was a mistake. The beast sensed his inattention and started thrashing wildly. My love's body was thrown side to side like a rag doll, but still he held on. His tail flicked forward as he struggled to regain control of the wild animal, and I screeched when that sword sliced right next to his clumsy tail fin.

No!

The poison of terror spread through my system, paralyzing my limbs as I watched. Mateo used his arms to bodily swing himself around so that his body was right next to the beast, not mounted atop her but aligned at her side. I breathed a sigh of relief. He wasn't mounted. But at least he wasn't a second from getting speared.

"Get back on her! Steer! Control her. Get her to the target. Remember to use those reins!" Felipe barked orders as if Mateo weren't about to be flipped over that beast's back and speared by its nose.

What in the hell are they thinking? I swam toward Felipe, but my movement caught the beast's eye. She changed directions and charged at me.

I hardly had time to be horrified, much less think, before Felipe had grabbed me in a burst of speed. The arena became a blur, the stands turned into stripes of stacked color, as we raced across it. I heard an angry low from the swordfish and Mateo's uncertain yelp, "Whoa!" and knew that we were still being chased.

Felipe made a sharp right turn and then suddenly shoved me behind something tall and dark and human shaped. A second later, with a crack, crunch, and crash, a metallic sword sliced through the giant dummy at our side, seaweed guts erupting from its leather skin and fluttering in front of my face.

My hand flew to cover my heart, which stumbled, stopped, and then haltingly started again. I was dizzy with fear and adrenaline.

But Felipe gave a joyous whoop. "You did it!"

I blinked, watching dully—trying to catch my breath as Mateo slowly unwound his hands, which were striped with red from how fiercely he'd hung on to the beast—as my guard and my true love embraced, clapping each other on the back.

Were they insane?

The beast gave a fearsome bellow and then a grunt from where she was still pressed up against the dummy. The sword on her nose waggled up and down. But the beast was stuck. I studied the target again and realized that his middle was made of a ship's mast. The blade had plunged right through that.

I grew queasy. That blade had been after me. And what about Mateo? He'd been practicing with this unhinged, violent swordfish all night? What was he thinking? What was Felipe thinking?

"The joust will be yours!" Felipe reassured Mateo with a pat on the back.

"I don't know about that, but I do think that maybe I'll know how to control the fish a bit better tomorrow," Mateo replied.

"Nah. Confidence. It's necessary. A tool even, I read that somewhere. You need to be confident. Bertie is the most vicious of all the beasts, that's what Posey told me. And she set all this up. If you're assigned any other beast tomorrow, then you'll be just fine. Easy as sinking a ship."

I turned my most Gela-like scolding face toward the fools. But I was scooped into Mateo's arms and swung in a circle before I could get a word out. "I did it! Avia, I did it!" He smashed me tight against him, and I reveled in the feel of being in his arms again.

It had been too long. And it felt so good, so right, like it was where I belonged. I never wanted to leave. But I still couldn't quash that inner need to scold him, to lecture him for doing something so dangerous, something that might have gotten him hurt. I pulled back and stared at his eyes, but his joyous glee was just too much. Tears swam in my vision, making him as blurry as if a strong current had just blown in and whipped across my face. My chest tightened as I felt the connection between us, and Mateo's elation soaked into me, washing away everything else.

He'd done it. He'd come to a foreign land—no, a foreign world—for me. He'd disguised himself, humiliated himself, looked like a bumbling fool to the other competitors. And then he'd spent who-knew-how-many hours here tonight, practicing so he could prove himself worthy enough to win my hand. Because we didn't live in a world where I could just give it to him.

I was so proud of him. And so humbled that there was someone in this world who loved me that much. Even if every other man in this tournament had selfish intentions, dreams of riches or power ... I knew one didn't. The man floating in front of me, posing as a silver-haired mer, he loved me. He'd loved me even without my magic, without anything else. He'd loved me when I'd simply been a normal-looking girl, a second daughter, a princess without any prospect of power, a human without magic.

I wrapped my hand around the base of his neck and used my wings to push myself up and forward, just enough to press my lips against his. Perfection. Delight. Euphoria. Nothing had ever felt more right. I deepened the kiss, opening my mouth slightly and tilting my head.

Mateo responded instantly with enthusiasm. His hands clutched at me before they drifted lower, curving around my ass and pulling me into him. My legs wrapped around his tail, near his waist, gliding easily over his smooth, surprisingly soft scales. I poured everything I felt into that kiss, trying to show Mateo how much it meant that he would want me, even changed and strange as I was, here in this wild world beneath the sea.

I felt heat travel up my thighs, lighting up my core. Bubbles tickled the skin of my legs, and the sensations were so intense that they couldn't only have been in my head—couldn't only have been the result of a kiss. My eyes popped open. I pulled away slightly and glanced down. Mateo's tail had magically transformed into legs. *But how?*

Mateo didn't question it as we sank slowly to the sand of the arena. His lips found the pulse at my neck and began to suck. My heart thudded and my eyes nearly closed as pleasure surged through me, but then I spotted him.

Felipe floated just behind Mateo, an open potion bottle in his hand. The exact same kind of potion bottle he used each day to give himself legs in order to make me more comfortable.

As Felipe watched Mateo's lips trail down my neck, the other man bared my breasts and began to suckle. I gasped as pleasure shot up my spine, and Felipe's eyes found mine. His pupils were blown out, and he stopped breathing. I recognized the one thing I'd always wanted to see in my guard's eyes as he stared at me.

Desire.

18

Always act like you will walk away from the fight. Then you can get in the first blow.

—Sultan Raj of Cheryn

"WHAT IN THE name of Sedara is happening?" Posey's voice echoed through the arena.

I yanked back from Mateo, startled, my arms flying up to cover my chest. My eyes landed on the half-flower sprite as she marched angrily in our direction, kicking up bits of sea dirt that swirled around her calves. Her petals stood straight up on her head, and despite the fact that her face was rotting because she was undead—and therefore unable to make every human expression—I could tell she was furious.

"I am in charge of this competition!" Posey snarled. "No one was supposed to know what it was. No competitor was supposed to have the opportunity to practice. I was supposed to ensure fairness." Posey glared at Felipe and jabbed a finger into his chest. The skin of said finger sloughed off sideways so that only her bone remained, jabbing him near the heart. "I trusted you," she growled. "I trusted you only had Her Majesty's safety on your mind."

"He acts under my orders." I tried to salvage the conversation, or at least prevent all her rage from melting Felipe where he stood. Posey's rage was rather volcanic.

The flower sprite turned her undead eyes to me. "You? You ordered this?" Her look of disgust could have withered a century-old tree.

I pressed my lips together and nodded. I debated telling her Mateo's true nature, about why he needed help. But the fewer people who knew about that, the better. Just as only three people on the planet knew about my injured heart. Though Posey knew exactly what would happen if I did rid myself of my heart to access my powers, because the same thing would happen to her. As part-sprites, we both could sacrifice our humanity to gain inhuman magic. She had chosen not to do so, as I would have if I hadn't hurt myself. But I didn't get that luxury any longer, not when rebels were attacking and I could help if I only accessed that magic. I decided to tell her a half-truth. "My future is determined by the outcomes of these competitions. I want to ensure that at least one of the men I marry loves me, not my crown."

Posey's rotting lips curled skeptically. She jerked her head to the side. "Majesty, a word, if I may?"

She trod away across the sand, and I straightened my nightdress with a pained glance at both Mateo and Felipe before I fluttered my wings and followed her.

When we reached the far side of the arena, she turned. "Are you sure about this? You really want the simpleton to win?"

"He's not simple! He just can't swim!"

Posey shook her head, her purple petals flowing around her face. "Well, at least ensure you also cheer for the smart ones." She marched off without another word, all the way to the swordfish, who had begun to sag against the dummy, resigned to the fact that her nose was stuck. The flower sprite put her hand on the swordfish's head, and immediately the creature made a little innocent sound like a bleating lamb. Ha. That fish was as far removed from a cuddly lamb as it could get. But the fish stilled as Posey tried to work it out of its predicament.

Felipe reached me a second later; Mateo swam clumsily behind him. "I need to escort you back to your room, Your Majesty. You need to get some sleep before the competition."

I nodded, suddenly exhausted. Yes, I had to fake enthusiasm tomorrow for thirty-two men, making each one feel special. I'd need my sleep in order to sustain my smile. I yawned widely. Too bad Lored hadn't yet gotten back to me about trading for coffee. I could have used it.

The water was warm and clear the next morning, and the mayor's palace was full of ripples as people swam about excitedly. Mer women swam through the corridors with elaborate creations of coral woven into their hair. All the talk was that this was the event of the decade. Men wore not only shell necklaces, but shell armbands too. The bright-colored skirts and pants of the tall sirens were so overwhelming with outlandish patterns that I felt like I was swimming inside a gaudy, tasteless rainbow.

The smiles I saw on every face were expectant and gleeful, like children in Evaness got on their birthdays. Gita had fled as soon as she'd dressed me so that she could get a good seat. Even my guards were smiling, well Ugo was anyway. Felipe was just as handsomely straight-faced and halfway sullen as ever.

Mayor Deacon greeted me with a hug, he was so excited. He only remembered himself when Felipe cleared his throat. The mayor pulled back, a blush coming over his striped features. Today, he'd worn a vest along with his pants, both of them in stark black and white stripes, perhaps to keep himself from blending in with the surroundings.

"You look absolutely ravishing, Your Majesty." He bowed by way of apology.

I grinned and took his hand. "Thank you. Would you care to escort me to the tent?"

Deacon grinned and tucked my hand into the crook of his elbow. "I'd be honored. But don't you want to eat first?"

"Oh, I'm too caught up in the excitement to eat," I replied as he swam me through the hall. I had to use my free hand to gather up my skirt, which today was made of narrow ribbons of red silk that flew in every direction when I swam. My top was the most daring I'd worn yet. Two red ribbons descended from my shoulders and tucked into the middle of my waistband, just hiding my nipples from view. My hair was styled up into a magnificent golden point, like the bud of a rose, with a white pearl crown nestled at the crest.

And I was nervous, though not nearly as nervous as last night; my fears about Mateo had eased a bit. My anxiety about all the men getting hurt had decreased even more this morning when Posey and Lizza had popped into my room. I hadn't been so relieved to see Lizza since she had saved my life. "Finally, you've returned from gathering potion ingredients?" I'd asked by way of greeting.

"Yes, and you'll be happy to know I found a few items that might work for you," she'd responded subtly, not mentioning my heart in front of the guards or Posey.

I'd nodded thanks. But knowing that the undead witch was here and would be available if any of my contestants were hurt eased my mind. Lizza had more magic in her rotting pinkie finger than all the other mages in my retinue put together. If anyone got hurt today, she'd be able to help, I didn't doubt it for a second.

Deacon led me down out into the stands of the arena, and I was overwhelmed. Thousands of sea people were there, and the rainbow rock denoting the rows was almost lost in the swirl of color from hundreds of heads. The warble and chirp of conversation reached my ears. Deacon and I paused at the entrance, and I spotted a local quartet. As soon as they spotted us, they began the national anthem. Like any good mayor, Deacon paused, waiting for the crowd to grow quiet and attention to turn toward us. Only then did he swim forward with me on his arm.

We cut a line right through the center of the sand, heading toward the dais where I'd watch the competitors. I smiled and used the royal wave I'd learned growing up. Deacon's smile and wave were broad. I received some nods, and polite applause filled the stadium, but there were also quite a few glares, which made my stomach churn. I hated that random strangers still didn't like me. Hated it. My grip grew a bit tighter on Deacon's arm, and his eyes followed mine.

"Don't worry about them," he said, patting my hand gently. "You can never please everyone. Trust me. The day before you arrived, I found a likeness of myself painted on the seat of someone's privy. I'll let your imagination decide where they'd painted my mouth."

Despite myself, I grinned. "What did you do about it?" I asked.

"Painted myself a hat, of course," he replied.

I dissolved into laughter, shaking so much that I clutched his arm for support. Tears came to my eyes. "Mayor Deacon, I do believe you are now officially one of my favorite people."

His grin was wide. "Glad to hear it." He leaned forward conspiratorially. "I'm certain that means you'll keep what I say next just between us."

"Of course."

"While those fools in the stands don't pose much threat, I would suggest keeping your head about you."

I leaned in, heart pounding. "Have you heard anything?"

He bit his lip and shook his head as we swam up to the tent I'd spotted the day prior. "No. But isn't it a bit odd that you were attacked on the way here? And that one of your competitors choked on a boot last night?"

I blinked, nonplussed. "I'm not seeing how those two events are related."

Deacon gestured toward the throne, which was a bright green elk horn coral covered in tufted cushions. I sat down, and he took the seat at my left side. "I've come to realize, over the several years I've been in this position, that sometimes, when things seem like coincidences, they actually are not."

His words sank me.

Was he right? How could they be connected? I supposed magic could have been a key. Was Humberto a target now because he'd stopped that hedge witch and her group? Did he need extra protection?

Worry brimmed in my gaze as I looked over at Felipe, who swam just off to my right, slightly behind me. My guard gave me a calm, confident look in response, as though this was within his control. I had no idea if he knew how much I'd come to depend on his confidence in the short time we'd been together, but I had. I couldn't be more grateful for everything he'd done for me.

Deacon excused himself before swimming to visit with some others further down on the platform. That left me with two spare seats at my side, and I turned to my guards.

"Feel free to sit if you need a break."

Felipe scoffed. He and Ugo took up posts hovering on either side of my chair as I stared out at the crowd and wondered about all the things that had happened since the start of the tournament.

My mages swam into the tent and took their seats along the sides. Lizza wasn't with them yet, she'd stayed with Posey in the competitors' preparatory room. But that reminded me. There was a third odd thing that had happened to one of the men in the tournament. Radford's odd fit. I started to rise from my seat, but Felipe quickly stopped me.

"Majesty, is there something we can get for you?" His tone was crisp and professional.

"I just wanted to speak to one of my mages," I told him.

He lifted his hand, indicating I should sit back down. "Any of them?"

"Carle, please," I requested.

He nodded and swam over to Carle. Seconds later, the dark skinned squi-shifter swam back to me. He was the oldest of my four royal mages. And he was the one I'd asked to check on Radford several times. Unlike the rest of the crowd, my mages were dressed in black pants today to identify themselves as magical healers in case they had to swim out onto the field.

"Majesty." He bowed his head.

I leaned forward in my seat as I asked, "Were you ever able to find a solution to the Radford situation?"

He bent his head down and spoke softly so that we wouldn't be overheard by the well-to-do of Reef City, those the mayor had invited to watch the joust from our platform so that they could be seen literally rubbing elbows with me. "No, Majesty. All I can say is that whatever happened didn't come from any potion bottle. It's not a spell any of us are familiar with."

I nodded my thanks, and he swam away, relieved to lose my full attention and thereby the attention of everyone around us. But I was left with a sense of unease. I knew my castle mages weren't the best, but wouldn't they at least recognize magic at work? Perhaps not.

My face was placid, and my eyes studied the crowd, but inside I fretted and my heart paced rapidly as if it were walking back and forth across the ground in agitation. There was no proof that what had happened to Humberto was anything more than an accident. But what had happened to Radford, and the attack, neither of those things could be so easily dismissed. Was Deacon right? Were these bad things related? Or was that just a paranoid flight of fancy?

Travelers were attacked on the road even in Evaness. It wasn't uncommon. And those rebels had been interested in more than just hurting me. They'd wanted the gold from the carriage. Maybe they were just victims from Mayi's reign? Maybe Radford had some enemy I didn't know about, some rival whale trainer who'd enchanted him to humiliate him? Maybe he'd used some random podunk spell that wasn't in the royal books. Maybe I was making molehills into mountains.

I sat back in my seat, trying to steady the lumbering thumps of my heart. I was an idiot to get myself worked up before the tournament had even begun. All I had was speculation. A lot of assumptions. And Queen Gela had taught me what assumptions made of people: asses.

My gaze was drawn down to the side when I watched a green sea turtle swim up from the stands and land right on my lap. The turtle glanced up at me, and I swore I saw a smile cross his face.

"Mr. Whelk! You impertinent bastard!" a familiar voice rang out.

I started to laugh, and I reached down to pet the turtle's leathery head as I asked, "Did your master put you up to this?"

Mr. Whelk simply let out an adorable *squee* and rubbed his spotted head harder into my hand. He was a fan of getting petted, it appeared.

Keelan strode up to the tent, his arms wide and the frown on his face as fake as a painted jester's. He wagged a finger at Mr. Whelk. "You naughty, naughty little turtle. You have no shame."

"I think it's his master who has no shame," I quipped. I bent down conspiratorially toward Mr. Whelk and asked, "Isn't that right?"

Keelan made his way over to me, eyes lighting up when he saw that I had no qualms about snuggling a very large turtle.

I noticed that he'd changed the lightning bolt of color in his hair to orange today. He slid into the seat at my right-hand side, the seat reserved for

Felipe. My guard said nothing, just moved over slightly.

"Queenie! Good morning. I apologize for Mr. Whelk. He was just so excited to see you."

Mr. Whelk abandoned my lap the moment Keelan was seated, utterly denying his master's words as he nosed at Keelan's pants.

I pressed my lips together, but a huge grin crossed my face anyway. "Well, go on. Give him the treat in your pocket. He's earned it."

Keelan pulled out what looked like a bit of pasta from his pants and held it up. Mr. Whelk snapped at it contentedly for a moment before I realized that the noodles were actually jellyfish tentacles.

Once Mr. Whelk finished his snack and wandered off toward Mayor Deacon, probably in search of more treats, Keelan turned to me. "You look ... well, there are no proper words to describe how you look." He leaned in close and brushed his lips against my cheek in a sweet kiss. "Now, I'm here so you can make good on your statement that I'm your favorite."

"Are you?" I couldn't help but laugh. "And how will I be doing that?"

"I'm here for a token. A lady always gives a knight a favor before a joust on land, doesn't she?"

His hand reached for mine, and his fingers played with the tips of my own, drawing the attention of those around us and making me—of all ridiculous things—feel nervous. I felt a sense of nervous anticipation, of giddiness, just like I had in Evaness when Mateo had led me down that dark corridor. I had the feeling that giving Keelan a favor would bond us somehow, like this moment was important. But if I gave him a favor, what would the others think?

I stared up into Keelan's amber eyes, weighing my options. Finally, I whispered, "What kind of favor do you want?"

His gaze trailed over me, and my stomach grew taut in anticipation, particularly when those playful eyes of his darted toward the tiny undergarments that Gita had placed beneath my ribbon skirt. But Keelan didn't speak immediately and looked down after a moment. "I'm so tempted right now," he said with a sigh. "I literally feel cleaved in two." He bit his lip as he met my gaze once more. "Part of me wants to take your underthings and parade around with them on display like my own personal banner. But the other, more serious, much smaller part of me knows that would actually be a horrid idea. So ... despite myself, I'd like to request that your 'favor' is to allow me to sit with you so we can get to know one another better."

My heart swelled. That was a favor I could grant. I tilted my head to study him more closely. A slight blush rose on his cheeks. Was he nervous? Was he worried that I'd say no? Who could say no? He'd been honest, funny, even sweet. I shook my head, and immediately he shot out of his seat.

"I'm sorry. I presumed—"

I stood and took his hand, guiding him slowly back down. Once we were both seated, I didn't drop his hand, but held it, to emphasize my point. "I love your suggestion. I'd be glad if you'd watch the first hour of the tournament with me."

He gave a shy smile that was so unlike his normal, confident grin that I couldn't help but love him all the more for it. "To be honest, this competition is as intimidating for me as it is for you," I confessed.

"Intimidating." He gave an exaggerated scoff and then immediately swapped his careless expression for one of wide-eyed seriousness. "It's terrifying."

"I'm terrifying?" I asked, wondering what he meant and which of his two responses was earnest.

"You're not evil, which is in itself terrifying because I worry that it'll pop up at any moment."

We both laughed, though we both knew there was a darker truth to his statement.

"But you're also ... not what I expected." Keelan shrugged. "I've never courted a sea sprite. But as a queen, I thought you'd be more demanding. Issue orders right and left." He lifted our fingers to make a hut, then flipped them over and interlocked them, waggling his fingers like seaweed in a current so that I was forced to waggle mine.

"Hmm ... you want more orders?" I asked as he started a game where his fingers tried to trap mine and I had to slide my own quickly away.

"Oh, no. Definitely not. I'm no good with orders."

"You were a soldier." Amusement colored my tone.

"Yes, and I quit." He quirked a brow.

"Is it that bad in the military here then?"

He shrugged. "It might have been. Before." His fingers trapped mine, pressing them down into my palm as he leaned close. "I have a feeling that it'll soon get better."

We stared at one another for a moment before there was a very pointed cough behind him. I looked up to see Sahar glaring daggers at her son.

"You're supposed to be stretching."

"Pfft." He shrugged a shoulder, but he did drop my hand.

"I thought you told me you needed time to warm up." Sahar didn't drop the topic but kept her furious gaze on her son.

"I am warming up ... to Queenie." His smile was all teeth, and an annoyed *humph* issued from Sahar's lips before she sat down next to him.

There was an uncomfortable moment before a loud horn signaled the start of the competition. I turned and realized that the stands had filled completely while I spoke with Keelan. Vendors now prowled up and down the aisles with clam kebabs and goblets, huge bladders full of bubble strapped to their backs. Siren children sat atop their fathers' shoulders. Groups of mermaids floated together; banners painted to cheer for whichever contestant was their favorite.

Keelan had at least three banners. I pointed one out to him, and he stood and pointed right at the girls in the crowd. Squeals erupted and he chuckled as he took his seat again.

"How do they even know which of you to cheer for?" I asked him as we stood for the opening announcements. He grabbed my hand again, this time subtly, as though he didn't quite want his mother to notice.

His answer was matter-of-fact instead of playful. "Traveling minstrels are making a fortune off us. They go from tavern to tavern. Even heard a few of us have sketches making the rounds."

Fascinating. "Some of you. Not all?"

"Well, I mean …" He slid his free hand through his hair in a mockery of arrogance before looking imperiously down his nose at me. "I stopped looking after I saw mine."

"Keelan!" Sahar scolded.

But I burst into laughter until the herald started to speak. Then I swallowed my amusement and turned a courtly face out to the siren who held an amplifying shell to his mouth.

"Reef City! I am delighted to welcome you to the ultimate quest! The attempt to win the hand of our fair Queen Avia and lead Okeanos to a new day! Thirty-two men are here today competing. Only twenty of them will make it to the next round. That's right! Twelve are going home! Their entire fate will be decided in two days."

The man was good. His speaking was crisp. He knew how to build momentum and suspense. I did fade out a bit when he explained the point system for the joust; it was far too complicated for me to follow. An impartial judges' panel sat on the far side of the arena. They were the ones who needed to understand the rules. All I needed to be aware of was that I got one exception. I could save one man if needed and keep him in the running.

I had a feeling I'd need that exception for Mateo, though I tried to quash it because that very thought meant I didn't have confidence in him.

The first round went off without a hitch. Two doors opened in the walls, and a green spark raced across the arena just before Julian and one of the other competitors gave war cries, charging at one another. I hardly had time to be anxious before the round was over. They swam, they clashed. There was a sickening squelch as Julian's swordfish speared the other man's. Julian's beast flicked his nose upward, sending the other rider tumbling through the waves.

Handlers scrambled out from all sides to help Julian contain his beast and then free its nose from the dead animal's.

"Round one is complete, ladies and gentlemen!" the herald took back up his shell to declare. "And with the judges giving Julian a near perfect score for that central hit, he'll be a hard one to beat! As we wait for the next contestant, let me remind you that all the swordfish slaughtered tonight will be distributed to the Reef's different quarters by the City Guard. Each citizen can collect their portion…"

His muttering droned on, but I was distracted when Keelan squeezed my hand and leaned in. "I'd better go. Watching makes me want to pace and shout obscenities."

"I don't mind."

"My mother would." He raised his eyebrow.

"Just one more round, please?" I really did need to ask him about that point system. I didn't want to sound like a dullard later when everyone around me buzzed about it.

"Fine. One. But my leg is going to be bouncing uncontrollably the entire time."

"Good. Fine. Now. Tell me about the scoring."

I convinced Keelan to sit there for four more rounds, explaining the rules to me. Once he left, Sahar took his seat over and—after a death glare—she began briefing me on the people who'd been invited into the tent, those that I'd need to rub elbows with when the tournament paused for lunch.

Sahar had just finished whispering about a very elegant woman who had an entire harem of brickmakers when a panel in the wall opened up, and Mateo emerged, sitting sidesaddle upon a swordfish that was at least twice as massive as the one he'd ridden last night.

Instantly, whatever question I'd had died upon my lips. My attention, which had always been split during prior rounds, turned toward the arena. Everything else dissolved as I watched him emerge. His arms were wrapped up in the reins while his head was crammed into a silver helmet topped by a plume of white ribbon that drooped sadly as the current died down. His swordfish's nose was encased in that hideous metal again, which glinted in the sunlight filtering through the waves. It looked twice as bright, twice as harsh, twice as deadly as last night.

My throat grew dry, and my heart gave a squeeze of protest. *No. He shouldn't do this. He should quit. Stand down. I should yell out and just declare his forfeit. I should use my exception before he has to go through with this.* My fear battled with the rage I knew I'd face from Mateo if I took away his chance. Our chance to be together. He'd never want to stay and look weak in front of the others. He'd hate me if I used the exception to metaphorically cut his legs out from under him. I squeezed my eyes shut for a moment and urged my body not to faint, not to be sick. If he could do this, then so could I.

A noise reached my ears, and my eyes popped open, unable to stop themselves from witnessing whatever was about to occur, even if it was tragedy. Out of the panel in the opposite wall emerged one of the competitors I'd taken no notice of—I'd spoken with him a few times but felt no connection, either good or bad. I knew who I would cheer for. I found Sahar's hand and gripped it as both men took their places at opposite ends of the arena.

Sound died down all around us.

Sahar looked at my worried expression, and her brow furrowed. "Don't worry. I know he's not the strongest competitor, but these sea boys have been racing around on mounts since before they could swim…" She trailed off when she saw how my eyes were glued to Mateo, how pale my cheeks had gone.

Shite. I was giving too much away. I needed to find a way to calm myself, to stop the blood pounding through my veins. But if I took my eyes off Mateo, what if that was it? What if something happened? What if this was the last moment I'd ever get to look at him? "Have you met him?" I nodded toward Mateo, trying to clear the tightness from my throat with a false cough. "I fear this competition is not quite within his skill set."

Sahar began to answer, but suddenly one of my mages shot out a bolt of green light from the middle of the stands. It arced across the arena, tail trailing through the water so that it resembled a sickly comet. The signal to start made both the swordfish rear slightly before they charged at full speed toward one another.

They created waves as they streaked toward one another, bolts of black and silver, features blurred by their speed.

I watched the other man, a siren, pull back on the reins and aim the nose of his beast—not at Mateo's mount ... at Mateo.

Thud. Thud. Thud. My heart galloped. What the hell was that man doing? Why?

Mateo's eyes widened as he tried to pull his mount up, to slide backward on the fish and curl his body low to avoid the sharp metallic blade. But with his poor tail control, he slid sideways toward the other swordfish. Right into the path of the blade.

The entire crowd gasped. Even the herald making announcements gasped into his shell, the sound reverberating around the arena.

All eyes were locked on the two men as the swordfish grew closer.

I felt as if I were watching my life flash before my eyes. My arms tightened so much that my muscles trembled. Every nerve on my face was on high alert, and goose bumps stood up on my arms. I wanted to scream, "Stop!" But whatever I did would be too late, and Mateo couldn't afford a distraction.

His arms struggled, and his silver tail thrashed, and he pulled himself up just as the tips of the two beasts' noses clashed. When the metallic sound rang throughout the arena, I felt my heart stutter to a stop.

My eyelids fluttered, and the edges of my vision blurred. I couldn't see if Mateo was hurt or not. As blood filled the water, darkness overtook me.

19

Be unexpected.

—Sultan Raj of Cheryn

I CAME TO IN A DAZE, only to find Felipe's arms wrapped around me. We were no longer in the tent, in the arena. We were in a hallway that was narrow and dark, lit only occasionally by a magical orb of light.

"She's awake," Felipe called out to someone I couldn't see.

"Mateo?" I asked, still in a daze.

"He's fine. Glancing blow to the arm. A healer will fix him up in no time," Felipe said softly, his thumb gently brushing back and forth over the scales on my elbow.

A rotted face popped up over his shoulder, wild frizzy hair making me blink, unsure if my eyes were focused or not. "Oh good. If she's up, she'll be able to chew her own lizard bits." I recognized Lizza's voice. The undead witch—the one who knew my secret—was with us. "Set her on the table. Then you go guard the hall or something. I'll deal with the queen."

I was set gently on what felt like a stone table. It was cold and hard against my spine, and I instantly wished he could hold me through this process instead. He couldn't. Because even though I knew Felipe suspected something was wrong with me, I couldn't let him know for certain. No one could.

But Felipe didn't immediately leave. "Are you alright?" His face held a look of genuine concern.

I had to lie to him. I had no choice. But what explanation could I possibly have for fainting for no reason at all? My sluggish brain couldn't seem to think of one.

"She's a swooner. Can't handle blood. She'll be just fine. Now, out you go, boy!" Lizza all but shoved him through the door, where Ugo hovered uncertainly. She shooed the guards out too. "You can stand outside just as well as you can in here. Move along then."

Felipe looked at me over her shoulder, and I gave a weak nod. I tried to sit up but hadn't the energy. He disappeared and I heard a *thunk* as Lizza slammed the door shut behind him before stomping back to me and stirring up sea mud around her calves.

I passed back out. When my eyes cracked open again, I had no idea what time it was, only that it must have been long enough for the mud to settle and Lizza to take a seat beside me. She saw me awaken and stood, her bones creaking as she leaned over to check my pulse.

"Well, you're quite the idiot, aren't you?" she asked conversationally.

"Excuse me?" My retort came out breathy, and I had to close my eyes for a moment. My entire body felt weak, dull—almost like I was floating.

Lizza didn't answer me directly, just shoved her hand under my breast and pressed an ear to my chest. A minute later she rose, shaking her head. "I'm surprised you can still speak at all. That thing's weaker than an undead dick."

"What? You said I had a month…"

"It's an estimate. As in a rough guess. Why the hell haven't you gotten rid of it already?" She waved a hand carelessly at my chest as she pulled open a pouch on her waist with the other and rummaged through it.

"I'm trying to decide who deserves it."

"Deserves? Deserves? Who cares?" Lizza grabbed a dead, headless lizard from her pouch and held it up. The arms of the poor decapitated thing drooped over her fingertips as she shoved it in my face. "Here. Eat this. All of it. I don't want to see you spitting out the bones either."

She shoved the lizard into my mouth before I could protest. The texture made me want to gag. But I knew she'd used it before to make me well, so I dutifully bit down. As I chewed, I tried to think of anything but what was on my tongue.

Lizza's scolding made it easier to focus on other things. "I should have just made you undead. That would have solved everything. I could still do it. You'd have a few pretty years before the skin started to fall off."

I couldn't speak with my mouth full, so I settled for shaking my head back and forth as frantically as my weak body would allow.

"You and your sister! Gah! Being undead is the best. Those stupid urges go away. Do you know how long it's been since I had my monthly courses? Neither do I —it's been so long I've forgotten." She pursed what was left of her lips in a smug grin. "You think about that for a minute."

No. I didn't want to think about that. I shouldn't have to. Fury at Mayi rose in my gut. If she hadn't shoved her heart into my chest ... Fury at Gela soon replaced it. If she hadn't kidnapped me ... I couldn't complete a thought. All I could do was wallow in a pit of anger that roasted my insides like lava.

I chewed for several more minutes in awful silence until I swallowed the last of the lizard. Energy surged through my body like a gust of wind or a wild spinning current. My heart started pulsing. The cobwebs in my mind cleared. After a minute, I was able to push myself up to sitting. I took a deep breath, both to steady myself and test my body. Perfect. I felt perfect. Like I had before this mess.

Lizza raised an eyebrow. "Well?"

"Well nothing. How long will that lizard last me?" I knew better than to get caught up in the strength flowing through my veins.

"It'll give you two, maybe three days." Lizza shrugged a bony shoulder. "You're farther gone than I thought you were."

Days? Only days? "You can't make more?" Panic made my voice tight and thin.

"I've got one more. But no, I can't make more in three days." Lizza shook her head.

It felt as though she'd dropped a boulder on me. It was a long moment before I could see past the black devastation that clouded my mind. I took several deep breaths, trying to stay calm. Two days. Maybe four with that second lizard. Six if I was lucky and her three day estimate was correct ... but I didn't feel lucky. "Then what happens?" I asked as I straightened the ribbons on my chest and feigned nonchalance, an emotion as distant from my current state as a star in the sky.

"Then, either you get rid of that heart or it'll get rid of you." Lizza's no nonsense tone brooked no argument.

There it was. Damn.

I clenched my fist. I'd known it already. But the hourglass by which I'd carefully been measuring out my remaining seconds had been smashed. There was no time left.

I nodded and strode past her toward the door, wings tucked down by my sides, a million thoughts at play in my head.

"Where are you going?" she asked.

I turned back to stare at her but found myself staring at the rough brain coral walls instead. "If I've got to pick someone to take this stupid thing, then I need to be out there, weighing my options. I need to see all the competitors in order to make the right choice."

"Competitors? Why would you give your heart to one of those men? Are you looking to maim them?"

I froze with my hand on the knob, not yet pushing the door open. "What do you mean?"

"You think handing a man your heart is going to be without issues? You've got a faulty one."

"Won't his own healthy heart override it?" I felt aghast as I dropped the doorknob and leaned back against the wall.

"To a degree. But he won't be the same ever again. And, if you give it to a man, not a woman ... just think how many more decisions we make with our hearts and not our heads. The emotions of it might drive him plumb mad." Lizza clucked. "I wouldn't give it away to anyone you liked."

"Anyone I don't like would never volunteer."

"Volunteer?" Lizza chuckled. "That's adorable. What did you think, we bring you both into the same room and you hold hands while I chant?"

I merely stared. In fact, I had been thinking something along those lines.

Lizza shook her head. "No. I do the spell. Poof, the heart disappears from your chest and reappears in theirs. Bing. Bang. Boom." She closed up her pouch.

"You think about that woman thing. Who might be able to handle it?"

A woman. Not a man. My entire premise had been to find husbands for that purpose! That, and to unite this kingdom, lessen their resentment of me. What the ever-loving sard was I going to do?

My thoughts immediately flew to Sahar. Or Gita. But did I really want to subject either of them to such a fate? I sighed. I couldn't.

I scrubbed a hand across my forehead. I'd known that I was selecting a victim. A person I'd want to keep at my side and control. But now I would be handicapping them too. I didn't know of any woman I could choose. I needed to stick with my original plan. I had thirty-two competitors who'd signed up for a royal life with all the trappings. Which of them should suffer that fate?

I'd hoped to choose one of my favored to get my heart, one who wouldn't mind being always at my side. But the thought of crippling Mateo or Keelan made me cringe. No. I needed to pick someone more middle of the road. Middle of the pack. I needed someone whose attachment would benefit me but perhaps wouldn't find themselves utterly ruined by my idiotic organ.

I yanked open the door with a frustrated sigh. Both my guards looked startled to see me up and about. I withheld an eye roll as I announced, "Magically cured. I'll try to cover my eyes next time there's blood." I hated the lie. But I hated the truth even more.

I opened my wings and started to swim back toward the arena, which had begun to swell with cheers. "Did they continue the tournament without me?" I turned to Ugo, still too emotionally unbalanced to look at Felipe. I didn't want his keen eyes to perceive the thoughts racing through my head.

"I'm sorry, Majesty, we didn't ask them to stop. And since technically the judges are still present ..." I waved off his apology.

"It's fine. Is there a way to get me back up to watch without everyone staring?"

Ugo visibly ground his teeth together, not wanting to tell me no.

I sighed. "Fine. Well. Let's go watch men try and plunge their fishies into one another, shall we?"

Ugo's eyebrows shot up.

"It was a joke. You can laugh." My tone was too harsh. He remained silent, and I mentally kicked myself.

"You don't have to go back out there yet," Felipe said softly, his hand touching my arm.

Ugo took the opportunity to escape. "I'll … go check the door." He swam down the length of the hall, disappearing into the darkness.

I turned to Felipe and shook my head as tears blurred my eyes. "Yes. I do have to go back out there." I shook my head as I stared at him. "The people already think I'm weak. The attack on the road. Now this? They're wondering what kind of queen they've gotten. How weak I am."

Felipe's hand tightened on my tricep. "You aren't weak."

I scoffed, trying not to let my voice break. "Oh no? It's normal—"

"Many women swoon."

"Many women don't wear crowns. They don't make life and death decisions. I need to be hard. I need to be strong."

"You are strong." Felipe's gravely tone was certain. "But strong and hard are not the same. Many men and many queens make that mistake. Sometimes, strength comes from flexibility. From going into a new situation, assessing it, trying to get input from others, even those who despise you …"

I gave a bitter laugh. "That has not worked at all. Watkins ... half those Reef City guilds, all those rebels still hate me."

"It will. Give it time." Felipe's features softened.

But his words made me want to throw something. Scream. Stamp my foot. "I don't have time!"

He looked at me oddly.

Shite. I shouldn't have said that.

I wrapped my arms around my middle and pressed my lips into a tight line as everything inside me shattered. Felipe stared at me a long moment before he swam forward and enveloped me in a hug.

First, I was shocked. Felipe had never crossed that boundary. He'd carried me, but only for protection's sake. He'd given me a pat on the shoulder ... but this? Professionalism was gone. This ... was the hug of a friend. Of comfort. His warm arms wrapped around me and melted that icy fear coursing through my veins. He rubbed my back as I trembled and as tears came to my eyes, and I allowed myself to be weak, truly weak, in front of someone else for the first time since I'd taken the crown.

I'd promised myself I wouldn't do this; after Mayi's darkness, I'd promised myself I'd be strong. But this hug, this comfort ... it broke me.

I sobbed in the dark corridor until my throat was raw and scratchy. When I pulled away and swiped at my eyes, Felipe gave me a soft, sad smile. "They'll come around. I swear they will."

For half a second, I wondered if I could give my heart to him. I wondered if I could selfishly bind him to me forever so that he could never leave. This perfect, sweet man who saw me. He was the only reason Mateo was in this tournament. He was the only reason I hadn't been crushed in that attack on the way here.

I stared up at him as my mind laid out each reason he was perfect for an existence full of miserable attachment to me. Dread and self-loathing started to swirl in the pit of my stomach when I didn't immediately dismiss those notions. But desperation was like stained glass, it colored my perception. I had to drag my eyes to the ocean floor before I called out Lizza's name.

I couldn't do that to him. I wouldn't.

Even if it means this country dissolves into war without an heir? The belligerent voice in the back of my head asked in a saccharine tone that belied its intentions.

Felipe was worth a war.

No sooner had I made that decision and forced my wings apart so that I could flee any other monstrous thoughts than I heard a terrible racket erupt from the arena.

Screams and shouts sounded as a crumbling crash reverberated through the coral. Ugo shoved open the door at the end of the hall and wave after wave of water came barreling through the tunnel, knocking me backward, shoving me into the sharp spines of the coral wall.

I pushed off from it, making my wings flit back and forth twice as fast as I normally did. I had to use every ounce of magical strength Lizza had given me to fight my way to the door. "What is it?" I asked when I finally got to Ugo's side.

He shook his head, shock written in the wrinkled lines of his forehead and the furrow of his brow. "It's the arena, Majesty. It looks like part of it collapsed."

20

Always have a scapegoat ready. The people require a blood sacrifice.

—Sultan Raj of Cheryn

I FLEW OUT of the corridor with fear pulsing in my ears as loudly as the screams that filled the arena. I emerged in open water where the sea was lit by a merry sun, and the water might have been light and bright if it weren't filled with mud and blood.

Sard.

My eyes found the other side of the arena where the crowd still ran for the exits. The coral rainbow stands had fallen in right above one of the competitor's entrance tunnels. The stands had sunken in; some people were still trapped among the rubble. The entrance tunnel itself was completely filled in with boulders.

Dismay whipped me raw as my hand flew to my chest. "Tell me someone wasn't in there. Tell me they were between matches," I ordered Felipe and Ugo.

But my guards didn't respond. They didn't know. They couldn't. Both of their faces reflected the shocked horror I felt.

To one side, the protestors who'd been carrying banners with Forsake the Crown were shouting, their anger as sharp as spears. Of course, the arena collapsing had to be my fault. Another stick in the pyre they were building for me.

Sard them! Couldn't they see people were hurt? Why weren't they helping?

I flickered my wings and kicked my legs, swimming hard through the muddy water, which was still soiled from the collapse, not caring how the particles clung to my skin or the waves fought against me and slowed me down to a pathetic crawl. The shouts and crying got louder as I approached, and my stomach sank beneath the ocean floor to hear them.

I emerged from the cloud of mud to see several of my soldiers, most of the competitors for my hand, and a few burly merman citizens dutifully shifting the coral. Gah! Close up it looked even worse. It looked like a mountain had collapsed. From the highest row to the bottom, an entire section of the stands as thick as the blue whale we'd ridden into the city had just crumbled.

I swam toward the nearest person I saw trapped, a siren woman whose leg was stuck. I reached for the boulder pinning her, and Ugo called out, "Majesty!" in a shocked tone.

"Shut up and help!" My manners had fled. Nothing else mattered in this moment but getting these people to safety. I shoved fruitlessly at the purple boulder, but it was nearly half my size.

A warm hand touched my shoulder, and Felipe gently said, "Let Ugo and me get it."

I grimaced but moved aside, cursing my uselessness. I'd seen Mayi form ice spears, watched her lift all the water in my cave, leaving me suffocating in the air at the bottom of the cave, helpless and gasping, until finally she let all the water crash down on me at once, slamming into me with a pressure so intense I'd been certain I'd die. This time, the memory didn't bring with it the normal bout of turmoil and emotion. I simply thought, *All that power. And I can't even move a stupid stone.*

I watched dully as my guards carefully lifted the stone enough for the woman to drag herself backward. Then they let it fall again, it was too heavy to keep aloft for long. As they picked the woman up and carried her over to several others laid out along the benches at varying heights, my eyes took in more of the scene.

My mages and random strangers worked together, tending to those who bled. Several tournament competitors were helping. I saw Mateo, Watkins, Valdez, Stavros, and Humberto in the crowd along with others. I noticed Julian helping one man with a dislocated shoulder. The man's scream when Julian wrenched his arm back into place made a shudder run down my spine, and I pulled my eyes up and away from the pair. Near the top of the arena, one of my mages held a snarling shark shifter at bay with a magical green shield. The shifter's tail already turned shark, his teeth long daggers. The blood in the water had clearly riled him up.

Shite. We were lucky there weren't more.

My eyes drifted away from him—the mage seemed to have it under control—and back to the entrance. Or where the entrance had once been. The highest peak of the rubble seemed to be right there. On that very spot. That was odd, unless the collapse had caused a miniature avalanche and rocks had rolled down to pile just there.

Mayor Deacon noticed me as he assisted a siren hobbling on one leg to a seat. He gestured for a mage healer before he swam over to me. His face had turned into blotches of rainbow to match the muddled rockfall behind us. Despite his bright colors, his expression was somber.

"What happened?" I asked softly.

He shook his head. "Uncertain. But I know I had my people check this arena three times before your arrival."

My throat tightened, and I could predict what he was about to say before he said it.

"I don't think it was an accident."

Self-loathing roared at me. Logic shouted. My stomach ached just like it had in the cave with Mayi after she had slowly stabbed me with ice only to magically heal me. Black specks danced in my vision because I knew, immediately, what had happened. "Protestors."

Deacon's nod was slow and steady—the opposite of my internal rant.

I should have halted everything after that attack on the road. I should have done more than question Watkins. I shouldn't have operated on the assumption that they'd attacked for gold because it was easy, or because no huge contingent of knights or soldiers would chase them through the open plains.

What a fool.

Dark thoughts rose like a chorus in my chest, blackly harmonizing all the ways I should have known. Deacon had been right. Things were connected. If I hadn't dismissed this hours ago, I would have seen it. Oh, this shite day couldn't get worse.

A hand clutched at mine, squeezing my palm, and I turned in a daze to see Sahar. Her eyes were wild, her hair unkempt, and her grip on my hand only tightened.

Immediately, I knew that someone had been in the doorway when the arena had collapsed. When her lip trembled, I knew who.

"No," I gasped.

She didn't respond. She seemed frozen but for the hand that threatened to break my fingers, snap my palm in two. I couldn't even imagine what she felt right now, because my own chest ached. I hardly knew him, but Keelan painted a bright spot in every day.

I met Felipe's gaze, and immediately he and Ugo swam down to the entrance and began shifting coral, trying to dig out some kind of opening. I kept Sahar's hand, not hugging her, not patting her back, because those gestures would signify that hope was dead. That Keelan was gone.

I watched for a moment, but floating and waiting felt wrong. My limbs twitched to yank back those smaller rocks, do what little I could. "We should help," I whispered jaggedly.

She nodded, but I wasn't certain she'd heard me. I pulled my hand from her grip and swam over, lugging rock after rock until my chest ached and the ribbon gown I wore was all but shredded.

The first time I found a hand, hope surged up only for it to be dashed against a rock. We pulled two spectators from the rubble, their faces blank, their chests still. And we weren't even down to the tunnel yet.

A third person, a squi-shifter, was found in animal form, still moving, but faintly.

"Hey, you!" one of the men called to a mage. "Here, now!"

The mage swam over in a hurry, and I could hear the clink of potion bottles as he checked his stores for whatever might heal the injured. Lizza appeared at my side then, clacking her teeth together as she surveyed the damage. "Not good. Not good at all."

I didn't respond because just then, two mermen heaved aside a big chunk of blue coral, and another hand drifted out of the rubble to rest gently on the sand. A golden hand. A siren's hand.

Sahar gasped behind me before swimming forward to dig at the sand on the ocean floor as the men around her shifted more coral away from the body.

I both hoped it was Keelan and hoped it wasn't. Because no matter how hard I stared at those fingers, they didn't twitch.

The ripples in the water blurred my vision. Or were those tears? Shock cushioned the edges of my thoughts with fuzzy clouds and kept the horror of everything from penetrating fully.

One last hunk of coral was lifted. A tournament helmet was yanked off. Keelan's signature lightning bolt streak hair came into view. I could instantly see why his hand hadn't moved; it was bent at an odd angle past the elbow, twisted sickly. Sahar gave a bitter screech of pain. She dragged a limp Keelan into her arms as she batted away the other rescue workers, cradling his long body on her legs as she rocked him. "My baby. My baby."

Like a dam cracking and bursting, all the shock that had been insulating me wore off, and the pain of the situation filled my mouth and rushed through my ears. I was drowning in it when I saw Keelan's face full-on for the first time.

His soft, golden skin was mottled with scratches and blood, abrasions turning the smooth surface into a patchwork of red. A lump had swollen on his forehead, and it looked like his nose might have broken. His eyes were closed. By all the afterlives, I hoped they weren't closed forever.

I turned to Lizza, my knees as limp as noodles. I stared wordlessly at her. Could we give him my heart? Would it save him? It would be a terrible fate, but wasn't death worse? My eyes asked the questions that my mouth simply could not. Not because I gave one shite about who might overhear what right now, but because I was so stricken.

Julian suddenly appeared between Lizza and me, before charging forward and picking up Keelan's hand. The scientist put his own fingers on Keelan's wrist, ignoring Sahar's attempt to bat him away. "Still has a pulse, but faint."

Lizza looked at me, letting her eyes drop pointedly to my chest. And then she shook her head, signaling that she didn't think this was the moment to give it to him.

"Do whatever it takes to save him," I ordered, voice as harsh as my violent feelings. I wanted him to take my heart but didn't. More than anything, I wished my stupid powers came with the ability to turn back the clock, to reverse everything. Because I felt certain now, without a doubt, that I was the reason all of this had happened.

"Undead?" Lizza croaked out the question.

It was on the tip of my tongue to say yes. But I hesitated. "Anything short of it. If it comes to that, his mother should decide." I watched Sahar lean protectively over Keelan and plant a kiss on his forehead. Her face screamed her pain though her tears were muted and soft.

If I could have switched places with him just then, I would have, because no mother would cry over me that way. And no mother who'd cry that way ever deserved to lose her son.

Lizza watched me solemnly for a second before she gave a nod and stiffly trod toward the others. She took Julian's hand and forced him to help her down. Her knees creaked as she knelt beside Keelan and reached out a hand to check his pulse.

I clenched my teeth together so hard that my face hurt as I watched. Hoped.

She'd brought me back. This couldn't be worse … could it?

Keelan's smile—the sight of him feeding Mr. Whelk a tiny jelly—it felt unreal that only hours ago, we'd laughed together. I hadn't even gotten to know more about him! I'd asked about the tournament rules like a fool.

Lizza glanced back at me and gave a brief nod. Did that mean she could treat him? That his injuries could be healed? He'd be okay? I sank to the sandy ocean floor in relief, settling on my knees, flaring my wings for balance, ready to sit in vigil as she worked her magic. But instead of treating him, Lizza snapped her fingers until Julian leaned back down to help her up. Then she turned and clomped back over to me.

Her face was as serious as a grave when she whispered, "Only one thing will save him."

"Anything."

She shook her head and reached into her pouch, pulling out a headless lizard.

Anything but that. Shite. Sard. Shite. I shoved my eyes shut. Squeezed them closed. Temptation danced like fire in my mind. Three days. I'd be giving up three more days. My heart shivered inside my chest, as if it knew and was scared.

"What about a spell to freeze him, preserve him—" Bloss had spoken of that sort of spell. It had been put on her castle and everyone within it.

Lizza barked out a rough laugh. "I'm no Donaloo. That crackpot had magic no other has ever had."

My fingernails sliced into my palms, and I could feel the plunk of my pulse. All I'd wanted, since before I'd started this damn tournament, was more time. But time was up. I had to decide, make a choice. All the moments of this tournament strung together and flashed before my eyes, like I was walking through a gallery. And I came to a conclusion. Quickly, before personal greed could burn away my good sense, I spoke. "Do it."

"Majesty. Are you sure?"

"Give it to him."

I didn't open my eyes until I heard the crunch of ocean sand under her feet, until I knew Lizza had turned back to follow my orders. But I couldn't help cracking my lids to watch as the undead witch pulled the last undead lizard from her pouch—my last hope—and fed it into Keelan's mouth.

Hours later, in my room inside the mayor's palace, I paced restlessly. The tournament's location had been moved to the open ocean, delayed until tomorrow for the all the remaining contestants. Sahar had nearly crushed me with a hug when Keelan had opened his eyes. The lizard brought him back. But his arm bone was shattered into so many pieces that I didn't think there's any healing it. Neither Lizza or Julian saw a way to restore it from the damage done.

Keelan's swelling, internal bleeding, those things were solved. But, just like my heart, the lizard's magic couldn't fix anything that was too far broken. Not forever. Keelan might have a useless arm.

Better than a useless heart, the bitter thought surfaced as I paced, but I waved it aside like a pesky moth. Cruel thoughts wouldn't make anything better. Though I had an idea of what would. And with that second lizard gone, a sense of urgency sprinted through my veins. My veins had nothing *but* urgency left. I needed to make a decision. And I'd lost nearly half a day to overseeing that rescue, to giving out speeches and hugs afterward, to promising to pay for funerals for those who hadn't made it. To checking on Keelan and a sobbing Sahar, who'd clutched my shoulders in gratitude.

"Your Majesty, I can't even tell you what it means to me. You've given me my life back," she'd cried.

I'd given her more than she'd ever know. More than I could ever admit. But I was trapped now, like a cornered animal. Time had me stuck in a corner, and my back was arched. My teeth were out.

Death crept nearer every moment. Unless I made a choice.

I'd had Sahar bring in the list of contestant names. I'd put it on the ground. I'd tossed a rock. But when the rock had landed on Mateo's name, I'd shuddered. No. Fate clearly didn't want me to choose one of them.

But who? Who could I give my heart to?

My mind shuffled through the events of the past few days again, trying to select someone.

A knock sounded at my door, and I called out, "Come in," as I gathered up my list and slid it under my pillow. The door opened from outside, and Mayor Deacon swam inside hesitantly, an apologetic look on his face.

"I'm sorry to disturb you, Your Majesty."

I shook my head. "It's fine."

Felipe pulled the door shut but remained out in the hall with Ugo. I'd banished them outside when I'd come in here to think, to decide.

Deacon knotted his fingers as he approached. "I wanted to let you know the City Guard has been asking around. But none of the typical protest groups, none of the known rebels, have been bragging about today's incident."

He didn't know who was responsible. There was no one to grab, imprison, punish. I fought against clenching my fist, because whoever had done this deserved punishment. Whoever had done this deserved to rot. "And what do you think?"

He shrugged. "They could be playing this close to the chest; it could be the first move of many. Or ... perhaps a lone actor with some agenda." He shook his head. "It's impossible to say really."

I gave a brisk nod.

"If I hazard a guess, you won't hold it against me, will you?" Deacon asked with a tilt of his head.

I froze and stared at him. He *did* have a theory. "Of course not."

The mayor turned and examined my room, his face turning a bright purple that matched the walls. "Well ... given the nature of the attacks on you and your competitors, I'd wager that whoever is doing this has inside access to you and them. A guard maybe. A maid. Someone ..." He shrugged as he trailed off.

His words hit home. I chewed my lip as I pondered what he said. I felt the truth of his statement in my bones. Hadn't Felipe said as much after the attack on the road? The route had been secret. Today, none but my staff, the competitors, and some guards had early access to the arena.

I glanced back up and met the mayor's eyes. He gave another sheepish lift of his shoulders as he said, "Well

… you know the old saying, keep your friends close, enemies closer?"

I gave a brief nod. It was the very reason I'd invited Watkins to the tournament.

Shite.

Deacon let out a relieved sigh and turned to leave. He'd swum all the way to the door before I called out, "Mayor Deacon?"

He turned. "Yes?"

"Can you have the undead witch Lizza sent to me, please?"

"Now?" he asked.

I nodded. "Yes. Now. There's something I need her to do." Lizza had said the man didn't need to be present. She'd said she could magic the heart from my chest into his. Well, Watkins had no idea what was coming for him. That arrogant shite—attacking everyone right under my nose as I tried, like a simpleton, to break through to him. Fury pulsed hot and bright behind my eyes as I made the decision not to give my heart to a good man.

Lizza walked in and as soon as she saw me, she knew. She shooed away my guards and locked the door behind her. "Who, Majesty?" she asked.

"First, confirm for me … the person I give my heart to doesn't have to know they have it, do they?"

Lizza's face tilted to the side. "No. But that's awfully risky."

It was. But, luckily, my worst enemy was the man I'd invited to join my tournament. An ass who thought he had the upper hand. But I was about to bind him to me and cut off his free will forever.

I leveled my gaze on Lizza. "I want you to give my heart to my worst enemy."

EPILOGUE

Raj

Hours ago, I watched her swim down the length of the arena, hand to her mouth, horror etched on her youthful face, an expression as beautiful as any I'd ever seen in my torture chambers in Cheryn.

I had longed to swim closer, to watch her as she leaned over the body of her newest favored and sobbed, but I'd known better than to do that. Gloating merely begot discovery … and I wasn't ready to be unmasked just yet.

Instead, I'd pretended to help a bit. Pretended to be concerned and sad and shocked. Playing the fool was such fun, more amusement than I'd had in centuries.

I hadn't even minded when the undead witch brought the stupid boy back to life. It just meant I'd get the chance to kill him again.

Him. And the others. One by one.

No one even suspected me, the fools. My disguise was so perfect, so complete, that no one would ever guess my real identity.

Inside, I grinned wildly as I swam back to my assigned room in the mayor's palace, though my face was the perfect mask of solemnity.

Breaking this little bitch was going easier than I'd imagined, given who her mother was and the queen who raised her. Both of them were as hard as diamond. I was a little disappointed actually; I had hoped this challenge would take a bit longer.

It had been too simple, too easy to wish the first man became an ass, whip another into bloodlust, crumble that arena.

Even a monarch in their infancy should have recognized my attacks for what they were.

But no, the little sea queen had been too blinded by the rebellion churning up the water. She hadn't even suspected ... It gave my victory a bitter aftertaste. I didn't want to be caught, but my brilliance was going all but ignored.

Such were the trials of genius. To be overlooked constantly by those with eyes too small to see the predator looming near ... They were like plankton to a whale, mere seal pups to a shark. The little queen had no idea that I was about to swallow her up.

I sighed as I entered my room, a brown coral husk that wasn't fit for a seahorse, much less a sultan, and turned the metal key on a small, fist-sized glass sphere floating in the water, lighting it. When I released the key, the heat of the magical fire inside the dome made it rise in the water, full of glowing orange light that filled the space like a tiny sun. My eyes followed the orb as it floated to my left side, farthest from the entrance, and bounced with a *clink* gently off the coral wall.

I leaned back on the sea sponge roll that I'd been given as a sleep mat and tucked my hands behind my head as I stared up at the ceiling, letting calm wash over me, a contrast to the ruckus I still heard outside, the gossip, the fury, the uproar.

I wondered what her next step would be, the little royal. Would she cry? Would she run back to her big sister?

The thrill that raced up my spine at that thought was nearly as strong as an orgasm. *I could toy with both of them together, turn them against one another ...*

There were so many possibilities.

Suddenly, pain ripped through me, sawed at me like a dull serrated blade. My chest heaved, and my hands flew up to clutch at it. I writhed as white-hot sensation traveled through me, throwing my heart repeatedly against my ribcage until both ached.

Had someone found me out? Was this a magical attack? I reached for my ring to wish it away, but another tormented arrow shot through me.

I bit down on a scream and rolled off my pallet when it felt as though a golden bar, a brick, a boulder was shoved into my chest cavity, forcing all my other organs to contract. Every thought was slashed to ribbons. My eyes rolled back in my skull, and my back arched as agony took over my entire existence.

I had no idea how long the pain lasted. I wasn't even certain if I passed out or not. All I knew was that when the pain finally ebbed away like the tide, I blinked in the darkness, the magic of my lantern extinguished.

A jolt of relief shot through me, followed by a strange glittering sorrow, an emotion I hadn't felt for hundreds of years. Elation followed like a bright dazzling sun. Then the more familiar fury. A strange softness, like a silk sheet, wove through me, an emotion I couldn't even identify. What was happening? Had someone wished for me to be driven mad by emotion? I'd protected myself against that centuries ago.

Or was I dying? Was the magic that kept me alive slowly disintegrating?

Instead of fear snapping at me, the only emotion that followed that thought was a mad giggle that bubbled up so strong that I couldn't resist it.

And as I brought my hand tentatively to my chest, which felt swollen and overly full, I felt my heartbeat, which had not settled or calmed at all. No, my organ beat out a rhythm in double time.

SURFACE: TANGLED CROWNS BOOK 5

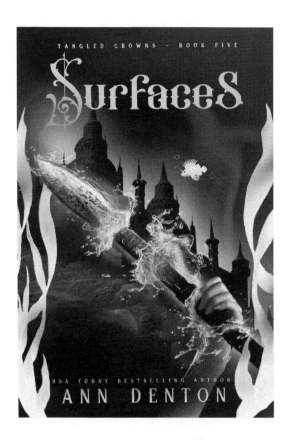

Surfaces - Tangled Crowns Book 5

Now Available at Amazon.com

AFTERWORD

Do you hate me with a passion right now? The evil part of me hopes so. It means that I've captured your imagination and made you wonder. And nothing makes me happier than knowing you're caught up in one of my books!

Thank you so much for reading! I can't wait to continue this story and bring you with me all over the kingdom of Okeanos! There are lots of secrets yet to unveil!!

Please consider leaving a review because reviews and personal recommendations are the lifeblood of indie authors. Without your help, I couldn't keep doing what I do. I'm grateful every day that I get to write beautiful words for you!

XOXO!

ACKNOWLEDGMENTS

A huge thanks to Rob, Rachel, Thais, and Raven. Thanks to my cover designer, Carol Marquess at Marquess Designs, and my amazing ARC readers.

And a massive hug to all my readers. This series is close to my heart and I'm eternally grateful to you for picking it up. There isn't a day that goes by that I'm not awed and grateful that you choose to read my stories. Thank you for your endless support.

ALSO BY ANN DENTON

Choose from books on the following pages based on your current reading mood.

The standalone or the first book in each series are listed by mood. The darkest reads appear first and grow progressively more light-hearted so it makes it easy to find just what you're looking for next. I also tried to add some basic mood info at the bottom of each series page for you.

ALSO BY ANN DENTON

FERAL PRINCESS SERIES
(Completed Trilogy)

A hot, dark shifter omegaverse with dub con, a steamy alpha, a loving beta, and a sassy omega who thought she was going to be an alpha female. She was sooo wrong, but when she's claimed by the pack alpha, make no mistake, she has something to say about it.

Defiant - Book 1

Mood - #DARK #DIRTY #ALPHA

ALSO BY ANN DENTON

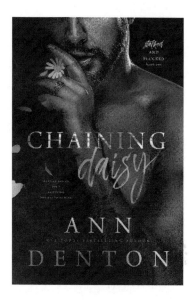

STALKED AND PLUCKED SERIES
(Series of Standalones)

A fast-burn, contemporary MF romance series with very morally gray men who stalk their ladies before claiming them. The series follows a group of college girls who are best friends.

Chaining Daisy - Book 1

Mood - #HOT #HOLYHELL #NEWKINKUNLOCKED

ALSO BY ANN DENTON

PINNACLE SERIES
(Completed Duet)

A medium-burn paranormal romance about a girl who gets herself sent to a reform academy on purpose, so she can recruit criminally-minded guys to pull off the magical heist of the century. (Reverse Harem)

Magical Academy for Delinquents #MAD - Book 1

Mood - #BADASS #FUN #SEXY GAMES

ALSO BY ANN DENTON

LOTTO LOVE SERIES
(Completed Duet)

A medium-burn, contemporary romantic comedy reverse harem about winning the lotto and doing whatever the hell you want with it, even if that means holding a Bachelorette-style competition for an entire harem of hotties.

Lotto Men - Book 1

Mood- #LOL #BLUSHING #NO WAY

ALSO BY ANN DENTON

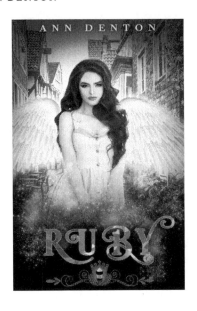

RUBY - JEWELS CAFE SERIES
(Standalone)

A medium-burn, fated mates reverse harem with an angel on her last strike, some nerds and a tech demon determined to help her, and Christmas miracles.

Ruby

Mood - #SWEET #AWWW #GIGGLES

ALSO BY ANN DENTON

DARK TEMPTATIONS SERIES
(Incomplete)

A fast-burn monster reverse harem in an alternate reality where monsters rule the earth. A human woman is captured and auctioned off to the Four Terrors who will haunt her nightmares and her dreams alike. Cowrite with Katie May.

Ravaged by Monsters - Book 1

Mood - #DARK #FATED LOVE #WILD SEXY TIMES

ALSO BY ANN DENTON

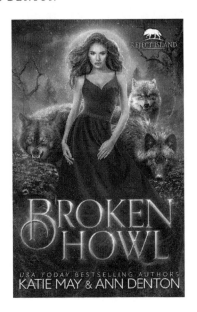

BROKEN HOWL
(Standalone)

A female omega rejects her mates so she can escape her abuser. She's sent to an island for rejects but her mates refuse to let her go…
Cowrite with Katie May.

Broken Howl

Mood - #CRYING #HEALING #FIGHTING

ALSO BY ANN DENTON

DARKEST QUEEN SERIES
(Incomplete)

The devil is a woman. And this is the story about she fell from Heaven only to rise as God's greatest enemy…
(A reverse harem spinoff of the Darkest Flames series)
Cowrite with Katie May.

For Whom the Bell Tolls - Book 1

Mood - #FURY #SOUL-DEEP CONNECTIONS #BATTLE OF WILLS

ALSO BY ANN DENTON

DARKEST FLAMES SERIES
(Completed Trilogy with a novella)

A medium-burn paranormal romance about a girl who tries a love spell on the hot guy at school and accidentally summons demons instead. It contains psychotic, alpha males, and student/teacher relationships. (Reverse Harem)
Cowrite with Katie May.

Demon Kissed - Book 1

Mood - #OOPS #NAUGHTY LAUGHTER #FORBIDDEN HEAT

ALSO BY ANN DENTON

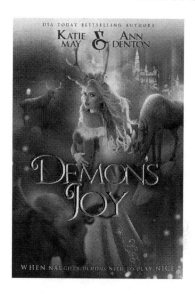

DEMON'S JOY
(Standalone)

Santa's daughter has to save Christmas from demons! And all she's got to help her are five funny reindeer. (A reverse harem spinoff of the Darkest Flames series) Cowrite with Katie May.

Demon's Joy

Mood - #SILLY #HOLIDAY CHEER #YUM

ALSO BY ANN DENTON

MAGE SHIFTER WAR SERIES
(Completed Duet)

A medium-burn paranormal mafia romance. A fae princess is taken captive by three shifter criminals.
(Reverse Harem)
Cowritten with Elle Middaugh.

Fae Captive - Book 1

Mood - #BONNIE&CLYDE #BADASS #HOT

ALSO BY ANN DENTON

HAMMER TIME
(Standalone)

A medium-burn paranormal comedy featuring Thor's daughter and a quest to save demigods from prison. Expect lots of ancient deities and potty humor.
(Reverse Harem)
Cowritten with M.J. Marstens.

Hammer Time

Mood- #PUNTASTIC #NOYOUDIDN'T #SNORT

CONNECT AND GET SNEAK PEEKS

Do you want to read exclusive point of views from different characters, make predictions and claim your book boyfriends with other readers, see my inspiration for these books, and hang with fellow RH lovers? Then join my Facebook Reader Group! I promise you'll love it!

Join Ann Denton's Reader Group

Facebook.com/groups/AnnDentonReaderGroup

ABOUT ME

I'm a shy lady who has always been obsessed with reading and travel and live theater. I've lived in four states and currently reside in Oklahoma, hence the nickname from my writer friends: Annie Oakie.

I have two of the world's cutest children, a crazy dog, and an amazing husband that I drive somewhat insane when I stop in the middle of the hallway, halfway through putting laundry away, picturing a scene.

Made in the USA
Middletown, DE
19 May 2024